England Expects

A Mirabelle Bevan Mystery

Sara Sheridan

CONSTABLE • LONDON

CONSTABLE

First published in Great Britain in 2014 by Polygon, an imprint of Birlinn Ltd.

This edition published in 2016 by Constable

A CIP catalogue record for this book
is available from the British Library.

ISBN: 978-147212-251-3

Typeset in Dante by SX Composing DTP, Rayleigh Essex
Printed and bound in Great Britain by CPI Group (UK) Ltd, Croydon, CR0 4YY

Papers used by Constable are from well-managed forests and
other responsible sources

MIX
Paper from
responsible sources
FSC® C104740

Constable
is an imprint of
Little, Brown Book Group
Carmelite House
50 Victoria Embankment
London EC4Y 0DZ

An Hachette UK Company
www.hachette.co.uk

www.littlebrown.co.uk

For Alan

Secret: a matter not meant to be known by others.

Prologue

*Murder is always a mistake – one should never
do anything one cannot talk about at dinner.*

8 a.m., Monday, 22 June 1953
Brighton

Joey Gillingham got off the train and checked his watch. He
had a little time before the meeting. Walking out of the station,
he angled his hat to keep the sun out of his eyes. It was another
scorcher. The paving stones were radiating heat already and
Brighton felt summertime sleepy compared to the buzz of Fleet
Street. Joey tucked his newspaper under his arm and headed
towards Cooper's. It was on his way. Then he remembered the
new place and changed direction. Three schoolgirls walked lazily
down the road in front of him sharing an illicit Kula Fruta on
their way to school and squinting into the sunshine. Sticky red
liquid dripped off their fingers and left stains like blood smears
on the pristine cotton of their summer blouses as they jostled to
make sure the division was fair. Joey smiled. Oxford Street was
quiet. A new sign glinted in the sunshine. Seymour's Barber.
He'd heard this new place was good. The glare obscured the interior of the shop from easy view as Joey poked his head through
the open door. Three black leather chairs with chrome trim faced
three square mirrors. The only nod to the old butcher's shop that
used to be there was the heavy block at the back, now displaying
an array of Brylcreem advertisements. *For the clean smart look.*
The air smelled of carbolic soap.

Joey shrugged his shoulders and entered. Why carry on to Cooper's when this new place looked all right? The shop was cool – a relief already. It took his eyes a moment to adjust.

'Morning, Sir.'

'A shave and a trim?' Joey enquired. 'I ain't got long.'

'Certainly, Sir.' The barber was dapper in a white jacket.

The man looked like he could land a decent right hook. He had the shoulders for it, but his eyes were too kind to make him any sort of fighter. Joey always said it was a pitiless profession.

The barber motioned him towards the first chair. 'Some tea?'

You never got that at Cooper's. It was a smart move. Not long off the ration, tea still felt like a luxury. 'All right, yeah, thanks.' Joey hung up his hat, took the newspaper from under his arm and settled down. 'Short back and sides. None of your Teddy Boy nonsense,' he instructed.

The barber grinned. 'You heard about that, then?'

'A mate told me.'

'I can do you a military cut if you'd prefer, Sir.'

'That's it.'

Joey checked his byline. When he saw his name in print it always reminded him of his English teacher at primary school. The bitch had said he'd no facility for words. 'I don't know what will become of you, Joey Gillingham. All you care about is sport,' she had sniffed disapprovingly. Joey smiled. Well, he'd done all right, thank you very much, Miss Prentice. More than all right. Joey Gillingham boasted several thousand readers, or at least the *Express* did. And he was about to up his game. In an hour he'd be onto the story of his life, and if he cracked it he'd be able to screw a bonus out of the paper.

Joey liked the money but he liked the recognition just as much. He'd been lucky to stumble across something big. Something out of his usual field. Brighton was like that – small and friendly. A bloke with his eyes open could pick up a lot. Joey reflected that 'investigative journalist' sounded better than plain old 'journalist' or 'sports reporter'. An investigative journalist wasn't a hack.

The barber swept a spotless napkin around Joey's shoulders and fastened it in place. Then he combed Joey's hair. Every customer was important to a new business. That was why he opened early – he always caught one or two blokes on their way into work or on their way home from the nightshift. It was worth getting up sharp.

'Right. Tea,' he said and disappeared into the back room to boil the kettle.

'Milk and one, if you got it,' Joey called and turned his attention back to the paper as the sound of heels on paving stones, squabbling children and distant traffic on the main road floated through the open door.

Joey didn't see the man. He paused for only a second at the doorway, checking right and left up Oxford Street. There was nothing distinctive about him – just a regular fellow sporting a shabby demob suit like thousands of others, with a worn brown hat cocked at an angle. No one noticed as he slipped inside out of the sun. As the man walked swiftly to the chair, Joey licked his finger and turned a page. This inattention was a particular irony because Gillingham was known to be unforgiving when a boxer didn't see a knockout punch. 'You gotta be on your guard all the time. Gloves up,' he always said. 'It takes less than a second if your opponent's on his game.'

The man was a professional. He moved silently, pulling a flick knife from his pocket and smoothly slicing the journalist's jugular without hesitation. There was no time for Joey to call out as his blood spurted onto the mirror. His body stayed upright in the chair. It always went too quickly, the assassin thought, as he calmly took off his jacket – a crimson spot had marked the sleeve. Coolly he folded it over his arm, dipped the knife into a glass of blue fluid on the old butcher's block to clean it and, checking the corpse's inside pockets, took what he wanted. Then, glancing in the mirror to alter the angle of his hat, he sauntered into the sunshine towards the station as if nothing untoward had taken place.

Chapter 1

*Choose a job you love and you will
never work a day in your life.*

Mirabelle Bevan swept into the office of McGuigan &
McGuigan Debt Collection at nine on the dot. She removed
her jacket and popped the gold aviator sunglasses she'd been
wearing into her handbag, which she closed with a decisive click.
The musky scent of expensive perfume spiced the air – the kind
that only a sleek middle-aged woman could hope to carry off.

Bill Turpin arrived in her wake. Like Mirabelle, Bill was
always punctual. He was a sandy-haired, reliable kind of fellow.
At his heel was the black spaniel the office had acquired the
year before. Panther nuzzled Mirabelle's knees, his tail
wagging. Mirabelle patted him absentmindedly.

'Glorious day, isn't it?' she said. 'Who'd have thought it after
all the rain? It feels like a proper summer now.'

'Nasty business on Oxford Street,' Bill commented, picking
up a list of the day's calls from his in-tray and casting an eye
down the addresses. 'That new barber's.'

'Tea, Bill?' Mirabelle offered without looking up.

'Nah. Always puts me off, does a murder.' His voice was
matter-of-fact. An ex-copper, he was used to dealing with
crime of all stripes. As a result, Bill Turpin never panicked
handling the ticklish situations that he encountered at
McGuigan & McGuigan. Debt collection was a tricky business
but it wasn't as bad as policing Brighton.

'A murder?' Mirabelle glanced over.

'Yeah. A slasher. First thing – just after eight. The fellow went in for a trim and got more than he bargained for. Poor blighter had his throat cut. I met the beat bobby on my way in. A murder right on the edge of Kemp Town. It's five minutes from Wellington Road nick and a spit from Bartholomew Square. There were coppers everywhere. They think the victim's from London – some hack.'

'Did the barber do it?'

'Nah. Poor fella was in the back. Just about had a fit when he found his customer dead in the chair. Must've only taken seconds. In and out while the bloke was reading his newspaper. They reckon it's got to be a professional job.'

'Did they find the weapon?' Mirabelle enquired out of habit.

'Well, it was a barber's shop, wasn't it? There were razors everywhere, though the murderer might have brought his own. Bit early to say. Where's the girl?' Bill looked around as if he'd only just realised that the third member of the office staff was not at her desk.

Mirabelle leaned over to peer out of the window. There was no sign of Vesta Churchill on the street below. 'Oh, she'll be on her way,' she said indulgently. Vesta was habitually late but she was a hard worker. Efficient to a fault, especially with paperwork, what was ten minutes here or there?

'Well, I suppose it's nothing to do with us,' Bill said, his mind still on the murder.

Over the last two years several murders had been personal to the employees of McGuigan & McGuigan. The day-to-day business of the firm was humdrum, but now and again Mirabelle had found herself embroiled in what Bill referred to as 'police business'. It was the upshot of being curious, she thought, and all three of them were certainly that. Bill was the most recently recruited to the firm and he had fitted in so well precisely because he was nosey. Nosey in a nice way, but still it was true – they were all curious about the world. More than that. McGuigan & McGuigan's little team was a tremendous minder of other people's business. Bill still acted like a policeman a lot of the time. He was slower to make assumptions than Vesta, and that, Mirabelle told herself, provided balance.

'They reckon the fella was down to see the boxing,' Bill said as he slid the day's paperwork into his inside pocket. 'Poor sod wrote a sports column for one of the red tops.' He shrugged and then whistled for Panther. 'Sounds like he got on the wrong side of someone serious, doesn't it? Well, see you later.' He tipped his hat and sauntered out.

Mirabelle looked at the kettle. There was no point in making tea for one. When Vesta arrived they'd brew a nice pot and chat about the weather. She lifted the first paper off the pile in front of her, sighed, and wondered what kind of person followed a man into a barber's shop to slit his throat.

Chapter 2

*Nothing flatters a man as much
as the happiness of his wife.*

Vesta Churchill walked down Lewes Road hand in hand with Charlie. She tried not to speak. People stared enough as it was without the pair of them arguing in public. Still, she hadn't finished what she wanted to get out and now her dark eyes flashed dangerously.

Charlie lifted his free hand and flicked a flake of pastry from his collar. He'd made croissants for breakfast in an attempt to seduce her. Unexpectedly Vesta was not to be won over by pastry – not in this matter. Initially he'd tried chocolate éclairs brought home from the kitchens of the hotel where he worked. After that there had been a Victoria sponge. Vesta, after all, was English. But no dice. She'd turned him down flat. Not only that but she seemed furious.

'Don't you see?' she hissed. 'We can't get married, Charlie. Think what would happen.'

Charlie had been thinking about exactly that. He'd looked at houses all over Brighton's suburbs and calculated that with the savings he'd put by, they'd have enough for a good deposit somewhere really nice or, if Vesta insisted, they could keep living in the bedsit and save up till they could buy a place outright. The acquisition of a mortgage, after all, might be too American.

'I want to make it official, baby,' he said. 'I love you.'

'It's a big change,' Vesta started. 'If we get married, everyone will expect things.'

'It doesn't have to be different,' Charlie cajoled her. 'We live together as it is. You'd just be Mrs Charles Lewis, is all. Your mama would be happy if we got married, wouldn't she? And so would mine. We're living in sin, baby.'

'But I like living in sin.' Vesta kissed him on the cheek. 'Can't we leave it at that?'

It turned out Charlie couldn't. He'd done his best to move things on as far as possible. He'd relocated from London to Brighton, leaving his well-paid job at the Dorchester for a worse paid one at the Grand, and he'd found a bar where he could play now and then – a dive in the Lanes that had jazz nights on Tuesdays and Thursdays. They weren't a bad bunch of guys. At first he'd taken a room near Queen's Park but then a bedsit had come up on the same floor as Vesta's in the lodging house where she stayed on Lewes Road. It was closer to town and there was a connecting door that they could unlock to double their space and effectively live together.

He still hadn't got over having to negotiate his tenancy. Vesta, uncharacteristically, had let him do the talking though she'd stood beside him while he made the arrangements with her recently widowed landlady, Mrs Agora. He railed against asking the old lady for permission but there was no other way. Vesta hadn't been prepared to lie.

'Is this how you people do things?' Mrs Agora had grumbled.Her hair was set in such a permanent wave that it appeared to be made of sheet steel riveted to her head.

'Do you mean Americans?' Charlie enquired.

Mrs Agora didn't flinch. 'You coloureds, is this how you do it? Because it ain't entirely respectable. Not here.'

Charlie swallowed the words that initially sprang to his lips. 'Well, ma'am,' he drawled, affecting his most charming accent, 'I've asked Vesta to tie the knot and she won't have me. So I guess living together will have to do. If you'll let me move in.'

Mrs Agora sucked furiously on a Capstan with her Revlon-red lips, all the while regarding the young couple as if they were a fairground curiosity. 'You sure about this, dearie?'

Charlie held his breath and felt a wave of relief as Vesta nodded curtly. He couldn't be entirely sure of her when it came to this – something was going on with Vesta and he couldn't figure out what it was.

Mrs Agora stubbed out her cigarette. She folded her arms. Vesta was a regular payer and never any trouble. This fellow had been hanging around for months. He'd fixed the wiring at Christmas when it had gone on the fritz. 'You'll do odd jobs now and then?'

'With pleasure,' Charlie grinned. 'And, lady, if we're still here next Christmas I'll bake you a cake.'

'I suppose you can't say fairer than that.' The old girl felt herself relenting. Lewes Road wasn't that respectable, after all, and the fellow was certainly handy. 'Any trouble and you're out, mind. I can't stand a ding-dong. Not since Mr Agora passed.'

Charlie gave the widow his solemn word and only later enquired of Vesta what on earth a ding-dong was. It was ironic, he realised now, that the only argument they ever had was about this. It made no sense. Women were supposed to want to get married.

He decided to sit on the pebble beach and soak up some sun once he'd seen Vesta into work. He was on the late shift. As they passed Union Road an ambulance pulled out, coming from Oxford Street. It was followed by a police car.

'It could be worse, baby.' Charlie nodded at the ambulance. 'The poor dope in there ain't even worth them ringing the bell. He's a complete goner.'

'It isn't that I don't love you, Charlie . . .'

'I don't understand,' he said, his voice rising with exasperation.

'Jeez, Charlie.' Vesta dropped his hand and picked up her pace. 'I like the way we live. I don't want to change and I don't care what anyone else thinks.'

Charlie looked round. There weren't many people. It was quiet, or quiet enough. He'd wanted to say this for days. 'We don't have to have kids yet,' he promised in a whisper. 'Not straight away. If that's what you're worried about, honey. I'll wait a year or two. I don't mind.'

Vesta looked distressed. A bus passed spewing oily fumes into the warm air. From the interior a little boy in school uniform jumped up and down, pointing at her through the window. He was saying something to his mother about the colour of her skin. Vesta didn't need to be able to hear the words to know what was going on. The bus's engine roared and her eyes fell to the ground in shame.

'Can't we leave it?' she pleaded, picking up her pace. 'Let's not discuss this in the street – wherever there's a quarrel there's a crowd. That or a body.'

'Vesta, sometimes you are weird, girl.' Charlie laughed, but seeing her eyes steady and serious he decided not to push the point. 'Let's leave it for now.' He grasped her hand again and squeezed it firmly.

It wasn't often that Vesta practically broke into a run as she approached Brills Lane. After pecking Charlie on the cheek she took the stairs at a lick, her red summer coat disappearing into the building like a magic trick. She hammered up to the office and threw her coat onto its peg.

'Morning,' she gasped.

Mirabelle looked up. The girl was chewing her lip as she skimmed the morning's mail at such speed that Mirabelle doubted she could possibly be taking it in. Mirabelle reached over and flicked on the kettle. 'Everything all right?' she said quietly.

Vesta dropped the papers and sat down with a bump. 'Mirabelle, if I get married, I don't have to give up work, do I?'

Mirabelle's lips parted in a delighted smile. 'Married! But that's wonderful news, Vesta. Congratulations!' Her eyes fell to the fourth finger of the girl's left hand.

'He bought a ring but I can't . . . He says he wants to be a family. A family!' Vesta let the tears trickle down her cheeks and she began to sob, unable to look Mirabelle in the eye. 'I . . . I don't want to spend all day keeping house. Every day. Even if it's a nice house. And kids! He wants kids – not straight away, but still. If you're married and you don't have kids everyone gets sniffy. It's not that I don't like children, but I'm enjoying things the way they are. It's nice that Charlie wants to look after me, but I don't want to be a housewife with no money of my own. I couldn't bear to be stuck indoors all the time, just cleaning and cooking. Oh God. You understand, don't you, Mirabelle? Marriage is just so . . . boring.'

Mirabelle sighed. 'Gosh,' she said, passing Vesta a clean handkerchief from her handbag. The truth was, she didn't understand. Vesta had been lucky enough to find love and here she was rejecting it. Mirabelle cast her mind back. All she had wanted, years ago when she had the chance, was to live with Jack. She gave up her job in a heartbeat to be with him when she moved to Brighton after the war. She hadn't been very good at keeping house but she'd done it. Her cooking was so terrible that Jack had come to an arrangement with the grocer's wife who, for a few shillings a week and the coupons, delivered a whole week's worth of home cooking straight into the refrigerator at the smart flat Jack bought for Mirabelle on the front at The Lawns.

'We can't starve,' he had exclaimed, 'and, darling, you heat things up perfectly. The main thing is that you pour my whisky just as I like it.'

A finger of Scotch and the same of water was not a taxing requirement, Mirabelle had joked. 'I should've gone to finishing school instead of Oxford.' She didn't mean it, not entirely. And neither did he, when he said, 'Well, thank God you've got other talents,' and pushed her onto the bed.

Now Mirabelle laid a comforting hand on Vesta's shoulder but she found it difficult to speak. McGuigan & McGuigan had been her last choice of occupation. The truth was she was here by default. If Jack was alive she'd never have taken the job. Not in a million years. She'd have been with him – every minute. Or at least she'd have been waiting for him to come home. The idea of being a family was heartbreakingly, tantalisingly marvellous.

'Vesta, do you love Charlie?' she enquired tentatively.

Vesta's eyes opened wide. She stopped crying. 'I adore him. It's not Charlie. It's all this other stuff.'

'You want to have your cake and eat it, you mean?'

Vesta nodded. 'Why not?' She sounded cross. 'Why can't I keep my job? My nice life? He gets to. Why's it always the woman who has to give up everything? It's not fair.'

Mirabelle considered this. It had never occurred to her. Vesta was certainly very modern. Perhaps that was what the war had done for young women.

'If you marry Charlie and you don't want to leave, I won't make you resign,' she said. 'It's custom and practice. It's not the law. I can't see how anyone would be able to take your place. I'd hate it if you went.'

'Really?' Vesta's eyes were bright. She flung her arms joyously around Mirabelle's frame, hugging her tightly. 'Oh, thank you, Mirabelle. Thank you. This girl I know was a teacher at Whitehawk Primary and they told her she had to go as soon as she got hitched, and one of her friends was a librarian and she got engaged at the same time and they chucked her out, too. But after the wedding the librarian was miserable and in the end she turned up to work every day voluntarily. She helped run the library till she popped her first baby. I don't know what happened after that. Women just disappear once they've had a baby. Missing persons – that's what it's like. And Charlie's in such a rush. He thinks he's being patient, but it's all so quick.'

Mirabelle held up a hand. Sometimes talking to Vesta was like directing traffic. It was extraordinarily easy to end up on a side road, miles from where you started. 'Well, if you want to stay at work, you'll be paid, of course. But I urge you to think about it.' Mirabelle realised her tone was that of an old spinster. I sound about ninety, she cursed inwardly. 'Look, Vesta, if you don't want children and Charlie does, it's bound to cause trouble. If you have reservations, you must be careful. Love is about making sacrifices. It's about changing your life for someone. At least a little.'

Vesta nodded. She dabbed her cheeks, blew her nose and solemnly returned Mirabelle's hankie. 'I know. It's such a big change. It's not that I don't want kids but maybe we could get a nanny? Can you imagine how that would go down?' She hooted with laughter. 'A black woman with a nanny!'

Mirabelle had a sudden and incongruous vision of a pale-faced woman in a Norland uniform taking orders from Vesta. Not that a Norland nanny would dream of taking on a black infant. They had a code, Mirabelle seemed to recall. There were rules, unwritten and otherwise. And Norland was a costly exercise. There must be other kinds of nanny, she thought.

'If I were you I'd speak to Charlie about it soon,' she said. 'It's the sort of thing you have to agree on.'

Vesta looked out of the window. A slice of sunshine was working its way up East Street. 'I wonder where he went. He's not working until lunchtime and he walked me into town. On a nice day like this perhaps he's sitting on the front. He likes it by the Aquarium. Charlie's a sucker for fish.'

Mirabelle smiled. Maybe Vesta loved the boy, after all. 'Why don't you look for him?' she suggested. 'You could see if he still has that ring.'

Vesta grabbed her handbag and pulled on her coat. 'I can't talk to him about it. I just can't. Thanks, though,' she said, her dark eyes shining. 'I hate parting on bad terms. I won't be long. I'll just give him a cuddle and then I'll come back.'

Mirabelle kept an eye on the street, watching from a height as Vesta hurried to the front. A wave of sadness washed over her as she stood by the window. She'd trade in everything for one more kiss, never mind the chance to get married.

Everyday things were reminders. Each time she drew the curtains at home she pictured how they'd sat in the window in the dark staring at the stars with only a bedsheet wrapped round them. Or last Christmas there was a snow scene in the window of the art gallery on North Street and day after December day she had thought how much Jack would have loved it. If only he hadn't died.

As Mirabelle sank into her chair she spotted the morning paper on Bill's desk. Without thinking she flipped it over and examined the sports pages. Sure enough there was a boxing match that evening – the reason the man who died had been in town. Brighton had a crack junior squad that had won every one of its bouts this year. The boys were being touted as boxing stars of the future. There was a picture of eight stocky teenagers, their hands swaddled in bandages, gloves hanging round their necks. They clustered around their coach – a fellow in a white vest, dark hair slicked back and a towel slung carelessly over one shoulder.

'My boys are unbeatable,' he was quoted. 'Individually or as a team, no one'll ever match them. What we have in Brighton this year is unique.'

Mirabelle smiled. Now that was confidence. Tonight's bout, which would feature two of these unbeatable Brighton youngsters, was set for 7 p.m. at the Crown and Anchor on Preston Road. If that's where the murdered man had been heading he'd certainly arrived in Brighton in good time.

It's not that far to Preston Road, Mirabelle thought, her curiosity stirring. She could nip up this evening and take a look.

Chapter 3

Women are like tricks by sleight of hand.

6.30 p.m., Crown and Anchor

The man on the door shifted uneasily as Detective Superintendent Alan McGregor flashed his warrant card. The pub was already filling up, and McGregor noticed that in addition to the usual Brighton crowd, there were a few faces he didn't recognise. Most of them were far too well dressed to be relying solely on ration coupons. Plenty of men would travel to watch a decent fight, and Brighton had hosted the top junior action of the season so far. Commentators were making wild claims for the future careers of the young crop of Brighton fighters. It put on undue pressure, McGregor reckoned. Still, he was keen to be here, and not only because it was where Joey Gillingham had intended to spend the evening. The Superintendent decided he might hazard a quid on the second bout. He liked a bit of hand-to-hand.

Inside, the pub was shabby but well kept. A clean smell of hops emanated from the bar. The front room was set out like a normal pub and that's where most people were congregated. McGregor knew it wouldn't take long before the crowd began to filter into the back room where a ring was pegged out with a few benches around it. At the bar, a man in a sharp suit with a dolly bird on his arm was trying to order a bottle of champagne, much to the barman's surprise.

'Don't you got nuffink decent?' he said, his East End accent thick as treacle.

'There's beer on draught and we got spirits.' The barman pointed sheepishly at the gantry.

The dolly bird pursed her startlingly pink lips and made do with a gin and bitter.

McGregor scanned the rest of the crowd. He eyed a huddle where illegal odds were being offered and then he turned his attention to the punters cheerily greeting each other as they arrived. It had been a hell of a season for the Brighton boys. Some of the men had brought their sons to the match. A group of kids in short trousers and long socks were drinking Vimto from the bottle as they headed outside. The boys were excited – rattling on about the fight and taking good-humoured pot shots at each other. There was nothing suspicious here, or at least nothing McGregor immediately felt related to the murder that morning. One or two of the men were spreading the news about Joey's death. He'd been well known in Brighton, particularly in these circles, so, McGregor reasoned, perhaps he'd be able to pick up something of use. Background.

The Superintendent sidled up to the bar and ordered a half-pint and a whisky chaser before he noticed Mirabelle. She was flushed from the sunshine, wearing a pale peach summer dress cinched at the waist with an elegant tan leather belt. As ever, she took his breath away as she removed her sunglasses and glanced around the pub, her hazel eyes adjusting to the low light. Her hair was down this evening – he hadn't seen it that way before. It looked silky as she shook it. Normally reserved, it was as if she'd relaxed in the sunshine. He'd hardly seen her since they'd had lunch at the Savoy last year after an inquest hearing. McGregor wanted to repeat the experience, but Miss Bevan always seemed so cool towards him that he'd ducked out of asking her again. There was nowhere like the Savoy in Brighton anyway, and after London's finest nothing else seemed good enough. At heart the Superintendent was actually rather shy. He lifted a hand in greeting.

'Miss Bevan. I had no idea you were interested in boxing. Might I buy you a drink? A whisky, isn't it?'

Mirabelle nodded. 'Thanks,' she said. 'Isn't it a wonderful day?'

McGregor's knee-jerk reaction was to say 'Not for Joey Gillingham', but he stopped himself just in time, telling himself that Mirabelle Bevan wouldn't want to hear about the case he was working on. What had been on McGregor's mind most was the unprofessional behaviour of some of his officers. His deputy, Robinson, had ordered Gillingham's body removed from the crime scene before he'd had a chance to inspect it.

'Cut and dried, boss,' Robinson had sniffed. 'I reckoned it was best to get on.'

By the time McGregor got to the scene all that remained was one traumatised barber, a vermilion spatter and a napkin soaked in Joey Gillingham's blood.

'There's no question about the cause of death, is there?' Robinson defended himself. 'It's hot, and there were kids on the way to school. I decided to get the corpse back to the mortuary. Seemed for the best.'

McGregor didn't doubt it, but he liked to see a body in situ. It was the usual protocol.

'No more slap-happy stuff,' he'd warned Robinson. 'I'm the DS. We do it my way, by the book.'

'You'll have had a busy day, Superintendent?' Mirabelle cut into McGregor's thoughts, lifting her drink for him to clink the glass. 'Talking to the *Express*, were you?'

'How did you . . .'

Mirabelle pointed to a man sitting on a bar stool. He was reading the *Argus* and Joey Gillingham's murder was headline news. *Express Journalist Butchered In Local Barber's Chair*, it read. McGregor blushed. He had been so involved he hadn't even considered the newspapers would make a meal of this morning's murder. There'd been too much to do. Now it sank in.

'They'll play it up for all it's worth,' he said. 'Journalists love journalists. They think their opinions are important.'

'Wasn't he important?'

'Sports writer? Not groundbreaking individuals as a rule, but every corpse is important, isn't it? Looks like this one had a few dodgy contacts but then you'd expect that. He was a gambling man. His editor said he was down for this.' McGregor nodded towards the boxing ring just visible through the back.

Mirabelle checked her watch. 'He arrived very early, don't you think?'

'Perhaps he was hoping to make a day of it.'

'Horrible affair.'

'At least it was over quickly. Poor fellow probably didn't know what was happening. If I had to choose how to go . . .' McGregor stopped. What was wrong with him? He sounded like a miserable old sod with a death wish. Mirabelle looked taken aback. 'Sorry,' he said.

She smiled politely and sipped her whisky, taking a moment to soak in the atmosphere.

'The boxing is in the other section. They've got changing rooms through there, too. It's a proper professional set-up, though tonight the fighters are junior amateurs. You haven't been before?'

Mirabelle raised her hands in a gesture of surrender. 'You got me.'

'You didn't know this one, did you? I mean, our victim?' McGregor's voice betrayed his nervousness. Mirabelle Bevan was in the disconcerting habit of being on first-name terms with a larger number of people who ended up dead of violent causes than the average member of the population. This, McGregor noted, did not stop him from wanting to become further acquainted with her.

'I don't read the *Express* as a rule. I'd never heard of the poor chap. The circumstances made me curious, that's all.'

'Mirabelle,' McGregor leaned in, concerned, 'I don't know who killed Joey Gillingham, but whoever they are they're violent, so please don't go poking about. I'm not sure you should be here at all.'

'All murderers are violent by definition.' Mirabelle didn't back down. 'Besides, the Crown and Anchor is a public place. It sounds as if the fight tonight will be terrific. I had no idea the local team was doing so well.'

McGregor downed his half-pint and lifted his whisky. At least he could keep an eye on her. 'Let's go through,' he said.

In the back room it was quieter. On the bench a fat, white-haired priest sat patiently, a large wooden cross on a chain rising and falling on the vast expanse of his cassock with every breath.

'Two of the kids fighting tonight are from the church youth club. Don't worry. The old crow's not here to administer the last rites. It'll be Queensberry rules.' McGregor was enjoying showing Mirabelle round. Usually she was so competent he had hardly any part to play but today she was hanging on his words. His heart lifted as she parted her lips to form a question.

'So,' she said, 'have you found the murder weapon yet?'

If there was one thing that was good about a sports crowd it made it easy to mingle. A match was always a good conversation opener. By half past nine Mirabelle had ascertained that Joey Gillingham was reasonably popular. He'd been a generous winner when his bets came in. Professionally, the general consensus was that his column had been firm but fair. He'd spent a good deal of time in Brighton this spring, not only on account of the boxing team's successes but also because of the racecourse.

'Joey liked the gee-gees,' a drunk man told Mirabelle. 'He wasn't a fella for the football. Not really. He preferred the horses and the dogs and, of course, this stuff.' He jerked his head in the direction of the ring.

'Sounds to me like he had a lot of friends in Brighton.'

'Friends? Everyone's a friend of Joey Gillingham, ain't they? Them boys knows what's what.' The man laid a sweaty palm on her arm and squeezed. 'They'll give you a tip sometimes, know what I mean?'

Mirabelle humoured him. She was getting what she wanted, after all. 'And he was a ladies' man like you, I'd guess?'

McGregor watched the encounter open-mouthed. Mirabelle seemed almost flirtatious. Still, the fellow spilled the beans.

'I never saw Joey with a woman. He was obsessed with the gee-gees, love. It was like a religion. There's normally hardly any women at the boxing. That means you're special, ain't you? Can I get you a drink? A lady like you needs feeding up.'

The man ran his eyes down Mirabelle's body and licked his lips. He dwelled on the swell of her blouse.

'Enough's enough, fella,' McGregor cut in, but Mirabelle was ahead of him and had already moved away.

The Superintendent quickly gave up curtailing her enquiries, realising with a guilty twinge that the men responded to her more openly than when he asked the questions. It was amazing. Mirabelle had an instinct for exactly what information to push for and she was formidable – steel-willed and smiling. She made an interrogation sound as if it was only a conversation. Between bouts the Superintendent fetched drinks, acting the solicitous minder rather than making enquiries of his own.

'Is that your old man?' he heard one fellow ask, nodding in his direction.

'He's my brother,' Mirabelle confided in a whisper and McGregor allowed himself a surreptitious smile.

When the young fighters stepped into the ring the Superintendent wasn't sure if Mirabelle would be able to watch them hammer it out, but as the bell sounded she took the violence in her stride and didn't flinch when the matches became heated. It couldn't be easy for a woman, watching the kids slug each other until they were swollen and bloody while the audience bayed for victory.

'You aren't squeamish, are you?' McGregor checked.

A look from Mirabelle dismissed the idea.

In the end, both the local boys won. Johnny Thwaite, a stocky, muscle-bound sixteen-year-old from Eastbourne, beat a seventeen-year-old called Davie Osler till the poor kid gave up. Afterwards, Thwaite, elated, climbed out of the ring to hug his father, a whiff of sweat and the tang of blood wafting off him, the heat of his body palpable on the air. He looked like he could go another ten rounds.

'Well done, Johnny,' the boy's father said, flinging his arms around his son. 'You slammed him. You'd have made your mother proud tonight.'

The fat priest, who it seemed had won money, came over and clapped the kid on the back.

Second up, there was Ricky Philips, a fourteen-year-old flyweight who was the favourite not only on account of his left hook but also because he came from Kemp Town. He knocked out a Jewish kid who'd come down from Shoreditch. One tight punch after another, and the crowd raised the roof on the Crown and Anchor. The MC was barely audible over the screaming until Philips triumphed, raising his hand in the air and taking a wide-grinned bow as the MC counted out the beaten boy to the jeers of the crowd.

McGregor watched Mirabelle, who remained impassive.

'It's not the first time I've been to the boxing,' she assured him and McGregor didn't ask again.

At the end of the night the fighters were taken off to have their wounds seen to and the priest climbed into the ring to say a prayer. The audience stood respectfully, heads bowed. Then the barman called time and McGregor helped Mirabelle into her light summer coat and walked her outside.

'I hope that boy gets back up to London all right,' she said.

'The Jewish kid? I'm sure he'll be looked after.'

'The last train must have gone though.'

Miss Bevan, McGregor noted, was kind-hearted even if she was ruthless in her enquiries. She tucked a loose strand of hair behind her ear as McGregor touched her arm to guide her towards his car. The air was still warm despite the fading light and a balmy breeze swept in from the sea. The roar of engines starting cut the silence as the well-heeled among the crowd headed home. One man walked into the blackness with his son on his shoulders explaining the Queensberry rules. Several more ran for the last bus, shouting the names of the fighters.

'I'll see you back home,' the Superintendent offered, holding open the door as Mirabelle slipped into the front seat.

'You've been down here a while now.'

'A couple of years, I suppose.'

'Has England been good to you?'

'It's a lot warmer than Scotland, that's for sure.' The Superintendent shrugged. 'But the golf courses are tamer. I miss losing my ball in the gorse. Scotland's a wildcat. She'd scratch you to death given the chance. Brighton's a softer place.'

Mirabelle raised a quizzical eyebrow. 'Softer? You really think so?'

'Yes. The odd homicide notwithstanding. Things seem less serious down here. I'm probably due a trip north. I don't want to lose my edge.'

'Family?'

'I don't have any family now. Only a few friends.' His mother had died the year before. The family home in Davidson's Mains had lain empty for months now. He couldn't decide what to do with the old place, and the family solicitor kept pestering him about it.

'Well, it would be a nice trip, wouldn't it? To go back to Edinburgh to see them. A holiday.'

The Superintendent stared out of the car window at an old bombsite. There were plenty of places where the detritus hadn't been cleared – years after the initial strike. On some sites no one had any idea what to build. They'd reconstructed the old viaduct on the London Road and the Odeon cinema when they had been hit. Out here where the railway line had been destroyed one night during an air raid, the ground was still strewn with bricks though the train tracks were long repaired.

'So,' McGregor asked, 'what do you reckon about our Mr Gillingham?'

Mirabelle sighed. 'If you're going to slit someone's throat you've got to be a committed killer. You've got to be harbouring a grievance or be commissioned by someone harbouring a grievance. I don't know, Superintendent, but Joey Gillingham was in Brighton very early and the racecourse isn't open today. So either there's a woman involved – and a man would slit the throat of his wife's lover, so I'd rule that out before anything else – or he was onto something connected with his work. Something dangerous. The second seems more likely – no one tonight associated Joey with women. No one had even seen him with one.'

'You think he was murdered over a betting scam? Match fixing?'

Mirabelle nodded. 'Perhaps he just owed a lot of money to someone particularly nasty. But then, even if you owe an awful lot of money a creditor doesn't usually kill you. They're not going to get their money back that way. It's far more likely they'll have a hard man beat you up – perhaps break a leg or a couple of ribs. Isn't that the way?'

'You would know,' McGregor teased. 'Miss McGuigan & McGuigan Debt Recovery.'

Mirabelle ignored the joke. 'Anyway, Joey Gillingham didn't die by mistake because a heavy went too far. Whoever killed him meant to do it. And I keep coming back to the fact that he was a journalist. So, my guess is that he was onto something, perhaps a betting scam, like you say. The racecourse or the boxing ring. Lots of the men tonight had taken tips from Joey. He had a sense of who was going to win and he was generous with his hunches. If I were looking into it, I'd check the race-course and the bookmakers. Does it remind you of when we first met?' she said and immediately wished she could take back the words.

Two years before, just after McGregor bagged the Superintendent's job, Mirabelle's boss, Ben McGuigan, had gone missing at Brighton racecourse. He'd discovered a money-laundering operation which had ultimately cost him his life.

McGregor smiled shyly. 'Well, a love affair aside, Mr Gillingham's editor didn't know any reason for him to be in Brighton by eight this morning, so I reckon you're right.'

Mirabelle shook her head. 'The editor wouldn't necessarily come clean. Justice for one of his stringers might not be his top priority. If Joey was in Brighton on a story, the paper would want to put another reporter onto it, not have the police all over everything before they had the chance to get their headline.'

McGregor considered this. 'Fair enough. And, of course, the reason Gillingham died might have been in the room with us tonight. Someone might have wanted to stop him getting to the fight.'

Mirabelle shrugged. 'It's more interesting, isn't it, why he was in Brighton so early? It doesn't make sense. That's where the mystery lies. For my money.'

The Superintendent had to concede she was right.

They had made it as far as the front. The sun was sinking below the horizon in a gorgeous peachy glow. As they passed the pier the strings of illuminations turned off, and the jetty plunged into darkness. The Kingsway was quiet tonight and the only pedestrian they saw was a policeman on his beat. They didn't speak again until McGregor pulled up at The Lawns.

From the front seat Mirabelle glanced at the long black windows of her flat on the first floor. 'I don't suppose there was any clue in his death mask?'

'I only saw him on the slab and by then his eyes were closed,' McGregor admitted.

'You didn't see him at the barber's?'

'No. Robinson had dispatched the body to the mortuary by the time I arrived. No harm in it – it was a hot summer's day and there were a lot of people around. It's a busy part of town. It wasn't as if there was any dubiety about the cause of death.'

An expression passed across Mirabelle's face – a silent question. He didn't answer it.

'And did Mr Robinson take a photograph of Mr Gillingham's corpse while it was still in the chair?' she enquired.

McGregor shook his head and said nothing.

'Thank you, Superintendent,' she said. 'I hope you catch your man.'

McGregor was about to speak, but Mirabelle had uncrossed her long legs, opened the car door briskly and was on her way up the steps before he could gather himself. He'd expected to have more time to say good night. It had been on the tip of his tongue to ask her to the cinema at the weekend and to dinner. There was a nice little place along the coast, though admittedly it wasn't the Savoy. She might have waited for him to open the car door like a gentleman. Her perfume lingered.

'Good night,' he called as the front door closed at the top of the steps. He wished Mirabelle wasn't so formal. He'd like her to call him by his first name. It had been a while since anyone had used it. No one down here knew him well enough.

His heart sank in the ensuing silence. He waited for the lamp to light the first-floor drawing room but instead of a warm yellow glow there was only a dark movement behind the glass. Mirabelle Bevan's pale outline was framed for a moment in the black window, a vision hovering above him in the darkness. Then she drew the curtains.

Chapter 4

The secret of getting ahead is getting started.

The next morning in the office Mirabelle waited patiently for Bill Turpin to settle into his chair. It was Tuesday and Bill always spent an hour or two on paperwork. Tuesday was the start of the midweek lull. For those punters who were struggling financially, any money earned over the weekend was long gone, and for most of them payday didn't loom till Friday. As far as clients went, Monday and Thursday were the days the agency was commissioned. The result was that Tuesday and Wednesday marked a quiet period in the office – time to catch up.

'Bill, I wondered if you'd heard anything else about Joey Gillingham?' said Mirabelle.

Vesta looked up from eating a slice of cinnamon toast. This was also a Tuesday occurrence. On Tuesdays and Thursdays Charlie's early shifts left Vesta bereft of a breakfast companion. It always made Mirabelle smile – twice a week the office smelled gloriously of coffee and toast, as it always had before Charlie arrived.

Bill took a deep breath as if he was reluctant to speak. 'Well, I don't like it. They're in a right old tizzy at the station. It's just a load of nonsense and it'll mess up the investigation. It already has.'

'What do you mean?'

Bill squirmed uncomfortably. 'Utter nonsense,' he repeated. 'It's a professional job – the bloke obviously got into bother with someone he owed money. I mean, look at his trade. And they're trying to cover it up 'cause of all that rubbish of theirs. Secret handshakes and the like. Next they'll be making out he was a saint. A sports writer on a red top. It ain't right.'

Vesta licked her fingers. 'What are you on about, Bill?'

'All that dressing up. It's just plain silly. I wouldn't demean myself. I done my duty in the war.'

Vesta stared at Mirabelle, her expression a question mark.

'Oh no!' Mirabelle burst out. 'You're not suggesting that Mr Gillingham was a freemason?'

'Not just him. They're all masons in the force. Every one of them. They got it sewed up tight – not just the police but the magistrates, too. Every constable and all the sergeants and higher than that and all. The only reason I got the job when it came up at Wellington Road was 'cause I was good with the police dogs and I'd mind the desk on meeting days. They'd never have let me go when they did if I'd joined their stupid club, but I ain't one for all that. I'm not a Papist either, mind. Secret languages – worse than Latin. Symbols chalked on walls like Guy Fawkes. Me and Julie are Church of England, see, and they say that's fine. But Church of England ain't full of secrets, is it? Church of England is up front. We're normal.'

Without blinking, Vesta folded the remaining crust of toast neatly into her mouth and took a swig of Camp coffee. 'What exactly is a freemason?'

'It's a boys' club,' Mirabelle offered. 'Like Bill says. They have meetings and dress up, and there are all kinds of ceremonies. If you're a mason you have to help other masons and sign up to their code of honour. They call it a brotherhood.'

'Like the Girl Guides? But for men?'

'Sort of.' Bill shrugged his shoulders. 'With secret signals. Private handshakes. Codes. I had it up to here for years when I was in the force. I can tell when a copper's got something going on with the masons and I could see it today the way they were all hush-hush about that body.'

'Are you sure?'

'Yeah. I know how it goes. Honestly, I get the knock with it. Drives me potty.'

'The knock?'

'You know. It gives me the creeps. Ain't you heard of anyone getting the knock before?'

Vesta shrugged.

'I thought everyone knew that. Don't they say it in London?'

'Well, not in Bermondsey.'

Mirabelle decided to interrupt the debate on the ins and outs of Sussex dialect. 'So, what you're saying, Bill, if I'm not mistaken, is that the police are hushing up certain aspects of Mr Gillingham's death because he was a fellow mason?'

'Yeah. I reckon so.'

Mirabelle looked vexed. 'But wouldn't they be even keener to catch the killer if Mr Gillingham *was* one of their own? I mean, if one of their brotherhood was murdered, surely they'd want to make sure justice was done? What is it you think they're hushing up?'

'They removed the body sharpish, didn't they?' Mirabelle nodded and Bill continued. 'Yeah. So that's my question. Why did they whisk him off like that? It's all them secrets – gotta be. I was thinking about it, and it can only be one of three things.' Here Bill held up three fingers, folding them down one by one as he elucidated. 'Either the dead man was a mason and they're hushing it up because somehow they reckon he'll bring dishonour to the brotherhood. Or, second, you got to consider what had the killer done to the bloke?' Bill shuddered. 'And, that, we'll never find out. Once something like that's disappeared inside the station, it's not coming out again. So, they're hushing it up because it's a dishonour to the poor guy himself. Or,' here he lowered his voice, 'maybe it was them that killed Gillingham. Maybe he'd threatened to reveal something and they had to get rid of him to cover it up. *A heart that conceals and a tongue that never reveals.* That's their motto. I'm saying that it might be the freemasons that did it, see? The police themselves.'

Vesta laughed out loud. 'Oh, come on! Policemen?' Then her face dropped. The year before, her childhood friend, Lindon, had died in a police cell. No one had yet got to the bottom of what happened. Vesta's voice trembled. 'A white guy? A professional? With a proper job? And you think they might have knocked him off?'

'I always said I should have joined the East Sussex Force, but Julie wanted to stay in town,' said Bill. 'So I joined Brighton and I found out pretty quickly it's like coming up against a brick wall. They won't let you in on nothing. That didn't bother me. I had the dogs to see to. I prefer dogs to anyone. But, still, if you want to commit a crime in Brighton and get away with it, pick the time of the masons' weekly meeting. There's hardly a policeman on duty for miles. You can get away with murder easy.'

Mirabelle found herself wondering if Detective Superintendent McGregor was a member of the lodge. During the war there had been plenty of freemasons in the service. What Bill said rang true. There had been times when she'd worried the War Office was undermanned because so many men had shipped up to Holborn for lodge meetings. It was perfectly respectable. The King had been a member, after all. Still, Jack hadn't joined. He'd been asked but he wasn't the kind of man to join a club of any sort – he barely crossed the doorstep of the Athenaeum though his family had organised his membership. Jack always made his own way.

'Freemasonry? Hobnobbing in aprons,' he'd said dismissively. 'It's only mutual self-interest, Belle, and the only things I'm interested in are you and me. Oh, and winning the war, of course.'

Still, there was no denying that plenty of brave men had

taken up the invitation and not all of them had prospered as a result. There was something touching, Mirabelle always thought, when she attended the wartime funeral of a mason and his loyal brothers crowded the service.

'Do you know where the lodge is in Brighton?' she asked.

Bill nodded. 'Queen's Road.'

'Strange. I've never noticed it.' She got up to fetch her coat.

'They don't let in women,' Bill objected. 'You don't want to go getting involved, Miss Bevan.'

Vesta's eyes flicked from Bill to Mirabelle and without hesitation the girl sprang to her feet. There was no question where her best prospects lay for a more interesting Tuesday. Abandoning the day's administrative tasks, she pulled on her bright red coat and reached for her hat, her hand hovering over the office umbrella before she decided the weather was set enough to leave it behind.

'Come on!' she said in reply to the flash of Mirabelle's eyes.

'I'm not going to the lodge,' said Mirabelle. 'I thought I'd call in to Bartholomew Square to see Superintendent McGregor.'

'And then have a look at the lodge?' Vesta called her bluff.

Mirabelle conceded with the tiniest slump of her shoulders.

'Well, then,' Vesta smiled, 'I'll wait while you speak to Lover Boy.'

Mirabelle's cheeks flared. 'Lover Boy? Really, Vesta!'

'Oh, Mirabelle, the lady doth protest too much, methinks.'

In reply Mirabelle flicked her eyes to inspect Vesta's bare fourth finger.

'I like living in sin. Turns out I'm the type.' The girl frowned as she pushed her boss out of the office.

As they emerged into the sunshine on East Street, Mirabelle put on her dark glasses. Crates of fresh cod had just been delivered to the fish and chip shop and crushed ice dripped down the sides of the stack, pooling on the paving stones. A warm breeze fetched up the street off the open water.

'You think there's a case here, don't you?' Vesta ventured.

Mirabelle nodded. 'Yes, I'm sure of it.'

'And you want to get involved?'

Mirabelle didn't respond. Sometimes Vesta wondered how Mirabelle's mind worked. Potential cases presented themselves on a weekly basis at McGuigan & McGuigan – and plenty of them might have proved profitable – but Mirabelle wouldn't touch a single one. She had a horror of divorce settlements and family intrigues. Yet something like this – something grisly and dangerous – and she homed in like a missile. Vesta admired her boss's sense of justice but at the same time it mystified her. As they turned left towards the police station Superintendent McGregor was just leaving. His tall frame ducked into a car at the entrance. Mirabelle waved and he raised his arm as he clambered inside with his hat pulled low over his eyes. She reached out, motioning him to wait, but the Superintendent didn't notice, the door thudded shut and the car drove away.

The women hovered on the pavement.

'Well,' Vesta sighed, 'perhaps you'll catch him later. What were you going to ask him anyway?'

'I want to know if he's a freemason.'

'How would you figure that out?' Vesta watched the vehicle receding down East Street. 'Do you know the secret code? Is it a handshake? Or a special word? There's a code word, isn't there, that you can work into the conversation?'

Vesta had a dramatic bent that in the past had occasionally proved useful. Still, Mirabelle did not approve of it. 'Don't be silly. I'm sure there are masonic handshakes – different for different lodges – but it's only between masons, and I'm obviously not one of those. No, I was simply going to ask him.'

Vesta looked unimpressed. 'He'd hardly just tell you, would he? Bill said it's a secret society.'

'Freemasons don't confirm they're freemasons, or at least they don't have to, but they aren't allowed to deny it either. They have a whole Judas complex. If I ask him and he says he's not a freemason, then he isn't one. There's nothing dramatic about it.'

Vesta's eyes narrowed. 'What's going on between you two, Mirabelle? Have you been seeing Superintendent McGregor?'

Mirabelle looked startled. 'Only last night.'

'Dinner, you mean?' Vesta pushed her. Not that Mirabelle ate.

'No. I bumped into him. I went to the boxing and he was there. That's all.'

Vesta took a breath. It gave her a moment to think. There was no point in quizzing Mirabelle more closely. If there was a medal for dodging questions, rather than dodging bullets, then Her Majesty would definitely award it to Miss Bevan. In the two years Vesta had known Mirabelle she still hadn't scratched very far beneath the surface. When anything personal came up, Mirabelle iced over. It vexed Vesta that, to her boss, the whole world was a crime scene. It was as if she was always on the lookout for something out of place to latch on to – a knot to unravel that took attention away from her tightly coiled emotions. Still, at least it meant she'd always talk about a case.

'What on earth do you think this is all about, then? I mean, if McGregor is a mason, why is it important? It's only a bit of dressing up. A funny handshake and a secret meeting. Unless you think Bill's conspiracy theory is right.'

'I don't know yet,' Mirabelle admitted, 'but it's intriguing, isn't it?'

Vesta considered this. 'Queen's Road, then?'

'Let's go.'

The walk only took a few minutes from Bartholomew Square. As they climbed the hilly streets Mirabelle looked at the shining new aerials mounted on the roofs. She rarely ventured very far up the roads that led away from the front. Up here, the Georgian horizon was punctuated with a forest of thin metal branches sticking up from elegant buildings in various stages of disrepair.

'Televisions,' Vesta nodded. 'Everyone and his mum got one for the Coronation.'

'Yes, of course.' Mirabelle had listened to the ceremony on the wireless as the summer rain beat on the window. It would have felt intrusive to have a screen with a moving picture at home.

'We saw it on Mrs Agora's new set,' Vesta enthused. 'Charlie baked biscuits – Coronation cookies he called them – and Mrs Agora had us in. It's like having another auntie. A white one.' Hot from the exertion of walking up the steep incline, the girl fanned herself with a piece of paper she had folded for the purpose. 'Is it much farther?'

Mirabelle pointed at the street sign. 'No, just up here,' she said, emerging onto the main street past the church. She looked left and right along Queen's Road. There were pubs as you got closer to the station, and some offices and private accommodation. When she thought about it, there weren't that many buildings that might house a freemasons' lodge. 'Do you think that's the place, over there?'

'I can't believe we never noticed it before. It's really not much of a secret society, is it?' Vesta laughed. 'I mean, if we can find it just like that.'

The lodge was a wide, three-storey stucco building in good repair. Corinthian columns framed the doorway, making it look rather grand, which was odd on Queen's Road – a street tainted by traffic fumes and rubbish from the station. To one side, a small brass plate announced the building's function, and the front door was fitted with a large pane of glass through which a shadowy hallway could just be seen.

'I always assumed it was a church building,' said Mirabelle.

Vesta eyed the door suspiciously. 'You said they wear something like a uniform?'

'I think it's only an apron. And they have badges of office. I saw a suitcase packed with bits and pieces once when I used to work in London – little plaques and tassels. One of the senior fellows had it in his office. But I expect it's a different drill in different places. If you want to keep things secret you need to let each group have its own way, you see. That's how guerrilla organisations work. In isolated cells.'

'Aprons! Bill's right. Seems silly to me,' Vesta snorted.

There were no lights on in the building. Mirabelle rang the bell and waited. The tinny sound echoed inside. Nothing. Then she knocked. Vesta looked at her high-heeled shoes with concern, clearly expecting Mirabelle to encourage her, in due course, to break in. It had happened before. The lodge was not an easy target. It looked solid and impregnable. The girl squinted into the bright sunshine and fanned herself more quickly. She was visibly relieved when the door opened and a stocky, elderly man dressed in a brown caretaker's coat peered into the sunshine.

'Yes, ladies?'

'Is this the freemasons' lodge?'

'We don't allow women . . .'

Mirabelle held up her hand. 'We have come about Joey Gillingham.'

The caretaker looked blank.

'He's the journalist who was killed yesterday,' Mirabelle explained. 'Is there anybody who might be able to speak to us about him?'

The man's hair was so white it seemed to glow. He fingered the collar of his brown coat. 'Are you from the *Express* or the *Argus* or something?'

'Debt recovery,' Mirabelle replied. 'McGuigan & McGuigan, Brills Lane.'

The man stood straighter. 'No one here will help you with that,' he said. 'The fella was murdered, weren't he? He'll hardly be cold yet. It doesn't seem fitting.'

'Still,' Mirabelle pushed him, 'I'd very much like to speak to somebody.'

The caretaker paused. He looked Vesta up and down. 'Debt recovery,' he mumbled. 'Wait here.'

The door closed.

'Well, he's not coming back.' Vesta grinned.

'He will. They're men of their word, the masons. Their first priority is loyalty to the lodge, over everything else, but they take honesty very seriously.'

'And what are you going to ask if we get inside?'

'Don't worry. I'll get a feel for things.' Mirabelle propped her sunglasses onto the top of her head. 'I always do.'

Chapter 5

Actions are visible though motives are secret.

Five minutes later the door clicked open again.

'You're lucky,' the caretaker said, standing back to let the women enter. 'He'll see you.'

Inside, the building was cool. There was a pervading smell of dusty books. The hallway was paved with black-and-white tiles. An ornate cornice skirted the ceiling and there were plaster reliefs on the walls that depicted a field ready for harvest and figures in Egyptian dress. Inside, the building seemed on too small a scale to house such finery.

The caretaker pointed towards a closed door – the first on the right. 'In there,' he directed and retreated into the darkness.

Mirabelle knocked and entered. The room was large and it was unoccupied. The walls were painted yellow and hung with three enormous oil landscapes and a portrait of Sir Isaac Newton. Vast navy-blue curtains framed the long windows. Two crystal chandeliers dropped from ceiling roses, their vague shadows cast over the full height of the back wall. The room must face due east, Mirabelle thought. The morning sunlight streamed in on a set of comfortable sofas and generously proportioned armchairs that looked as if they had been in place for years. Dust motes whirled in the sunbeams. On a table there was a jug of water and some glasses.

'Do you think they'd mind?' Vesta asked, and without waiting for Mirabelle's reply she poured a glass and gulped down the water. 'Would you like some?'

Mirabelle shook her head.

Vesta perched on the edge of one of the sofas. She could feel the warm chintz along the back of her calves. 'It's very nice. It doesn't feel secretive or sinister at all. I can't see anything dangerous happening round here. Do you reckon Bill's just jealous? Perhaps this crowd never asked him to join – maybe that's his real problem.'

Before Mirabelle could fully consider this idea, the door opened on a balding man in his sixties. He was a rotund fellow, wearing a navy suit and a tie that sported an embossed military insignia that Mirabelle recognised as that of the IX Corps. Thin red veins were visible on his cheeks and he was limping heavily. He raised a hand, half in greeting, half to encourage the women to have patience.

'I say,' he said, 'we don't often have lady visitors. I'm John Henshaw, the chap in charge today. Don't mind this.' He indicated his leg as he settled himself in an armchair. 'Gallipoli. Got promoted to captain for it before they pensioned me off. Takes me a little longer to move around.'

Mirabelle joined Vesta on the sofa. 'The Dardanelles campaign,' she said. 'An honest foe. You must have been quite young, Captain Henshaw.'

This made the fellow grin and lean forward conspiratorially. 'Quite. I was straight out of school. Keen as mustard. By now I've had one leg for longer than I ever had two. I try to walk normally but sometimes I require a wheelchair. My wife says I *am* the resistance in that regard but I prefer to be on legs than wheels, and that's that. Thank you for waiting. Well now,' he regarded the women carefully before continuing, 'seeing we're playing a guessing game, if I didn't know better, from the look of you two ladies, I'd hazard that you were soliciting for charity. We hand out a good deal over the year – we like good causes here at the lodge. I'm informed, however, that you're debt collectors.'

'Yes. McGuigan & McGuigan.'

'Well, I never. And what can I do for you?'

'Joey Gillingham. The incident in Oxford Street yesterday. The fellow who was murdered. As I understand it, he was a freemason.'

'And the poor chap owed a client of yours money, Miss? Is that it?'

Mirabelle let the unanswered question settle into being a fact. Vesta looked away. She didn't like it when Mirabelle stretched the truth.

'I'm Mirabelle Bevan, and this is Vesta Churchill, my partner in the firm,' Mirabelle continued.

Captain Henshaw rubbed his chin. 'I'm afraid I can't give out details about our membership but what I can say is that Mr Gillingham was not personally known to me and I've been a member here for some years. How about that?'

'So he wasn't in Brighton on masonic business when he died?'

Captain Henshaw sat back. 'I couldn't possibly say what the chap was up to. How would I know?'

Mirabelle wondered what Captain Henshaw might do if she pushed him. She decided to try. 'As you can imagine, in our profession we have close connections with the police force, many of whom, as I understand it, have close connections here.'

'That's hardly a secret.' An edge crept into Henshaw's voice though he was still smiling. 'What specifically is it you want, Miss Bevan?'

'Mr Gillingham, or, at least, his body, appears to have meant something to the officers who first arrived at the scene of his murder. They removed his corpse without waiting for the senior officer to examine it. That concerned me.'

'Some members of this lodge are police officers, Miss Bevan. But it does not follow that everyone here has intimate knowledge of police affairs in Brighton. I myself, for example, am an accountant to trade. There are always dark stories of conspiracy about the freemasons but we're a simple bunch. Perhaps you ought to ask the policemen who attended the scene of the murder, if they were familiar with Mr Gillingham. I only read about the affair in the evening paper. I'd say I know a good deal less than you do.'

'But if it's a matter that pertains to the lodge, they won't tell me any more than you will. That, as I understand it, is one of the first rules of freemasonry.'

Captain Henshaw ignored this comment. 'Tell me, to whom did the chap owe money?'

Mirabelle played with her sunglasses. 'Captain Henshaw, if you think freemasons have a stringent code of secrecy, it has nothing on the code of honour between a debt collector and her clients.'

A shadow of a smile played on Vesta's face. Mirabelle really was something.

Captain Henshaw sucked his bottom lip and contemplated his next move. There was a flash of steely anger in his gaze – but only a flash. He took a deep breath. 'Well, that being the case, it seems to me you require Mr Gillingham's solicitor to register the debt for probate,' he parried. 'The poor chap came from London, I understand, so perhaps you should direct your enquiries there. As far as I'm aware he was not legally represented in Brighton. I'm sorry – there's nothing more I can do. It might have been better if you had been collecting for charity. I should have liked to have been able to help.'

Captain Henshaw hauled his leg into position and eased himself up in order to bring the meeting to a close. He grimaced as if this caused him some discomfort. Vesta wondered if it was painful, but then how could the leg be painful if it wasn't there?

'Takes a minute to get my balance,' he said.

She was about to form a question, to ask about his injury in a roundabout way, when there was a thump from beyond the room – as if something heavy had fallen elsewhere in the building.

'What on earth was that?' Henshaw was becoming annoyed. First these women arrived asking questions and now there appeared to be a disturbance. 'I don't know what's happening today. Giles! Giles!'

'Giles would be?' Mirabelle enquired.

'The caretaker,' Henshaw snapped as he struggled to keep his leg from buckling.

'I'll go and look for him if you like,' Vesta offered.

'No, you can't,' Henshaw objected. 'Visitors are only allowed in the hallway and in this room . . .'

Here he was interrupted by another thump, this time followed by a much louder crash. It was clear that the noise was coming from the room next door.

Mirabelle held out her arm. 'Let me help. We'd better go and take a look.'

Captain Henshaw reluctantly put his hand on Mirabelle's sleeve and found his balance. They made their way into the hallway while Vesta went ahead to open the door of the adjoining room, but before she could turn the handle Captain Henshaw withdrew his hand from Mirabelle's arm and motioned for the women to stay at a distance.

'I'm all right,' he insisted. 'I'll take it from here.'

Mirabelle and Vesta remained behind him as he turned the handle.

At first none of them noticed anything odd – or at least nothing that might have caused the noise. The room was in shade, but they could discern ceremonial chairs laid in rows around a central square. The walls were decorated with murals – the night sky in one corner and the sun in the other with a wheatfield just like the one in the hallway. The windows were small and set high on the wall. The modern chandelier edged with brass lilies was not lit and neither were the large candles on Corinthian columns that skirted the main meeting area. Everything seemed in order, almost church-like, Mirabelle thought. Then a low moan grabbed her attention. The noise had a ghostly quality because it was difficult to tell where it came from. Vesta felt the skin on her arms prickle.

'Stay there. I'll see to this,' Captain Henshaw barked as he limped inside and closed the door abruptly on the women.

Mirabelle let out a frustrated sigh. She peered towards the rear of the hallway, wondering if the caretaker might appear. The silence settled.

'This is a very odd place,' whispered Vesta. 'I've changed my mind. I think Bill might be right. Perhaps we should leave.'

Mirabelle regarded the girl as if she was a madwoman and was about to give Vesta her views about quitting the building just as something appeared to be happening, when another noise could be heard from behind the closed door. It was a high-pitched wail – an animal sound – and was followed by scraping as if Captain Henshaw was moving chairs across the wooden floorboards. Mirabelle's eyes flashed.

'I don't think you should . . .' begged Vesta, but Mirabelle already had her hand on the door handle.

Inside, Captain Henshaw was in the far corner. He hadn't realised the door had opened because his attention was fully employed in trying to lower himself towards the floor. This was a difficult operation, and Mirabelle realised the noise they had heard was the sound of his artificial leg scraping against the floorboards as he attempted to bend down. The fellow would probably be better in a wheelchair, she decided. His wife was right.

Then, from the corner, there was another wail, which this time could be identified as a woman calling out, 'Please. No. Please.'

Mirabelle didn't hesitate. She stepped inside and, at last, with a clear sightline she made out a body on the floor.

Captain Henshaw looked up. 'She's done for, poor old girl,' he said sadly. 'I'll see to it,' he insisted, waving Mirabelle off. 'You aren't allowed in here.'

Mirabelle ignored him. She dodged between the chairs. The body was writhing in small involuntary movements. As she got closer she could see it was an older lady, who was overweight. Her hair was dyed an extraordinary shade of auburn, which, Mirabelle could not help noting, was far too young a colour for a woman of her age. She was wearing a green tabard and white flannel gloves. Her body twitched as if undergoing an electric shock. Her eyes flickered open and shut. Then her hand flopped to one side like a dying fish on a dry deck.

'Get out. There's nothing to be done,' shouted Captain Henshaw. 'You can't just barge in. Give her some dignity, won't you?'

'Don't be silly,' said Mirabelle firmly. 'This woman needs proper medical attention. The poor thing's having some kind of fit. Look, there's foam on her lips.' She crouched to take her pulse. 'Vesta, call an ambulance,' she shouted towards the door, where the girl hovered uncertainly. 'There's a telephone on the table in the hallway.'

'What is it?' Vesta gasped. 'What shall I say?'

'There's a woman here and she's dying.' Mirabelle glared at Captain Henshaw. He'd wasted valuable time by not calling for help straight away. 'Hurry, Vesta,' she urged. 'Dial 999.'

Chapter 6

To investigate a problem is to solve it.

Superintendent McGregor would not normally have taken the call. An old lady having a stroke was hardly an investigative priority when you had a journalist with a slit throat on your hands. He'd made good progress today. Gillingham's sister had arrived from the family home in Gravesend to identify the body. She had made a statement to the effect that the previous week her brother had a big win on the flat at Brighton. Miss Gillingham was a blowsy blonde whose hands were covered in flaking skin – a misfortune that had not discouraged her from painting her nails pillar-box red. She said Joey had been winning a good deal of late and quoted with ease the details of some of his successful bets. McGregor mentally calculated how large Gillingham's debts would have to be for this good fortune not to alleviate them. It seemed unlikely, on balance, and the Superintendent shifted his expectations of the motive for Gillingham's murder accordingly.

'He wanted to buy a house up west,' said Miss Gillingham. 'He said he was going to find a nice girl and settle down proper. He was saving up.'

While she didn't know the name of her brother's bookmaker, she had certainly memorised details of his winnings, which if the figures worked out as she claimed, was not an inconsiderable amount.

'This week he laid five pounds at five to one to win on the two-thirty at Derby and that came in,' the girl dictated as if by rote. 'And another fiver at eleven to two on the four o'clock. We need to find the betting slips for those two. They'll be in his notebook. And he's got more coming up. Joey's good at picking winners. He keeps the slips inside the cover with a paperclip. They're mine now, Superintendent. I'm his heir and I want to claim the money.'

'What notebook?' McGregor asked.

Miss Gillingham frowned. 'He always carries his book. In his jacket pocket. Joey never goes anywhere without it. He noted down everything. I want that notebook back, Superintendent. All his tips are in there – the form for the weeks coming up. Joey wrote down everything.'

Miss Gillingham pulled a handkerchief from her pocket. It was canary yellow with a line of tiny black cats cavorting along the edges. The memory of her brother's note-taking was seemingly too much to bear as her face crumpled and thin rivulets of mascara dripped down her cheeks.

McGregor took a deep breath. If Joey Gillingham had been carrying a notebook it constituted missing evidence. 'We didn't find anything like you're describing on your brother's body,' he admitted. 'I can have them go through his things again.'

The Superintendent knew there was no point in this – apart from reassuring the crying woman. Gillingham's pockets had contained a roll of banknotes, some coins, a return ticket to London, a pencil stub, a house key and a packet of Player's cigarettes. Nothing else. Why hadn't he considered this? The girl was right. Joey had been a journalist. In all likelihood the assassin had removed the item from his body. And that altered matters. It provided a decent motive, especially now that it seemed Joey wasn't in the red. Maybe whatever Gillingham had written down had proved important enough to see him killed.

'What kind of information did your brother take down, Miss Gillingham?' he asked. 'I mean specifically.'

The girl stared. 'I don't know. Everything. Odds. Tips. Interviews. Quotes. Anything he could use.'

It was at this point that the call from Queen's Road came in.

'It's a suspected stroke, Sir, and that Miss Bevan is there,' Sergeant Simmons reported.

McGregor nodded. Simmons was right to inform him about Mirabelle's presence. The rate of corpses piled around that woman was astonishing. If someone was ill in her general vicinity, it would be best to check it out. He arranged for Simmons to finish the paperwork and have Miss Gillingham dispatched back to the railway station in a police car while he set off for Queen's Road.

The lodge wasn't far and the walk would afford him time to think. As he passed through the double doors at Bartholomew Square he wondered what Joey Gillingham might have noted that was worth killing him for? It had to be some kind of scam, and that meant the racecourse was the most likely place to turn up information. There was a meeting at Freshfield Road later that week. McGregor made a mental note to ask around and put together a team to work the bookies.

In the meantime, in the glare of the midday sun, the Superintendent worked through the options. He was so busy thinking things through that as he turned onto Queen's Road it took him several seconds to realise that there was an ambulance parked at a strange angle to the kerb. McGregor's mind shifted. This was his priority now. He could see that the front door had been left slightly open and he crossed the main road quickly, pausing on the doorstep for only an instant before he pushed the door wide to investigate the shady interior. He stepped inside, through the hallway and into a room to the rear. There, several figures were gathered around a writhing body with a straggle of unnaturally bright hair. A fresh-faced medic with a First Aid cross on his arm was trying to bring the woman round by slapping her face with some vigour.

McGregor tried to work out the layout of the building. This room faced westwards, and the placing of the windows meant it was impossible for it to be overlooked. It was set out for a meeting. What on earth was Mirabelle doing here, he thought as he watched her on her knees intent on helping the medic. Vesta sat hunched on a chair. Beside her, an old man with a wooden leg was straining to see. He looked upset. The medic struck the woman again and the older man flinched.

'Come on!' the boy admonished the twitching body. 'Wake up!'

'Is that really necessary?' the old man snapped.

The woman's cheek was scarlet.

'She's taken something, don't you see? It'll be too late by the time we get her to hospital. We've got to wake her up and get her to vomit,' the medic explained, lifting the woman's eyelids and making his diagnosis. 'I've got an emetic and a stomach pump in the van.'

Captain Henshaw's eyes hardened. 'It's too late,' he spat. 'Can't you see that? Don't you have any experience at all? How would you like this kind of treatment if you were dying? People you don't know crowded round?'

'We've got to try, Captain Henshaw.' Mirabelle's voice was steady. 'You can't be sure.'

'I've seen enough people dying to know when it's too late,' Henshaw puffed. So far, objecting to the intrusion had proved useless and the old man was clearly livid. 'Making the old girl sick won't help.'

The medic wasn't listening and as his plan of action unfolded, Henshaw realised that he was about to make the woman vomit here, in the meeting room of the Provincial Grand Lodge of Sussex. It was an eventuality that the old man hoped to avert.

'Could you fetch a bucket, do you think?' he asked Vesta. 'There's a wastepaper bin next door, where we were sitting.'

'Sure.' Vesta sprang to her feet, nodding to acknowledge McGregor as he stood in the doorway.

No one else had noticed the policeman. Captain Henshaw sighed, his leg rigid before him as, without waiting for Vesta to complete her mission, the medic pulled open the woman's mouth and inserted his fingers into her gullet, with a cheery, 'This might make her sick. If not I'll fetch the flush kit from the van.'

Captain Henshaw looked up and finally noticed the stranger at the door. From his seat, he put out his hand as if this might arrest the man's progress. It had been a morning of intruders, and as far as he was concerned McGregor had wandered in casually off the street.

'You can't come in here, old chap,' he said with conviction, tearing his eyes away from the medical procedure and directing his attention to the Superintendent.

'Police.' McGregor pulled out his warrant card.

'These are private premises,' Captain Henshaw explained. 'That's the thing.'

McGregor ignored this comment and the captain did not push the point. After all, the room already contained several people who patently weren't masons and really shouldn't be here.

'Who is she?' McGregor nodded towards the prone figure.

'Mrs Chapman. She's our cleaning lady,' said Henshaw, misty-eyed. 'Poor old girl. She's had it.'

Mirabelle raised her eyes and caught McGregor's glance before turning to the captain. 'And you allow that kind of thing, Captain Henshaw? Women in your meeting hall? Even if they're staff?'

Captain Henshaw shrugged. 'Mrs Chapman is not one for idle gossip. She's worked here for years. I was only a novice when we first took her on, fresh from my service days. The place has to be kept clean.'

Mirabelle's eyebrows rose. Then she returned to helping the medic by holding Mrs Chapman's head. So far Henshaw was right. The old woman was unresponsive. The twitching and moaning had all but stopped.

'I'll get that kit,' the medic said, rising to his feet.

But before he could, Mrs Chapman's body took a startlingly deep breath. It sounded as if the woman might suck the air out of the entire room. Her back arched violently, and then she fell back. Mirabelle had a sudden vision of an equation being solved, as if everything had found its natural balance. The room felt peaceful. She laid her hand on Mrs Chapman's glove just as Vesta returned, apologising for taking so long, with a small wastepaper bin.

The medic checked the woman's pulse. 'Well, that's it, I'm afraid. She's gone.' He pulled a sheet from his pack to cover the body. Vesta put the bucket on the ground with a decisive bang.

'I knew,' said Henshaw regretfully. 'You can tell, you know. I've seen the whole system collapse like that before.'

'Really, Sir?' said McGregor.

'The trenches, my boy. I don't believe in heaven or hell, but the front line at Constantinople was a good approximation of torture in a fiery pit. A regular Bruegel. Mrs Chapman was done for. I could tell by the way she was moving. All you people achieved was to make it worse for the poor old thing.'

Mirabelle let go of Mrs Chapman's hand. If she was dying she knew she'd rather that the people around her tried anything to bring her back. She motioned the lad to wait for a moment as she checked beneath the eyelids.

'Her pupils are dilated,' she said. 'Most irregular.'

'We'll do a post mortem,' McGregor cut in. 'I was told it was a stroke.'

'A stroke. Well, I can tell you now,' said Mirabelle, 'this poor woman didn't die of a stroke. She was poisoned. Her pupils and all that fitting – it's nothing like a stroke. I think her heart gave out in the end.'

'You're right. She's definitely taken something,' the medic confirmed as he smoothed the sheet covering Mrs Chapman's frame. He dropped his voice. 'Poison for sure. Some women find it hard these days. Was she a widow?' The lad directed the question to Captain Henshaw.

'She was. Her husband was in the RAF. Air Sea Rescue. He was a career serviceman, but it's been over ten years since he died. That was right at the start of the war. But . . .'

'It's tough on the widows. The grief can take them any time. We see a bit of that, these days. A lot of women reckon it's easier just to take something and pop off. Sudden, like. I've seen it before.'

'In the middle of cleaning a room?' Mirabelle sounded outraged. 'If you've taken hemlock you don't polish the silver till you go. Look, the poor thing is wearing polishing gloves and her cleaning uniform. It's not logical. If you miss someone so badly you can't go on, you curl up in a ball before you kill yourself. You want to be private. Quiet. Close to them. You do it somewhere that means something. You don't go to work and decide to kill yourself while you're in the middle of a domestic task. You disappear from the world, don't you see?'

An uneasy feeling crept over Mirabelle's heart. Did it sound as if she knew too much about the mind of a suicidal woman who had never got over a bereavement?

'This lady was poisoned,' she finished. 'She didn't kill herself. I'm sure of it.'

'Some toxins take a while to work.' The medic defended his corner. 'She could have popped something hours ago and thought it hadn't taken. Then perhaps she perked up, came into work and was struck sudden.'

Mirabelle looked dubious. She turned to Captain Henshaw. 'You say she's been employed here since 1918?'

'As long as I can remember,' he said sadly. 'Twice a week. Mrs Chapman has always been very reliable. She cleans the Pavilion, too. For the council. That's how we found her – I mean, when we first took her on. Perfect arrangement, really. She was part-time for them and part-time for us. She's a country girl – a hard worker. They recommended her highly and they were right.'

'But Brighton Pavilion's been closed for years,' Mirabelle pointed out. 'Ever since the war.'

Captain Henshaw was becoming annoyed. 'It's a former royal residence. It has to be maintained. And what the blazes has it got to do with you? Nosey parker. I knew the minute I saw her there wasn't any hope.'

'Perhaps I could walk you out, Miss Bevan, Miss Churchill.' McGregor decided to take charge before the witnesses came to blows. It was standard procedure to separate people as quickly as possible. Besides, he had questions of his own for Mirabelle and Vesta. As he directed the women towards the door, the phrase 'herding cats' came into his mind. 'Miss Churchill,' he motioned.

Captain Henshaw watched Mirabelle and Vesta fall into step. 'We need to have Mrs Chapman's body collected, don't we? By an undertaker. The old girl deserves some respect now, at least. I'll ask the caretaker to telephone.'

'Leave all that to me, Captain Henshaw,' McGregor said firmly. 'I want to speak to Miss Bevan for a moment, but I'll see to Mrs Chapman. If she's been poisoned, this is a potential homicide scene. I'll send for my boys. We'll be as quick as we can but we'll need to keep the body in situ for a while, I'm afraid. And we'll need to interview anyone else who was in the building this morning, too. So, please ask the caretaker to make himself available.'

Henshaw exhaled sharply. 'I'm going to phone the Chief of Police. This room is sacred. I don't think you understand.'

'I understand perfectly well, and the Chief won't say any different.' McGregor called the old man's bluff, though Mirabelle thought she detected a shade of uncertainty in his voice. 'If the woman was murdered, we'll need to inspect everything. Don't touch anything you don't have to,' he insisted as he held the door open for Mirabelle and Vesta. 'The medic will need to stay here, and if you could fetch the caretaker I'll interview him next.'

Henshaw didn't object. Instead he hoisted himself to his feet and limped in the direction of the door. 'All right, I'll get him,' he said. 'I might as well do something useful.'

Chapter 7

Practice forms a man to do anything.

'What are you two doing here?' demanded McGregor. He had bundled the women into the sunny reception room at the front of the building, which now seemed rather eerie. Mirabelle cast her eyes over the intricate carved wooden feet on the sofas and armchairs and wondered if Mrs Chapman had polished them with her white gloves earlier that day. She did not want to sit down.

'It's a free country,' Vesta managed to get out.

McGregor cast her a stern look that quashed all hope that that kind of reply would be adequate. 'A woman has died,' he said flatly. 'And they don't allow lady members in the masons, so how do you explain your presence?'

'We were interested, Superintendent.' Mirabelle's voice was smooth. 'That's all.'

'Interested? Interested in what? Next time you're *interested*, let me know and I'll send a uniformed officer to avert the homicide.'

'Well, if you're going to be like that . . .' Mirabelle took her sunglasses from her handbag, arming herself for the sunshine as she turned towards the door in a perfumed swish. She'd had quite enough of aggressive men for one day.

'No,' McGregor caught her by the wrist, 'I didn't mean to be unreasonable. It's only, what were you interested in *exactly*? I don't understand. First you were at the boxing last night and now this.'

Mirabelle looked pointedly at his hand, which was still

grasping her arm. The Superintendent quickly removed it. 'You're not a freemason, are you?' she said.

McGregor shook his head. 'My father didn't hold with it.' His voice was solemn.

'I thought not. I hoped not, actually, given how things stand. Well, I'm sure this won't come as a shock to you. You might not hold with the tenets of freemasonry, but most of the Brighton police force does.'

McGregor laughed. 'Some of them, probably. Everyone's allowed a hobby. It's the same at home. What's that got to do with anything? It's only a few police officers in a gentlemen's club.'

'It's rather more than a few, Superintendent. If my information is correct, which I believe it is, it's by far the majority of the Brighton force.'

'Even so, there's no law against it. The old duffer in there is pretty unfriendly but he's upset. The masons are harmless, Mirabelle. What is it you think you're on to?'

'Joey Gillingham's death, of course. And now Mrs Chapman. She's your second corpse with a link to this place, or at least a link to freemasonry.'

'There's no link between Gillingham and the masons.'

Mirabelle sighed as if her patience was being tried. 'I beg to differ. My guess is that's why your men removed Joey Gillingham's body yesterday and Bill Turpin thinks so, too. It's a logical explanation. Something about the body struck a chord with them because they were freemasons. I don't know what it was and I don't know why they felt they had to act, but I think it's why they whisked Joey Gillingham away.'

'Robinson?' McGregor sounded incredulous, but his eyes were thoughtful, as if he was working through the idea. 'Well, it would certainly explain how he's managed to hold onto his position all these years. He's a terrible detective, if I'm honest. Are you sure?'

'I'm more sure now. I don't believe in coincidences, and if

some poor woman dies in suspicious circumstances the day after Joey Gillingham's body is removed for what I believe are masonic reasons, and that woman dies in a masonic lodge, then my money is on there being a connection between the two deaths, or rather murders. It's something to do with the masons.'

'But Joey Gillingham can't have known Mrs Chapman. She's just a charwoman. These are two completely different crimes, Mirabelle, if that's what Mrs Chapman's death even turns out to be. One murderer's a slasher. The other's a poisoner, and that's only if the poor woman didn't do it herself. I can't see any concrete connection between the two victims and certainly not anything masonic. I mean, a cleaning lady from Brighton and a sports journalist? How would a cleaning lady even meet Joey Gillingham? Why would he be interested in her? I think you've got it wrong.'

Vesta stepped forward, furious. 'Because she's a cleaner? Or because she's old? My mum's had jobs as a cleaner and for that matter she's probably about the same age as the woman in there. They're people, you know – cleaners and old ladies.'

'I'm sorry,' said McGregor. This was all going wrong. It seemed he always sounded like a fool in front of Mirabelle Bevan. 'What I meant was that Joey Gillingham was a single chap in his late twenties and he lived on the other side of London, in Gravesend. Mrs Chapman was, what, in her fifties? She was a cleaning lady from Brighton. I doubt the two of them knew each other socially. I doubt they had a romance. I doubt . . .'

'Where did he stay?' Mirabelle cut in.

'What?'

'When Joey Gillingham came to Brighton where did he stay? Did he ever board somewhere?'

McGregor conceded it wasn't a bad idea. 'All right. I'll have someone look into it. But I'm not convinced, Mirabelle. And, in the meantime, you two need to let me do my job. If you could just remain in Brills Lane and collect a few outstanding debts it would be tremendous. You stick to your patch and I'll stick to mine.'

'Will you keep me informed?'

'This is police business,' McGregor objected. 'You can't go poking your nose in. It's not for busybodies or amateurs. Sorry, but it isn't.'

Mirabelle flashed her most charming smile. He remembered her using this technique the night before at the Crown and Anchor when she wanted information from unsuspecting men. Well, if that was how she wanted it, he'd play along. He might as well get something out of this apart from a half-baked conspiracy theory. A vision of Mirabelle dressed for dinner flitted across his mind's eye.

'All right,' the Superintendent changed tack, 'I can't say you're not helpful. Thanks for tipping me the wink. How about I keep you informed and you promise to keep out of the investigation? Why don't you let me take you for a drink this weekend? I can fill you in over a whisky or two and perhaps dinner?'

Vesta looked on incredulous as Mirabelle paused and then unexpectedly succumbed to the request. 'You know where I am,' she said. 'May we go now?'

Five minutes later the women were heading back towards the seashore. The sun was at its height and the hot dusty air from the traffic made the heat almost unbearable.

Vesta fanned herself furiously. 'You know where I am,' she mimicked Mirabelle's simper. 'That man is creepy, Belle. Busybody, indeed, and amateur. Hardly! Where would he be without you? He hasn't got a clue. Next thing you know, he'll want you to look after him. You'll see, he'll get his legs under the table and that'll be it. You'll be cooking him breakfast, lunch and dinner, and ironing his shirts, too.'

Mirabelle wished fervently that Vesta would sort out her difficulties with Charlie. It would make life, if not less complicated, then certainly less accusatory.

The girl continued, scarcely drawing breath. 'He tells you to go back to the office and you act like a puppy that's been told off. Do you remember when Panther first arrived and Bill used to give him a row? That's you – creeping back to Brills Lane. What's wrong with you, woman?'

Mirabelle pushed her sunglasses to the end of her nose and scrutinised Vesta. 'Who says we're going back to the office?'

A smile spread across Vesta's face. 'You don't fancy him then?'

'Don't be ridiculous,' Mirabelle scolded. 'I feel terribly sorry for the chap. Poor Superintendent McGregor had a dreadful time during the war. He'll probably never get over what happened to him.'

Vesta froze. 'Gosh. What was it?'

Mirabelle's wartime tales left Vesta breathless. Occasionally over tea and a biscuit they would get on to the subject of wartime heroism – the men who broke out of Nazi internment camps to join their compatriots or the bravery of those fighting in the field. Mirabelle looked on it as an education for the girl. Vesta had been too young during the fighting to realise what her hodge-podge of childhood memories actually meant.

'This is your history. Your generation's freedom is what we were defending,' she would say. Vesta had cried over some of the stories Mirabelle told her about women who had won posthumous medals. She seemed to have an endless supply of heroic tales of extraordinary derring-do, though none detailed her own wartime experience, over which she continued to draw an impenetrable veil. Vesta had given up asking anything personal. Mirabelle had signed the Official Secrets Act and that was that. She wouldn't talk about it.

'Even if I told you, you'd find it very boring. Really. I only worked in an office,' she always said. 'We all did our bit.'

Now Vesta's curiosity about the Superintendent was aroused. 'So, what happened to McGregor? I mean in wartime.'

'It's really none of our business,' said Mirabelle coolly.

Vesta did not give up. 'Did he go into enemy territory? Was he a spy? Did he kill people?'

'No, no. Much worse than that. He stayed at home, you silly girl. Don't you see? He had to stay at home while everyone else fought for their country. There's something wrong with the poor man. His chest. His feet. His eyes. Who knows? Maybe it's his heart. We should feel very sorry for Superintendent McGregor, Vesta. He'll never get over it. He didn't get to feel useful. And if I'm not mistaken he's also been recently bereaved. Poor fellow has had a dreadful time.'

'How do you know that? Has he taken you out for dinner already, Mirabelle? Really, you can tell me.'

'Honestly, Vesta.' Mirabelle turned up Old Steine. 'Will you stop using your imagination and use your eyes. Since January he has been wearing a plain gold ring on his pinkie. Most men wear a signet ring, but McGregor's looks more like a wedding ring – one slim enough to have belonged to a woman. My guess is that he's lost his mother. Can't you see the change? He seems sad, or sadder than usual.'

Mirabelle had a nose for bereavement. It was as if she was a bloodhound for heartache. The girl cursed her inattention – she hadn't even noticed the ring. 'What do you think is wrong with him, then? Why didn't they let him fight?'

'I haven't the faintest idea,' said Mirabelle as she cut off the main road. 'And I have to admit I'm relieved we're here, so we don't have to pry into the poor man's business any longer.'

Vesta looked up. 'Here?'

In front of her was a wrought-iron gate, behind which an overgrown pathway led to the entrance of the Royal Pavilion.

The building seemed to grow out of the jumble of plants that crowded its foundations. The curved white onion domes of the roof were like those of a fairytale castle. The fretwork that decorated the outline was like lace edged in soot and there were holes in the plasterwork. Sure enough, looking down, small lumps of dusty white stucco littered the ground. An illegible shred of paper pinned to the front door by a single nail was the last vestige of instructions to callers. Vesta squinted at it from a distance through the railings.

'Of course we came here,' said Mirabelle. 'Mrs Chapman worked at the Pavilion. That's what Captain Henshaw said.'

'But it's closed.' Vesta gestured expansively. 'The place has been closed for years. The gate's locked.'

'It's a former royal residence,' Mirabelle calmly repeated Captain Henshaw's words as she drew a lock pick from her handbag and grasped the gate's mechanism. She had been given an SOE set of picks as a gift from an old colleague the year before. Now she inserted the file and expertly flicked it inside the lock, as she continued to explain her reasoning. 'Someone has to clean this old place. Well, that was Mrs Chapman, I suppose. But it has to be looked after. It's not open to the public, but someone must be here at least part of the time.'

There was a click as the bolt inside the lock drew back and then a long creak as Mirabelle opened the gate.

'Come along,' she said, 'let's see if we can find them.'

Chapter 8

The richest legacy is honesty.

Charlie decided to deliver a plate of choux buns to McGuigan & McGuigan on his way home. Often on a Tuesday he'd pop in with a few treats that he managed to smuggle out of the Grand at the end of his shift. Some days it was slivers of cheese pastry or delicate strips of sponge cake. Today it was perfect little choux buns, filled with whipped cream and glazed with caramel icing.

'You fancy a cuppa, son?' Bill offered, getting up. He was glad of the interruption. It had been a slow day. Panther looked up sleepily and, not interested in Charlie, let his head drop back onto his paws.

'Where are the ladies?' Charlie asked.

'Couldn't rightly say,' said Bill, plugging in the kettle. 'They went out a while ago.' He checked his watch. 'Is that the time? They've taken it easy, I expect, in the sun.'

'Well, if they aren't here, perhaps we can have a special cuppa.' Charlie drew his hip flask from his pocket. He always had a slug of decent brandy to hand. 'Chef's privilege,' he said.

'Good idea, son.' Bill smacked his lips.

Charlie settled in the chair on the other side of the desk. He drummed a rhythm on the edge of the wood with his fingers.

'Tuesday's always quiet,' said Bill, letting the pot brew before he poured two cups and held them out for Charlie to add a generous tot with one hand while he offered Bill the plate of buns with the other.

61

'Is that real cream inside?' Bill asked, putting down the tea.

Charlie grinned. 'We've got a lot we shouldn't have in the kitchens at the Grand. We get away with plain rations in the restaurant, but room-service people want black market. If we make too many buns, then someone's got to have them. I always make too many buns,' he admitted. 'Matter of principle.'

'My Julie would kill for these. She's a baker – lovely scones – but we ain't had cream in a long time. So, are these on the turn?' Bill sank his teeth into the pastry nonetheless.

'No, man.' Charlie slurped his tea. 'They're just right. But my boss thinks they're on the turn. That's the main thing.'

The men were so occupied with their gastronomic break that they didn't hear the steps on the stairs. When the visitor reached the office landing, a vague outline hovered in the hallway, just visible through the frosted glass. The shape disappeared towards Halley Insurance and then reappeared. A few seconds later there was a tentative rap.

Bill looked up guiltily and placed the illicit plate of buns out of sight on Mirabelle's chair. 'Come in,' he called, wiping his mouth.

The girl who opened the door was slim, blonde and in her early twenties. She wore a short grey summer jacket and a small straw hat decorated with silk daisies and a trail of lace. She appeared uncomfortable in her clothes, as if this wasn't her everyday wear and she had dressed up especially. Under her arm she held an ochre clutch bag, so that her elbow was jammed uncomfortably into her side. Her lipstick was slightly smudged.

'Oh,' she said, unable to take her eyes off Charlie, 'I didn't think . . . that is to say . . . I heard there was a lady in charge. A police constable put me onto this place, up at the station.'

'Don't mind Charlie, Miss.' Bill's voice was as smooth as toffee as both men got to their feet. 'He's only visiting. Can I help you?'

The girl's eyes fell on the two empty desks. She didn't move beyond the frame of the door.

'Miss Bevan and Miss Churchill are out,' Bill explained. 'Is it a debt to be collected?'

'Are you Mr McGuigan?' the girl enquired, glancing back at the sign painted on the door.

'No. I'm Turpin. Bill Turpin.' He held out his hand.

The girl hesitated before coming into the room to shake it. She was wearing lace gloves. 'Yes,' she said. 'It concerns a debt. But I don't know who owes me the money.'

Charlie brought forward a chair and Bill took a pencil from his top pocket as she sat down.

'That's unusual. So, if you don't know who the debtor is, Miss, at least tell me how much money we're talking about?'

The girl looked as if she might cry. She shifted in the chair. 'That's the problem. I'm not sure. I don't know what he'd put on and what he hadn't got round to yet.'

'Put on what?'

'The horses, of course. And I don't know all the odds neither.'

Bill smiled patiently. He sipped his tea. 'Would you like a cup?' he offered. 'There's a hot drop in the pot. It's fresh.'

The girl shook her head.

'Well,' he tried again, 'it sounds complicated. I think we'd better start at the beginning. What's your name?'

'Ida. Ida Gillingham.'

Bill felt relieved that at least the girl could answer one of his questions. So far she had spoken entirely in riddles. 'Gillingham,' he spelled it out as realisation dawned. 'Ain't that the name of the fellow . . .'

'My brother,' Ida interrupted. 'Yes. He's the man that got murdered yesterday. I just confirmed his identity for the police. They've got him laid out, you see.' She reached into her clutch bag for her now crumpled yellow handkerchief. 'I'm all right,' she sniffed, smearing the last of her lipstick onto the linen as she blew her nose, 'but Joey's notebook's been nicked. He had all his betting slips in it. Joey picked winners and I'm his only living relation. That book is my legacy. The police tried to send me home. They ain't bothered about Joey's slips or the money he was going to lay. But I ain't going till I've found out what happened. Joey's winnings belong to me. He would have wanted me to have them. The bookie'll have to pay out. He'll have to.'

'Betting slips are bearer bonds, Miss Gillingham. It'll be difficult to claim money without having the slips in your possession. Do you know when the notebook went missing?'

'I dunno. But Joey always had it on him. Something's fishy, innit? I mean, whoever killed him might've taken it, but I wouldn't put it past the coppers either. It's worth a lot of money, that notebook – not just the bets laid but the tips, too. You can't trust the Old Bill, can you? Most everyone's on the make these days.'

Bill nodded. 'I can ask around. I know the force, and if someone's taken it I'll see what I can do.'

Ida considered this. 'What'll that cost?'

Bill looked serious, as if he was offended by the question. 'I won't charge you if I don't get my hands on it. How about that? And when I do, it's fifteen per cent of whatever we recover on your behalf. That's our standard rate. And if you've got a good tip on the gee-gees, Miss, I'd be glad to have it and all.'

'That's fair. You got a deal,' she said.

'Good. Now, where can I get hold of you?' Bill had his pencil poised.

'I dunno. Is there somewhere round here? Somewhere to stay?'

Charlie stepped in. 'My landlady's got an extra room, if you like. It's not too far. I'll walk you over there, Miss Gillingham. Come and meet Mrs Agora.'

Ida looked perturbed. 'Is she a spade an' all?' she said bluntly.

Bill almost choked on his tea. This made Panther sit up and take notice. The sky could fall in and Panther wouldn't pay any heed but if Bill sneezed the world might be coming to an end. The dog lumbered out of the corner. Ida reached out to pet him.

'Mrs Agora is as white as they come. Like milk,' said Charlie. He never took offence. It was just the way people were. Besides, it'd take too much time if he got hot under the collar at every ignorant remark.

'Well, I dunno,' Ida said.

'While we're asking questions of a personal nature, Miss Gillingham, could you tell me something about your brother?' said Bill. 'It would help with my enquiries.'

'What do you want to know?'

'He was a writer?'

'A journalist. Yes. He worked for the *Express*.'

'Did he belong to any clubs that you knew of? Did he attend meetings?'

Ida shook her head. 'Only race meetings. What're you getting at?'

Charlie held out the plate of pastries to Ida. 'Go on. You've had a difficult day.'

Ida peered. Her nose twitched. 'Cream cakes,' she said delightedly and then removed a glove, revealing the flaking skin on her fingers.

Neither man commented as she scooped a bun into her mouth. Bill took a sip of his tea without taking his eyes off her. 'So, he wasn't a mason, then?'

'What's a mason?'

'Secret meetings and that? Did you ever see him with badges of any sort? Reading books about symbols? Was he interested in that kind of thing?'

Ida hooted at the idea. 'Joey never read a book in his life. He wasn't a reader, he was a writer.'

'What was he interested in then?'

Ida licked her fingertips. 'Horses. Dogs. Fights. Anything he could bet on. Joey liked to win. I never seen him as happy as when he got a payout. He'd rather win a fiver than earn one. It was all about winning for him. He was like that since we was kids. We used to play cards for our sweet rations. He won most of the time. Rummy.'

'Was he superstitious?' Bill pushed.

'No,' Ida said very definitely. 'Joey didn't believe in anything except himself. Not really.'

'What was he like when he lost? On the horses or the dogs?' That was always the telling thing – what people did when things didn't go their way.

'He wasn't happy about it. You shouldn't speak ill of the dead, but let's say he wasn't happy and leave it at that. We stopped playing cards years ago. As soon as we weren't kids any more. We was orphaned, you see, but we stuck together. Joey looked after me. When I left school he paid the bills and I kept house. Lucky for me, he won most of the time.'

'You've no other family, Miss?'

Ida shook her head curtly. She stood up, pulling on her lace glove. Then she slipped the clutch bag back under her arm. Charlie wondered if now her brother couldn't take things out on her, her skin might heal.

'On second thoughts, why don't I contact you?' she decided, eyeing Charlie. 'I've got a funeral to organise, and Joey must've had a bank account, mustn't he? I better have a look for it. There's so many things to see to, Mr Turpin. Yeah. I won't stay. I'll ring you tomorrow. What's the number?'

Bill handed her a card. 'Don't worry, Miss. I'll find out what happened to your brother's notebook. I'll do my best.'

'I hope so,' said Ida. 'There's tips in there, and if we miss the races we need to lay money on, it's just cash down the drain. I'm trusting you, Mister.' She snatched the card from Bill's fingers and hurried out of the office as Charlie lazily lifted another little bun to his lips.

Bill shook his head. 'Sorry, Charlie. That kind of rudeness isn't illegal but it bloody ought to be.'

Charlie grinned. 'No skin off mine, man. You want me to come with you? I got nothing else to do today.'

Chapter 9

Look at yourself before condemning others.

Having knocked on the front door and elicited no reply, Mirabelle and Vesta took a turn around the Pavilion's gardens. Amid the tall grass and copious weeds, the roses were in bloom and a trail of vibrant laburnum dripped over the overgrown flowerbeds. At the edges, patches of mallow sent a peppery trail through the hot air. Closed for years, the Pavilion had been carefully secured. The doors were bolted, and most had been padlocked for good measure. All the windows were boarded up. Even with her standard issue lock picks, Mirabelle couldn't find an easy chink in the building's armour beyond the garden gate.

Vesta stopped to fiddle with her shoe. 'These heels were not designed for long grass,' she said. 'You're not going to find an easy way in, Mirabelle. You can't go housebreaking in broad daylight. It's a palace.' The girl waved towards Old Steine, only a few yards away over the Pavilion's perimeter fence.

'Ha!' said Mirabelle triumphantly, pointing at the side of the building. 'There's someone living in it.'

'What do you mean? There can't be. Look at the place.'

Vesta's curiosity saw her risk her heels once more as she joined Mirabelle back in the long grass. Almost hidden from view by an enormous clump of red ivy was a television aerial sticking up like a prong from a makeshift fissure in a boarded ground-floor window.

'Crikey,' said Vesta.

'It can't have been there long, can it?'

'Well, they're not answering the door. Who do you think's inside? Queen Victoria's lost grandson?'

Mirabelle did not grace this quip with a response; instead she extracted herself from the undergrowth and led Vesta back round the exterior of the building. They were almost at the front door when a man in a blue uniform unlocked the gate at the end of the path.

'Oi, you two,' he said as it swung open. 'What do you think you're doing?'

Mirabelle turned and squared up to him. 'Do you work in the Pavilion?' she said.

Answering a question with a question usually worked. The man adjusted his cap and altered his tone slightly as if he had only just realised he was speaking to a lady. 'Of course I work here. Parks and Recreation. I check the gardens. The public aren't allowed in, Miss.'

'I need to speak to someone who is responsible for this building.' Mirabelle stood firm, with Vesta behind her.

'What about?' The man fingered the whistle that hung from his top pocket on a short chain. It was only Mirabelle's demeanour that stopped him blowing it.

'It's about the woman who cleans the place.'

The man's moustache twitched. He leaned to one side, looking around her. 'There ain't no job for you here, love,' he said, enunciating the words with slow clarity in Vesta's direction. 'One of the council cleaners has done this old place for years. Nice old bird.'

'Oh, for heaven's sake, who works in the building? Who is responsible for it?' Mirabelle persisted.

'The council owns it, Miss. Then there's the restorer.' From his tone of voice it was clear that the man did not rate restoration work highly. 'The restorer's the only one who works here full-time. Making a list of the repairs the old place needs.

Course, they'll never be able to pay for it. I reckon they'll end up tearing the whole thing down and building something useful. People could do with something useful, not this white elephant. Amenities, like.'

Mirabelle eyed the overgrown vegetation. 'Well, you're not helping. This garden is neglected. Shouldn't you at least cut it back?'

'Summer, innit?' he said defensively. 'We send in a team once the leaves is finished. They do it all at once. This isn't a functioning public park. It's a plot, is all. I'm here to check it for safety. Once a week.'

'And is there anyone else?' Mirabelle enquired.

'From Parks?'

'From anywhere. What about this restorer?'

The man walked to the front door and fumbled with the chain in his pocket. He drew the whistle to his lips and blew it several times in succession. 'Takes a moment, dunnit? It's a big house and there ain't no doorbell. They built the walls thick in them days. They probably had some poor blighter sitting at the door all day in case of callers. S'only way to do it. No one would even hear the whistle on the upper floors, never mind a bell.' He took a deep breath and blew again.

'The gardens are very pretty,' said Vesta. 'The flowers are gorgeous. It just needs a little looking after, doesn't it?'

The man apparently found it impossible to address himself to Vesta in the matter of anything other than a cleaning job, so he ignored her comment and kept his eyes on Mirabelle. 'Wouldn't you be better making an appointment through the council? They won't let you in, but I'm sure you'd find someone who could help you at City Hall.'

Then, suddenly, behind him there was the sound of the door unbolting from inside the Pavilion and the man stepped aside. There, stood a slim woman in her early twenties wearing linen trousers, a brown shirt and round spectacles perched on her nose. There were smudges of dust on her cheek and she had tied a pretty green scarf around her auburn hair, some of which escaped at the sides.

'What is it?' she said, her voice like cut glass as she eyed the park keeper. 'Problems with the willow tree again?'

'It's this lady. She wants to talk to you.'

Mirabelle stepped forward and held out her hand. 'How do you do? I'm Mirabelle Bevan.'

The woman paused as if considering whether to indulge herself in a handshake. 'Daphne Marsden,' she finally announced, as if saying her name constituted a weighty decision. 'Excuse my appearance.' She ran a palm across her thigh and limply shook Mirabelle's fingers. 'Trousers are so much easier when one is up a ladder.'

Her smile revealed a gap between her front teeth. The girl's skin was as white as alabaster, and underneath her eccentric attire you could just pick out the makings of a classic beauty. Mirabelle removed her sunglasses. In an American military handbook she'd read some years ago it stated that people were likely to be more helpful if they could see your eyes when you talked to them.

'This is Vesta Churchill,' she gestured, 'and I'm afraid we've arrived with bad news. Might we come in?'

Daphne moved forward, blocking the doorway. 'Where are you from?'

'It's a private agency,' Mirabelle parried. 'This isn't an official visit. We have some news for you, Miss Marsden. That's all.'

Daphne stood her ground. 'It's not entirely presentable inside, I'm afraid. It's not presentable at all. People expect a royal palace, but the place is riddled with damp and we've had problems with the roof. There's fallen masonry in the Music Room. The Royal Pavilion isn't open to the public, Miss Bevan. It's dangerous, you see.'

Mirabelle stared pointedly at the man from Parks and Recreation. 'I think it would be better if we spoke to you in private.'

The keeper got the message and indicated to Miss Marsden that he'd be round the back if she needed him as he walked off smartly.

'When he said a restorer, I expected a man,' said Mirabelle and smiled. 'That's terrible of me, isn't it? Good for you, I say.'

Daphne brought out a packet of Camels from her trouser pocket and offered them to her visitors. Both said no, thanks. The girl flicked the bottom of the packet so that a cigarette popped up. She placed it between her lips and lit it. She seemed more relaxed now that the park keeper had left.

'I don't think a man would take this job.' She exhaled. 'There's no money in it, so they're stuck with me. Not many people think this kind of building is important, but I do. It's a hopeless case, of course, but it's still our history. Heritage isn't all about saving the countryside. I mean, that's what everyone goes on about – saving England's past and preserving the country – but these town buildings are just as important as watermills and ancient stone circles. And they're falling apart. If we don't save this one, they'll tear it down and build a bus station, you'll see. That's what that chap wants. Him and his like. Anyway, I'm doing my best to prop up the old place, but it's a bit of an uphill struggle.'

'Are you from the National Trust or Historic Monuments?' Mirabelle enquired.

Daphne smiled. 'The Trust. Fighting the octopus,' she declared. 'Historic Monuments don't really *do* women.'

Vesta frowned. 'What octopus?'

'The octopus. Haven't you seen it in the papers?'

Vesta shook her head.

Mirabelle prompted the girl. 'The octopus of development. Its tentacles spreading over England . . .'

When the daily newspaper arrived, Vesta always leafed through it, but she clearly wasn't taking in a thing. Now Mirabelle came to think of it, Vesta spent a good deal more time on the *Picture Post* than *The Times* or the *Argus*.

Daphne folded her arms. 'So, what's this news, then?'

'It's your cleaning lady,' said Vesta quietly. 'I'm afraid it's most unfortunate. She's dead, Miss Marsden. She died this morning.'

Daphne put her hand to her mouth. 'But Mrs Chapman was here only yesterday. The old girl seemed in such good spirits. She'd had a bash at the Dining Room. We're trying to stop the carpet going mouldy. What on earth happened?'

'That's the thing.' Mirabelle decided to take over. Vesta had been a little blunt, but the girl seemed able to take it. 'It looks very much as if Mrs Chapman was poisoned. That is to say, murdered.'

Miss Marsden seemed to take this information in her stride. She flicked the ash of her cigarette so that it sprang into the overgrown box hedge beyond the doorway.

'Poisoned? Don't be ridiculous. Who on earth would want to do that?'

'That's something I was hoping you might help us find out. Do you mind if I ask if you have any connection with the freemasons?'

Daphne smiled at the suggestion. 'Mrs Chapman certainly did. She cleaned the lodge on Queen's Road. There are only funds to have someone two days a week here, you see. The council makes a small allowance and whatnot. I don't know why you're asking me about the freemasons. I doubt they've had a fit of equality. They don't admit women.'

'No,' said Mirabelle. 'It's only because that's where Mrs Chapman died – at the lodge. The police are there now.'

Daphne glanced involuntarily behind her. It was a fleeting gesture, but Mirabelle thought it was telling.

'The police?' Daphne checked.

'Yes. Of course. I mean, when there's a murder, the police are always involved.'

'But that's absurd.' Daphne's eyes were hard. 'I mean, she was quite elderly. Probably her heart just gave out or something. You must be mistaken.'

Mirabelle and Vesta just stared.

The girl stepped back inside the door as if she was retreating. 'The police, indeed. They'll be at home up there at the lodge, anyway.'

'You seem well informed,' Mirabelle pushed.

'George IV was a mason. A Grand Master, in fact. Brighton's always been knee-deep in that kind of thing. Policemen, magistrates. Historically speaking, *gentlemen*.' The girl was babbling. 'Anyway, thank you for letting me know. I'll write a note to the council to inform them Mrs Chapman won't be back. Poor woman. They'll have to find a replacement, won't they? And there'll be a funeral, I expect. I shall telephone and find out.'

Daphne retreated another step as Mirabelle's mind flicked through the available information. Miss Marsden was behaving quite strangely, but she didn't want to jump to conclusions. The girl might not be paid much but she was wearing a well-tailored silk blouse. The television aerial hidden at the rear of the building meant she was here at night. She didn't like the idea of the police poking around and wasn't entirely comfortable at the idea of the local council becoming involved.

Mirabelle spoke as the idea fell into place in her mind. 'They don't know you're living here, do they? The council thinks you're coming in and propping up the old place, but you're living here and you don't want them to find out. Not him,' she pointed in the direction the keeper had taken, 'not the council, and certainly not the police.'

Daphne bit her lip. 'I don't know what you mean. That's actually none of your business. You've no right to come here and snoop.' She made to close the front door.

Mirabelle inserted a perfectly timed foot. 'No one has a television set at work, Miss Marsden. It's quite a luxury for a girl with not much money. It means you're here in the evenings and it means you have resources – perhaps not your own – but enough to provide an item like that and yet somehow not cover your rent.'

'Blow it.' Daphne paused to consider the situation for a second before she made the decision to come clean. 'Is it that obvious?' She sighed. 'Oh, all right. My uncle bought the television. He thinks I rent a place down here and he sent it from Harrods so I could watch the Coronation. My family are quite well off, you see. He sent me this silk square, too – just this season's colour. He doesn't have anyone else to shop for.' She touched the edge of the green scarf. 'It's kind of him. Really, I ought to try to find a proper job but I want to do this. It's important, but it doesn't pay. Not more than peanuts, anyway. They really won't find anyone else to do it, you see. Not easily. Are you going to tell on me?'

Mirabelle shook her head. 'No. Someone should be trying to save the old place.' It was a shame. At least a few people still cared about what happened – about history and what was right. The girl was well educated, but so many families these days couldn't afford to keep up their daughters' allowances. Unmarried girls who would never have considered taking a job in the days before the war were earning their keep if they wanted to leave home or, in Daphne's case, earning pocket money and making do.

Mirabelle hadn't had to take on McGuigan & McGuigan. She'd had an inheritance that afforded an allowance and the flat Jack had bought was in her name. But if she only kept house, she knew that her spirits would fester in no time now he was gone. She had that in common with Vesta, though for different reasons. Perhaps she had it in common with Miss Marsden, too. They all needed something to keep them occupied – something worthwhile.

'What is it that you actually want?' Daphne asked. She sounded angry but then Mirabelle couldn't blame her.

'We want help,' said Mirabelle simply. 'Vesta and I are curious about what happened. We'd like you to tell us everything you know about Mrs Chapman.'

'I don't really *know* the woman,' Daphne insisted. 'I only see her twice a week and direct her attention to where I think she might best be able to help.'

'You knew her better than we do,' Vesta cut in.

'Please.' Mirabelle held Daphne's gaze.

Daphne considered for a moment. The women hadn't threatened her directly but they had her over a barrel. 'All right. You'd better come in,' she conceded. 'Just as far as the long hallway. That's relatively safe. You need to be careful. There aren't any lights.'

Chapter 10

Friendship is a slow ripening fruit.

Bill and Charlie left the office with Panther at their heels. Charlie turned towards Bartholomew Square, choosing the shady side of the street, but Bill jerked his head in the other direction and into the sunshine.

'Wellington Road nick. We're much more likely to turn up something there,' he said, and they set off down East Street and along the front.

The Promenade was packed. The good weather had attracted a crowd of midweek visitors from London. For weeks England had been engulfed in grey cold drizzle, so when the sun finally came out, everyone wanted to make the most of it. Ponytailed girls sashayed past groups of boys in short-sleeved shirts and flannels, perched, captivated, on the railings. Around the pier the tantalising aroma of fresh baking rose on the hot air. At the shore, a pair of toddlers paddled in the water while their mothers stood patiently, brandishing thin towels in shades of overwashed grey. The deckchair attendants were doing great business, dispensing chairs and change to those who didn't want to sit on the scalding pebbles. Older couples watched the sea, dozed in the sun or read the paper. On the Promenade, two fresh-faced girls took photographs of young couples posed with the pier behind them, to be printed and picked up later.

'Gillingham's sister seems to care more about the money than she does about her brother,' Charlie mused.

'Death affects people in different ways, mind you,' said Bill. 'You never can tell what it'll throw up. You think people will do one thing and usually they do another. Something like that isn't always suspicious. It's just the way it takes them. In fairness to the girl, it sounded to me as if things swung both ways in her house and Gillingham cared more about the money than he did about her. Families, eh? My guess is that he battered the poor kid. You know, when he lost on the gee-gees.'

Charlie sucked his teeth in disapproval. 'Yeah, I thought that, too. You gotta treat the ladies right.' His mother, a formidable sparrow of a woman from Delaware, had imprinted this mantra on her son's consciousness along with the absolute necessity of eating good food, by which she meant copious quantities of cornbread and fried chicken.

'Yeah,' Bill grinned, eying Charlie up and down. 'You gotta treat the ladies right. Your lady, in particular, son.'

'Hey,' Charlie put up his hands as if surrendering, 'I want to marry Vesta. I asked her over and over. She ain't having none of it. I almost went up to London to see her father and ask his advice but I don't want to drop her in it. I don't know what to do, man. It's a sin – this living together. I know it's wrong. I just can't figure her out. She won't say what's on her mind. I thought all women wanted to get hitched, like they was keen on it, but not Vesta. I guess they broke the mould after they made her.'

'If it's a sin and it bothers you, you should move out.' Bill kept his eyes on the street ahead. 'No one's making you stay against your conscience.'

'I can't do that.' Charlie sounded genuinely shocked. 'After I've taken advantage of her? That would be worse than anything. Besides, I love her, man, and that's that. I just got to find a way to get her to see sense, that's all.'

'Have you bought a ring? A proper ring. A diamond?'

Charlie delved into his pocket and brought out a small black velvet box which he flipped open with his thumb. Inside there were three diamonds perched on a plain gold setting. 'I bought it from an antiques shop in the Lanes. I carry it with me all the time, just in case. I keep thinking she'll weaken.'

'You bought it from that fat bastard with the gold chains hanging in his window?'

'Sure. That guy's got connections with the London auction houses. I asked around. He goes up twice a week just to buy stuff. I took my time choosing this ring. It came from some swanky family who was clearing out. I saved up for it. And now I'd like to see it on Vesta's finger, but I tried everything, man. Everything. I sang to her. I *sang*. She wouldn't have none of it.'

Bill cast a sympathetic glance at the lovesick chef. 'Are her parents married?'

Charlie nodded. 'Yeah. I don't know anyone more respectable. I doubt the Churchills have a dark secret. I don't think there's anything she can't bear to come out. Though there's something on her mind, Bill, that's for sure, and I can't figure out what to do to make it right.'

The men fell into companionable silence as they approached Wellington Road. Bill bypassed the front entrance of the police station and headed to the rear of the building. He rapped on the back door.

A gimlet-eyed sergeant peered through the spyhole and let them in. 'Blimey. Ain't seen you in a while, mate,' he greeted Bill warmly.

'This is Charlie Lewis, Jim.' Bill indicated his friend. 'Charlie, meet Jim Belton. He's in charge of this nick. Isn't that right, Jim?'

Sergeant Belton stood back to let the men enter. 'I'll get the kettle on.'

Charlie regarded the policeman. There was something absurdly tidy about him. The buttons on his uniform gleamed. His shoes gleamed. Even his face gleamed. Charlie wondered how Bill had ever fitted in. Bill's hair stayed in place, but the rest of him looked like he'd fallen into a whirlwind. He always had an untied shoelace or a missing button or a tie that had twisted.

Bill smiled at his friend. 'Nah. Charlie and I just had a cuppa back at the office. Helluva day for it.' He pulled out a white handkerchief and mopped his forehead. 'Tell you what though, Panther could do with a saucer of water.'

'Always looking out for the dogs, eh? Good for you, Bill.' The sergeant went to the sink and filled a small bowl with water. As he put it on the ground, Panther fell on it, slurping furiously.

Bill laughed. 'Thirsty, are you, boy? Listen, Jim, I wanted to ask a couple of questions about that hack that got done in. Were you on duty? Did you see his body come in?'

'Yeah. I was on duty, at least. They took him over to the mortuary, though it was the boys from Bartholomew Square that handled it.'

'But you're closer here.'

'It's just how it got called in.' Belton shrugged. 'You know what the boundaries are like. There's always arguments. The super calls it our very own turf war.'

Bill put his hands in his pockets. 'So it was the boys from Bartholomew Square that itemised the bloke's possessions, then?'

'I suppose. Yeah. What's this about? Did he owe someone money?'

'Kind of. The thing is, they're saying that the bloke's notebook's gone missing. His sister's in a right old tizzy. The fella had all sorts inside including a few winning betting slips. Seems he was a demon for the horses. A sports hack – it ain't surprising. And the lady, that's to say, the sister's sentimental, like, about the slips that ain't been cashed in.'

'I can't see the boys over at Bartholomew Square . . .'

'Can't you?' Bill interrupted. 'Not a bent copper on the whole force? Not one of them tempted by slips that've got to be worth fifty, sixty quid, maybe more, and some solid betting tips besides?'

'You want me to check?' Belton sighed. 'I can ask around. Winning betting slips, eh? Off a dead man. Whoever'd do that would have to be a right chancer. The bookie'd know, wouldn't he?'

'Well, he'd probably take a cut then. The slips are missing, so someone took them. You're thick as thieves with Simmons, aintcha? He's in charge of the desk over there, and if anything got nicked on his watch he'll know. Discreet, like, Jim. Be careful.'

Belton nodded. 'Leave it with me,' he said. 'Mum's the word. Hey,' he addressed Charlie, 'ain't I seen you playing drums down the Lanes? On a Thursday?'

Charlie grinned. 'Sure. Every week. Tonight and Thursday.'

'Great stuff,' enthused Belton. 'Best night of my week, a Thursday. The wife's sisters come round and I get out sharpish. I'm glad to meet you, mate. I love a spot of jazz. You working for those women, too, then? It's turning into a hive of industry at McGuigan & McGuigan. Looks like the debt collection business is booming.'

'Nah,' Charlie said shyly, 'I'm just a friend.'

'Don't go knocking it, Belton,' said Bill. He knew his old colleagues thought it was hilarious that he was working for a company where there were two women in charge. He got teased in the pub about it regularly. 'Miss Bevan and Miss Churchill are smart as whips, and they're fair with it.'

'Bit of a change from the force though.' Belton laughed.

'Laugh all you like, mate.' Bill folded his arms. 'They got lady police officers all over these days.'

'WPCs.' Belton emphasised the letters. 'And we ain't got any. There's two at Bartholomew Square. They deal with the missing children off the beach.'

'Matter of time,' Bill said sagely. 'They'll get promoted. Things are changing. There'll be lady sergeants. Inspectors, even. Detectives. Mark my words. It's coming your way.'

Belton grimaced. 'Not on my watch, sunshine. The lads'd start a revolution.'

Bill smiled and shrugged as if to say that Belton's approval was by the by.

Chapter 11

Trust not too much to appearances.

The air was cool inside the Royal Pavilion. It was hard to believe the sun was splitting the stones outside. Vesta shivered as she followed Mirabelle and Daphne Marsden up a short flight of stairs, through a lobby and into a long corridor with a grubby threadbare carpet. Mirabelle peered at the ceiling. It was made of coloured glass and absolutely filthy. The dust of decades of neglect peppered the skylights, and the watery, tinted light made the place seem even more shabby.

Lighting another cigarette, the girl led them up the hallway past vacant Chinese plant pots and gilded mirrors towards a pool of bright natural light at the foot of a staircase. The balustrade appeared to be constructed out of bamboo, but on close inspection Mirabelle realised that it was intricately carved wood. At the bottom of the steps there were two sofas upholstered in fraying blue silk.

'The old place wasn't built to survive without staff,' Daphne explained. 'Queen Victoria neglected it before she sold it to the council. She hated it here. Too many kids to make it workable, I expect, even as a holiday home. And the bedrooms are small for a royal residence.'

Vesta stared at a life-size burnished ebony statue of two black men wearing turbans that she could just make out in the shadows of a room that led off the hallway. It was as if they were waiting to give service, perpetually frozen. She shuddered and forced herself to look away. 'Has it been left just as it was?'

Daphne shook her head. 'It used to be properly habitable. And it used to be fully furnished. Queen Victoria retained the contents when she sold it but she gifted things back now and then. In the late nineteenth century they did some restoration work – not the kind of thing we do today but it propped the old place up for a while. Then it was used as a hospital. Occasionally I find things from the early days in the cupboards. There was a day dress that must have belonged to George IV's daughter, Princess Charlotte. It was sewn with gold thread. I sent it to London – to a friend at the Victoria and Albert Museum. For safe keeping and whatnot.'

Mirabelle took in the state of the sofas. A copy of an illustrated magazine, a tattered *Complete Works of Alfred Lord Tennyson* and an overflowing gold ashtray that looked like it was the butter dish from a very fancy dinner service betrayed the fact that Daphne spent at least some of her day here. She tried to imagine what the place would be like at night with its long unlit corridors and looming artworks. 'Don't you get afraid on your own?'

'Ghosts, you mean?' Daphne snorted. 'I don't believe in that kind of thing. And as for intruders, well, the place is pretty secure. The only thing that makes me nervous is the falling masonry. Now that really could do some harm. I keep out of the way when there are high winds. Afterwards I sweep up whatever's fallen and keep it. One day there'll be money for a stonemason and we'll have it all reinstated. The Music Room needs a lot of that kind of work.'

Mirabelle nodded. There was nothing to be afraid of here. The girl was quite right. Still, she was plucky. Mirabelle admitted to herself that she wouldn't relish staying in the old palace alone with no light other than a candle. The place teetered on the cusp of grandeur and squalor. It was an uneasy accommodation.

'I have storm lamps,' Daphne conceded. 'And there's running water. The water closets work. It's a lot better than you'd expect.'

'Where do you sleep?'

'There's a camp bed,' the girl said. 'Look, do we have to go through all this? I thought you wanted to know about Mrs Chapman.'

Vesta perched on the edge of one of the sofas. 'But how do you cook?'

Daphne let out an exasperated sigh and dropped onto the plump cushion at the other end of the sofa. This sent three small white feathers sailing onto the floor where they joined several more. The sofa had evidently not been moved and the cushion had not been repaired for some time. The girl stubbed out her cigarette in the butter dish.

'George had extensive kitchens built when he commissioned the early renovations from Henry Holland in 1787. I keep my Primus there – I didn't want the house to smell of tinned soup. The kitchens don't function but they have adequate ventilation – you can open the skylights with a stick. I try to use the old place respectfully. I don't eat in the dining room, if that's what you're about to ask. At the weekends I visit friends. The railway station is very convenient. You can get practically anywhere from Brighton these days.'

Mirabelle hovered at the bottom of the staircase. She wanted to have a look around. 'Do you know where Mrs Chapman lived, Daphne?'

Daphne's features betrayed relief at the spotlight being off her illicit activities. 'Miles out. Patcham, I think.'

'Do you know if she took in lodgers?'

'I haven't a clue. She never mentioned anyone. Honestly, I only saw her twice a week – Mondays and Thursdays. I'd let her in. When she first started, she dusted. Can you imagine? In all this disarray she got out a feather duster and some beeswax and off she went. As if that would help. Anyway, I redirected her attention. Less dusting, more of the important stuff. Lately I've had her do some of the donkey work on the textiles. She's saved a few early curtains. Not originals – George IV got rid of those – but there are a couple left from his first round of renovations. The place is rotting, you see, as well as falling apart. I had Mrs Chapman dry the fabric and treat the mould. The old girl was working on the carpets. She wasn't bad. You have to have an eye for detail. A lot of restoration work isn't difficult, it's just slow and repetitive. Mrs Chapman wasn't interested in the place's history but she got caught up in the job. She wanted to see it done correctly. So textiles became her bag.'

'Did Mrs Chapman know that you live here?'

Daphne eyed Mirabelle. 'Come off it! You think I knocked her off because she caught me camping? What's your interest in this, if you don't mind me asking? You aren't just some kind of ghastly busybody, are you?'

'At the least.' Mirabelle smiled. 'You're the second person to call me a busybody today. Let's just say I don't like seeing people die unnecessarily. And you haven't answered my question. Did she know what you were up to?'

Daphne shrugged. 'I sleep in one of the Yellow Bow Rooms at the back of the building. The Duke of Clarence's, if you must know. It's where I keep my clothes. Mrs Chapman has never been there, though. She brings a sandwich that she eats wherever she's working. She's never voiced any suspicions about my presence. Why should she? I didn't chat to her much – she was only the cleaning lady. I issued instructions and kept an eye on her work, that's all. She came in, did her seven hours and left. It's not as if we were friends.'

Vesta's eyes flashed at the implication, but she managed to bite her tongue. 'When was Mrs Chapman here last?'

'Yesterday. She arrived at eight thirty in the morning and left at four.'

'Is there anything poisonous she could have come into contact with in that time?'

Daphne considered. 'You mean, might she have accidentally ingested poison while she was here? Well, there's lead paint in some of the rooms, but she'd have to have licked the walls for that to have an effect. And there's none in the Yellow Bow Rooms, before you ask. Some of the cleaning fluids are probably toxic, and the stuff I use to treat woodworm definitely is, but she was cleaning carpets the last few times she was here so she was only handling carpet shampoo. So, no, there's nothing poisonous that she could have swallowed inadvertently unless she ate some of the mushrooms that are growing where the wood is rotten. She wasn't stupid. And, in any case, if she'd done that, she'd have been ill yesterday – that kind of thing is pretty immediate. I don't think she was poisoned here. Honestly, are you sure the old girl didn't just eat a dodgy sandwich before she popped off? If she was poisoned at all.'

Vesta shifted uncomfortably. Mirabelle's steady gaze held Miss Marsden's pale eyes without blinking. She wondered if anyone really cared about anyone else these days. Things had changed a good deal since the war.

'Mrs Chapman died in a fit on the floor of the lodge on Queen's Road. Her heart gave out and she stopped breathing about an hour ago. I was holding her head,' she said. 'Her pupils were dilated. She was frothing at the mouth and then she fell unconscious. That isn't caused by an iffy sandwich, Miss Marsden. That's chemical poisoning. That's deliberate. It's strange that you don't appear to care. The poor woman was probably murdered.'

'That's unfair. It isn't that I don't care about the old stick. Of course I'm sorry she's dead, but if it's murder, isn't it really a police matter, Miss Bevan? I mean, if Mrs Chapman was poisoned they'll find out how when they do a post mortem. I still don't understand what you're doing here. Not really.'

Mirabelle ignored the girl's comment. If the fact that she had been present when the old lady died didn't explain her presence adequately there was little she could add. She changed tack. 'And she hadn't come into money of late?'

Vesta got up from the sofa and wandered to the door of the darkened room. She peered past the slave figures. 'She doesn't know, Mirabelle. Miss Marsden doesn't pay attention to insignificant details concerning insignificant people. Servants, that is.'

Daphne rolled her eyes. She flicked another Camel out of the carton and lit it. 'All right,' she said. 'I don't know if Mrs Chapman had suddenly come into money. But she turned up for work so she can't have come into that much money, can she? Look, I'll show you her apron if you like – her dusters and whatnot, if you care so much.' The girl's voice was sarcastic now. 'She used a cupboard at the other end of the building. They're the only things she kept here.'

Mirabelle and Vesta turned towards her in absolute unity. 'Yes,' they chimed together.

Vesta grinned at Mirabelle. 'Maybe we're both busybodies,' she said.

The Pavilion might have been on a small scale for a royal palace but it felt labyrinthine. Daphne lit a storm lamp and set out along the gloomy corridor once more. It was clear she had expected the women to refuse her offer.

At the far end of the hallway there was a concealed door that was flush with the sweep of the wall. Daphne opened it. The light from the storm lamp sliced into a void of pitch black. Mirabelle could just make out some chipped paintwork and a stone floor. Compared to the ornate decoration of the public hall this corridor looked positively monastic, though it smelled less damp. There was perhaps less to rot away.

'The servants' side of the operation,' Daphne explained. Their heels echoed now they weren't walking on carpet. 'No one wanted to see the staff at work, so there are passages to keep the business of the house out of the way.'

Mirabelle heard Vesta tut in the dark. 'So they had everyone sneaking around?'

'Yes,' Daphne continued breezily. 'You see it all over the place. Like most stately homes, the Pavilion is really two houses intertwined – the service house and the royal one. Buckets of coal and housemaids were kept off the corridors. In some houses they had the servants move entirely underground, but this place already had its foundations in place when George took it over. Over a hundred people lived here – residents and staff . . . Now it's only me.'

She led the way into a pantry. Mirabelle could just make out a wall of pale wooden cupboards behind a plain scrubbed-pine table. Lifting the lamp high Daphne opened one of the doors and continued. 'I think this room was for the footmen. It's convenient for the front doors and the hallways. The rest of the cupboards are empty. This is the one Mrs Chapman used.'

Mirabelle peered inside as Daphne held up the lamp. A grey apron with posies of lavender printed onto the fabric hung on a solitary hook. To one side there was a feather duster, a pile of rags and a bucket. The cupboard smelled faintly of bleach. Mirabelle reached in and checked the pocket of the apron. It was empty.

'Nothing much to see.' Daphne's voice was drenched in told-you-so.

Vesta, however, fell to her knees. Beyond the main beam of light, the bottom of the cupboard was lined with something. She reached in and pulled out some tattered sheets of paper, holding them up to the lamplight. The sheaf was patterned with newsprint and stiff with dirt. There was an indent and smears of mud where Mrs Chapman must have placed her outdoor shoes.

'It's a racing paper,' Vesta said triumphantly, reading the text sideways. 'From May this year. Well, well. Our Mrs Chapman liked the horses. That has to be how she knew Joey Gillingham. We've found the connection.'

Chapter 12

A tragedy need not have blood and death.

That evening, when Mirabelle locked the office door, it was almost seven o'clock. By five, everyone else had been ready to leave. Bill wanted to chase up information about Joey's notebook on his way home and Vesta was being picked up by Charlie. The young couple planned to go for a walk in the evening sunshine before it was time to disappear into the maze of the Lanes and Charlie took his place at his drum kit. All afternoon there had been snatches of music from the direction of the pier – songs from the American hit parade, Mirabelle guessed. The notes rose high on the heat and seeped into the houses, flats and offices opposite the seashore and just behind. Vesta's ankle beat out the rhythm, one high-heeled shoe dangling from her foot as she kept time.

'We're going to pick up fish and chips.' The girl checked her vermilion lipstick in the mirror of a compact her mother had given her when she left home three years ago. Much of the inlaid diamanté had fallen out and the design of intertwined roses on the surface was scratched. As she got up to pull on her red coat she turned. 'Won't you come with us, Mirabelle? It's such a gorgeous evening.'

'Come on, ladies.' Charlie checked his watch. 'There'll be a queue at Shackleton's by the time we get there – best fish and chips in town.'

This started a debate with Bill who swore by Bardsley's, especially for the haddock. The extra walk, he said, was worth it.

Mirabelle sighed. All this banal talk meant nothing. Two people were dead. 'I'm not hungry,' she said and waved them off. 'I'll finish here.'

As the door closed and the sound of footsteps descended to the street Mirabelle could still discern the tenor of Vesta's voice, the men a bass line below her, debating the quality and quantity of chips in their chosen establishments and the merits of salt and vinegar in differing proportions.

Alone at last, Mirabelle leaned back in her chair and shut her eyes. God, she could do with a whisky. She had spent most of the afternoon trying to piece together the jigsaw that had landed on her desk. As yet there was too much that was uncertain, and Bill's intermittent comments and Vesta's fanciful attempts to construct a whole picture out of what could only be described as intriguing scraps had made it difficult for her to focus. Jack always said a good agent had to keep an open mind and stick to the facts. There had been times when Vesta seemed to wilfully ignore not only one but several facts simply to make a theory fit. Perhaps that was why the girl was so good with paperwork. She could make connections between people and events that seemingly weren't connected at all. It had stood her in good stead when she worked at Halley Insurance down the hall, and even here at McGuigan & McGuigan the skill proved occasionally useful even if it wasn't what was required at this stage of an investigation.

Mirabelle considered Joey Gillingham, his notebook and his sister on the one hand and Mrs Chapman, her interest in horse racing and her cleaning duties on the other. After almost two hours, there were still only two things that appeared to hold the murders together – the masons and the horses. The nub of the matter, she realised, might be either of these or, indeed, both. Certainly, the journalist and the cleaning lady had connections at the racetrack and possibly at the lodge. But they had died so differently. A murderer usually killed by one method or another – slitting a man's throat was quite a different matter from poisoning an old woman. Perhaps it indicated two separate murderers who may or may not be working together.

Mirabelle pulled on her summer jacket, turned the key in the lock and walked down the stairs and onto the street. Outside, the air was still thick with the heat of the day and there was a palpable air of excitement in the streets. She pulled out her sunglasses and began to walk up East Street. This was not her habitual route home but she had a call to make.

Bypassing Bartholomew Square police station and casting only a cursory glance at the dark window of Detective Superintendent McGregor's office, she disappeared into the lanes beyond the Victorian edifice. In the sunshine the ramshackle buildings looked more like the remains of a medieval village. The sounds of heated discussions and gales of laughter emanated from the pubs.

When Mirabelle first arrived in Brighton these streets were the narrowest she'd ever seen. In places the russet pantiles of one house kissed those of another across the cobbles. These, however, weren't the smallest lanes in Brighton. This way and that, passageways the width of a garden gate snaked off, and now Mirabelle disappeared down one. There wasn't enough room for two people to pass. Where a pedestrian encountered anyone else they had to slip past sideways. There was no proper pavement either, just a rough stone gutter down the side of the beaten earth.

Mirabelle kept her eyes down. It was easy to trip on the uneven surface. She didn't like to think what it must be like at night – the street lighting at either end didn't extend over the pathway. But that was why Fred had decided to locate himself here – tucked conveniently out of the way, only accessible once you knew where to go. The passage was used by drunken old men out of their minds on Blue Billy – a lethal mixture of methylated spirits and Brasso – and by young lovers looking for somewhere to go in the half-light on their way home. The police rarely came here.

About two thirds along, Mirabelle stopped. To the left there was a row of tiny cottages – all but one abandoned. This, she knew, was far too picturesque a description – the cottages were slums. The wooden frames of the filthy windows were split and rotten, and the doors were spattered with mud as high as the handles. The roof had caved in on one, and the stench from privies concealed behind the facades pervaded the air. Mirabelle slipped her sunglasses into her bag and knocked on the green door.

The man who opened it was more dapper than might be expected. In his early forties, he wore an immaculate white shirt tucked into a pair of tweed trousers and stood six foot in his well-polished brown brogues. The scent of aftershave, a breath of sandalwood, emanated from his person. His eyes brightened when he saw who was standing on the doorstep.

'Miss Bevan.' He stepped back, running his hand over his greying hair. 'Please come in.'

Mirabelle glided over the threshold. Inside, the room was lit by three gas lamps. The atmosphere was dank, as if the summer sunshine had never penetrated the cottage. Mirabelle couldn't see the walls because there were boxes piled as high as the ceiling. In fact, the room was almost full. Apart from a few passages between his illicit stock and a small area he'd cleared so he could sit down, the place was at full capacity – all of it black market.

'Fred,' Mirabelle nodded in greeting, 'good evening.'

'I'm glad to see you.' Fred smiled. 'You've come for a bottle of malt?'

Mirabelle shook her head.

'I ain't got more of those chocolates, I'm sorry to say.'

The chocolates had been for Vesta's birthday. She perched on the edge of a pile of boxes that appeared to contain tinned orange juice on the bottom layer and behind her a loosely woven basket of fresh eggs.

'Well, perhaps I will take some Glenlivet if you have it, Fred, but it's not really what I came for.'

Fred disappeared among his stock. 'I got lovely bottles of French perfume. Shalimar,' he called. 'Difficult to come by. You can't pick up this stuff even in Burlington Arcade these days.' He peered from behind the boxes but Mirabelle shook her head. She wore Chanel. Always had.

'Stockings, then? Silk. Fine gauge. American.'

Mirabelle's eyes fell to her calves. She hadn't worn stockings today – not only because of the weather, but because she was running out and didn't want to waste what she had. It mattered less in the good weather. Or perhaps her standards were slipping. She considered this as she enquired how much they were.

Fred appeared holding a bottle of whisky which he laid on top of a wooden packing case cum shop counter. 'Daylight robbery, of course,' he grinned, revealing toothy gaps in his smile. 'You need a nice fancy man to see you right, Miss Bevan. You shouldn't be paying for all this yourself. Mr Duggan wouldn't have wanted you to be on your own.'

Mirabelle froze. Fred was one of the very few people who knew about her affair with Jack. He'd been one of Jack's agents in the early days. Jack always said he was a survivor. 'Fred's the cream,' he said. 'It's effortless for him. He'll always rise to the top, doesn't matter where you put him. War or no war, Fred'll always do all right.'

When Fred had gone missing in the south of France in 1942 Jack had refused to give up on him and, sure enough, he surfaced seven months later, arriving back in England off a ship from Bilbao. In an attaché case he carried a German code-book he'd picked up in mysterious circumstances and in a leather trunk he'd smuggled a nine-year-old Jewish boy who had been orphaned.

'I couldn't help myself,' he'd said with a beaming smile. 'Now you're gonna want to debrief me, aintcha? The old Marylebone Hotel, eh? Well, let's get on with it. You best check I'm not a double agent now I've a kid to look after.'

He was irrepressible. Some of the situations Fred had faced might crush another man, but Jack said he was an ideal agent – solid as they came. And despite his Cockney accent he spoke French as if he'd been born there.

When Fred turned up in Brighton earlier that year, Mirabelle wasn't surprised he was pushing goods on the black market. He'd always had that edge – right and wrong were relative to him, not absolute. He was some kind of magician. That's probably how he'd survived. She'd bumped into him coming out of a pub on the Lanes.

'Miss Bevan!' he'd greeted her delightedly, as if the last time he'd seen her had been a jolly social occasion perhaps a week or two before. 'I didn't know you was in Brighton. How's Mr Duggan? Has he made an honest woman of you yet?'

It had been difficult to tell him about Jack's death but what else could she say when he asked after his old spymaster?

'Oh, I'm sorry, love. I'm so sorry,' he said. 'You come and visit me. I got a place just round from the Black Horse. Past the pub and turn down this little path you'd miss if you didn't know it was there. Ignore the tramps – they ain't no real bother. Green door. I got whatever you're after.'

If she hadn't known him from her wartime days she'd never have considered it. As it was, Mirabelle had wanted to buy Vesta a box of chocolates for her birthday and a bottle of nice whisky for herself. The truth was that she missed the antiseptic taste of a clean malt. The whisky generally available was an anodyne blend that scarcely tasted like the malt Jack used to drink. What really drew her in though was the connection to her old life. It was difficult to resist. She'd known Fred for years – far longer than anyone else in Brighton. In 1940 – thirteen years ago now – Jack had taken Fred and Mirabelle for a drink in a hotel on Berkeley Square just as the Dunkirk fiasco had erupted. When every other Allied soldier was coming back to Blighty, Jack dispatched Fred in the opposite direction. The drinks had been their way of saying goodbye. Jack hadn't seemed to mind letting Fred know about his affair. He'd introduced Mirabelle as his best girl and she had blushed. After all, there wasn't a polite name in English for 'mistress'.

'You make a nice couple, don't ya? Bet you keep it a secret, eh? Mrs Duggan and all. I got a wife myself,' Fred admitted. 'We don't get on neither. Still, you gotta make things work the best you can.'

Now Mirabelle directed her gaze to the bottle of whisky Fred had left on the counter. She wondered what had happened to Fred's wife. Not that she'd dream of enquiring. Fred seemed perfectly happy, but then he always had.

'I'll take three pairs of the stockings,' she said. 'And it isn't Glenlivet in that bottle, is it?'

Fred winked at her. 'It's the nearest I've got, Miss Bevan. From Speyside. Straight up. I've been drinking it myself – you know I love a tipple and there's nothing like Scotch. This one's cask strength. It'll knock these stockings off.' He giggled good-naturedly as he leaned down and took three packets from inside a tea chest and laid them beside the bottle. 'You got to add a finger of water to open up the taste. When you do, it's lovely. Now would you like it or not?'

Mirabelle nodded as Fred brought out a large brown paper bag.

'Can't have people seeing now, can we?' He popped Mirabelle's items inside. 'You sure you don't want some eggs? You could do with feeding up, Miss Bevan.'

Mirabelle shook her head. Buying luxuries on the black market was one thing but she didn't want to pick up day-to-day items from Fred's stock. Someone, somewhere might be doing without. 'It wouldn't feel right,' she explained.

'However you reason it,' he said, lifting a solitary hen's egg from the basket before wrapping it in half a sheet of newspaper and popping it into the bag. 'Have one on me, eh?' He held out his hand for payment.

Mirabelle passed him a note and waited as he counted the change from his pocket into her hand.

'So, what else is there? Come on. You got something on your mind.'

'It's that fellow who had his throat cut. In the new barber's? Did you hear about it? I thought you might have met him.'

'Joey Gillingham? Yeah. Sure.' Fred looked serious. 'He was a right one for the horses. I've met him a few times at Freshfield Road and up in London. I gave him a half-bottle of brandy once when he tipped me a winner on the dogs at White City.'

'I wondered if you'd heard anything about his murder? Anything that hasn't been in the papers?'

Fred rubbed his chin. 'I could put myself in the way of hearing something if you want. Is there anything in particular, Miss Bevan?'

'Are you a freemason, Fred?'

Fred's face betrayed his surprise at this question. It was, Mirabelle noted, the first time she'd ever seen him look surprised in all the years she'd known him.

'I used to be, Miss Bevan. Used to be. When I was a young man, between the wars. These days I don't believe in nothing. Not God and not worshipful brotherhood either.'

'Joey Gillingham's murder might have had something to do with the masons. I don't know what. Perhaps he was a freemason. Perhaps he got caught up in some masonic activity – something questionable. The police who found his body were certainly brothers. They removed the corpse from the scene of the crime very quickly. I want to know what they saw and why they did that.'

Fred didn't say a word, and Mirabelle let the idea hang in the air for a few moments before she asked her second question. 'Joey had a notebook, Fred. It's missing.'

'Now that's interesting.'

'Joey's sister, Ida, is a client of the firm where I work, McGuigan & McGuigan. She's asked us to recover his notebook. It contains racing tips and betting slips. Miss Gillingham believes the police removed it from Joey's body for that reason – for their own profit.'

'The Old Bill?' Fred snorted. 'Nah.'

'Why not?'

'It couldn't have been a random snatch, that's why. If Joey's book's gone missing whoever nicked it must've known him or at least known a bit about him. If a policeman took the book off his body after the fact, it was a sneak crime – opportunistic like, wasn't it? No point in that.'

Mirabelle cocked her head to one side. 'But surely it was worth some money? Everyone who knew Joey seems to have got a good tip from him.'

'Yeah, he tipped winners all right. But you couldn't get that kind of information by nicking his notebook. No blighter would be able to read it. Joey's notebook was written in code – something he'd come up with himself. You wouldn't have known what was in the notebook unless you knew Joey and even then you wouldn't be able to read it without knowing the cipher. Who nicks a notebook full of gibberish on spec? No one.'

Mirabelle rested the contents of the paper bag in the crook of her arm. 'Now that *is* interesting,' she said. 'Thank you.'

Fred moved to open the door. The warm breeze that entered was enticing, as if the outside world was calling her away.

'There's been another body,' she slipped in before she left. 'A Mrs Chapman. She was a cleaning lady in Brighton but she liked the horses. I think there's a connection.'

'Throat cut?'

Mirabelle stood half in the warmth and half out of it. It was a strange sensation. Neither here nor there.

'No,' she said. 'Mrs Chapman was poisoned. But there's a connection. There has to be. I just don't know what it is yet. She was an odd-looking old soul. She dyed her hair bright red. Have you ever seen her?'

'I'll ask around. And, Miss Bevan, I meant what I said about Mr Duggan. He wouldn't want to see you alone. He adored you, he did. Loved you to pieces. And he'd want you to be happy.'

Mirabelle stiffened. Outwith his spying activities, Fred said whatever came into his mind or at least whatever he thought was right. It was sweet of him to notice her sadness and to try to help, but as she walked into the sunshine and gestured good-bye with her free hand she couldn't find the strength to reply. He was right, of course, but how did you let go of someone as perfect as Jack? Someone as good. Someone who had been taken away so unfairly. It was an impossibility. Not a day went by when Mirabelle didn't wish she was gone, too. Except occasionally when she found a case to distract her. And even then she missed him. Casting a long summer shadow as she instinctively turned for home, Mirabelle waited until she was out of sight before pulling a handkerchief from her handbag and dabbing away the tears that were rolling down her cheeks.

Chapter 13

Things do not change; we change.

10 p.m., The Lanes

It was getting dark by the time Vesta left the pub. The smoky atmosphere was overwhelming – from her place by the makeshift stage she could barely make out the door. The pub was packed and the music jumping. In a side room, away from the band, a few people had cleared the tables and chairs so they could dance. In a dark corner right at the back, couples didn't so much move to the music, as smooch to it. By contrast, at the bar a line of men in suits drank steadily with their eyes fixed on the musicians, taking in every nuance.

Charlie had been at his drums now for almost two hours, lost in the rhythm. He'd stay there until long after closing, Vesta thought, as she headed uphill through the balmy half-light and away from the excitement. The syncopated rhythm dogged her as she made her way up the street. It lapped like warm water at her ankles, trying to tempt her back, but something was on Vesta's mind and she'd decided to see what she could do about it. As she passed the Royal Pavilion the air cleared of music, and the only sounds were occasional passing cars and snatches of conversation as people walked towards the front. Above her, the palace's onion domes were silhouetted in the failing light and she couldn't help wondering if Daphne was curled up inside, wrapped in a blanket and watching the news on her television set. It seemed an odd way to spend a summer's night, but Mrs Agora had become attached to her television and watched it every evening. Perhaps it became normal – less of a treat – once you got used to it.

'It's a comfort,' the old lady insisted. 'I know I'll get square eyes, but I don't mind,' she chuckled. Occasionally Vesta caught Mrs Agora humming the theme tune from *Café Continental* as she cleaned the communal hallway or came through the front door with her basket of shopping. That said, the old girl still tuned into the wireless for George Elrick, whom it was impossible to overtake in her affections. '*Housewives' Choice*,' she said contentedly. 'He's got such a lovely voice. There's no one quite like dear George.'

Continuing up the hill, Vesta reassured herself that this little trip was hardly out of her way. The street gradually emptied. A tabby cat padded along the warm paving stones of the main road and then cut up an alleyway, bounding over a stretch of wall. The smell of lilac floated across Vesta's path, vying with those of fried food and car engines.

At Queen's Road Vesta loitered on the corner. All but dark now, an amber glow seeped from behind curtained windows on the upper floors of several of the buildings. Bedsits, she thought. The shops were closed now. At last she let her eyes fall on her destination. The lodge was lit by a white light over the entrance and the pane of glass in the front door betrayed a dim illumination that warmed the dark wood of the hallway. By contrast, the windows of the reception room where she'd sat earlier that day were black. She'd been thinking about this all evening ever since the idea occurred to her. There had to be more information to be got from the lodge – in the shock of Mrs Chapman's death the women had missed a trick. It was easy to overlook people in service. That must be why the butler usually did it in the detective novels that Mrs Agora so enjoyed. In real life Vesta knew what she needed was more information. She walked across the road, took a deep breath, rang the doorbell and waited. As the caretaker emerged from the door at the rear of the hall, her stomach lurched. Just do what Mirabelle would do, she told herself, and took another lungful of air.

The man peered through the glass and then opened the door tentatively. 'What do you want?' He squinted along the empty pavement. 'Where's your friend?'

'I'm on my own tonight, Mr Giles.'

'That's Mr Tupps to you, young lady. Mr Giles Tupps.'

'Mr Tupps. Of course.' She hovered awkwardly. Having been rude enough to get the man's name wrong, it felt difficult to continue.

'Well?' he said. 'It's late. I'm closing up.'

'I've never seen anyone die before, Mr Tupps,' Vesta blurted. 'Mrs Chapman was my first. I have some questions. I thought you might be able to help.'

'Me?' The caretaker's eyes widened. 'What do you mean?'

'You must have known Mrs Chapman better than anyone. That's what occurred to me. You've both worked here for years, haven't you? And I thought that probably you had, well, experience. You seemed like you did. Like you knew things. You'd seen it all before?'

The old man nodded slowly. 'I seen plenty of people die.'

'In the war?'

'In the Great War, yes. This time round, I was a warden. Up in London. I seen folks die there, too. We moved back down after the peace, see – I was born here in Sussex. Lots of places didn't see a single bomb. Not us. I got a cousin up north said he wouldn't have guessed there was a war at all. But we was hit hard up the Smoke – harder than down here and all. Everyone dies, don't they? You just got to hope it's quick. You best come in,' he gestured, standing back to allow the girl to pass.

'Won't they be bothered? The freemasons, I mean?'

'There's no one here, love. I'm just finishing up. Why don't I get on the kettle? We can have a cuppa.'

Vesta opened her handbag. 'I have these,' she said, pulling out a small paper bag. 'They're Jelly Babies.'

'Well, I never. I haven't seen them in a while. Peace babies we used to call them.' A hint of a smile played around his lips as he reached into the bag. 'Sweets are off the ration, then? Nobody's offered me a sweet in years. Very nice of you, young lady. I don't mind if I do.'

Vesta followed the old man downstairs. At the back of the hallway there was an unsettling display of unsheathed swords that Vesta hadn't noticed before. She stayed close to Mr Tupps as he opened the door to the back stairs. The lights were on in this part of the lodge. The kitchen was tiled floor to ceiling with pale green crackle-glazed tiles. The room stank of stale wine bottles and cigarette smoke. There wasn't any food to be seen. The old range was so pristine it looked as if it had never been used. Mr Tupps put on the kettle as Vesta looked around. Two deep Belfast sinks were plumbed in below the barred windows that overlooked the back of the building. The garden was little more than a yard from what Vesta could make out, but it was cultivated, and not with the fruit and vegetables that were customary. Mr Tupps, it seemed, had been growing flowers. Eerie white and yellow trailing fronds sprouted luminous in the blue moonlight and seemed all the more exotic for it. They almost covered the back wall. She sat at the kitchen table as Mr Tupps made two cups of tea and plonked one down in front of her.

'Get a fright, did you?' he asked.

Vesta considered this. She'd only seen Mrs Chapman at the very end, but that final moment when death took her hadn't exactly been shocking, more unexpectedly mundane, like an engine cutting out. Death, she thought, ought to be more of an occasion, more dramatic. 'It seemed too easy,' she said quietly.

Mr Tupps nodded. 'Yeah,' he said and took a noisy slurp of tea. 'I know what you mean. You think people are tough. That death should be impossible. And then it just lands. Like snow. The long silence. You'd think she was frail, poor Elsie, but she wasn't. And still, she switched off in the end,' he clicked his fingers, 'just like that. You had a question, you said?'

'I'm sorry. You must have answered a hundred today. I mean, what with the police.'

'That didn't take five minutes, girl. They wanted Elsie's address and her next of kin. The fella asked me if she had any enemies. Elsie Chapman – I ask you.'

'What was she like, Mr Tupps?'

'I've known the old girl for thirty years,' he said. 'Longer. I knew her before the war even when we was just kids. She was in with the bricks here. Been cleaning for the lodge since she was a slip of a thing. I still see her that way, like she's sitting at that table, right where you are now, having a cuppa. Four lumps she took – after the first war and before the second. Funny. She struggled when the sugar ration came on. She never got used to the taste. Complained it was bitter every time but she still drank it. She was sweet, Elsie – sweet enough herself, I used to say. When she was younger she had her pick, you know. Elsie had admirers even after she was married. I don't approve of that, course. I never looked at her that way. Still, after a while you don't look at people at all any more. You're too young to know about that, but you get a feel for a person. You recognise your friends by their atmosphere and Elsie had a good atmosphere. You knew what she was about. When her looks faded it didn't bother me none.'

Vesta thought about Charlie. The way he felt. If she closed her eyes he was as easy to feel as he was to visualise. She wondered if his smell would change over the years – the trace of tobacco and baking bread that lingered on his skin. 'Is that love?' she asked.

Mr Tupps sat back in his chair. 'Elsie!' he hooted. 'I didn't love Elsie. Don't be ridiculous. Oh, she was a looker all right, in her younger days. Difficult, I think, for women who've relied on that, when they get, well, past it. But I was never in love with her. Hang on, you ain't thinking of me, is you? You got a fella in mind?'

Vesta nodded regretfully.

'Soft on him?'

'Yes. He's asked me to marry him.'

Mr Tupps lifted his cup in a toast. 'Well, you get on with it, girl. It's institutions like marriage that are most important when it gets down to it. You get on with it, I say. Best days of your lives, those days. My missus always said that. And it's my missus I'm in love with. Been that way since the first day I saw her. At church. It's still that way and she's been dead five years.'

'I met Charlie in a church.' Vesta smiled. 'Or, at least, a church hall.'

'Well. There.' Mr Tupps settled down as Vesta tried to haul her mind back to the matter in question.

'Mrs Chapman liked the horse racing, didn't she?'

'Yeah. Elsie'd have a flutter. Her kids are grown and gone, and with Arthur dead she could do whatever she liked. The kids are the next of kin, of course. Two up in London and one girl married a fella from Eastbourne. They'll have told them by now, I expect.' He sighed. 'She liked the gee-gees. It's a bit of excitement, isn't it? That's what she used to say.'

'Did she win?'

'Sometimes. She was brought up on a farm so she could read a horse. When she won she sent the money to her youngest girl. Elsie always said she didn't need nothing herself. It was just a flutter, like. But she wanted to help little Eleanor. The girl is studying to be a secretary. Elsie was proud of that.'

'So she went to the racetrack, did she?'

Mr Tupps sucked his teeth. 'I dunno about that. Sometimes, I think. More'n that she read the form in the paper and then if she fancied she'd lay a bet with a fella she knew. That was more like it. Under the counter. She was a surprising old bird.'

'Did she read the *Express*? Mr Tupps, did she know Joey Gillingham?'

'Who?'

'The journalist who died on Monday? He wrote the racing column in the *Express*. Do you think Mrs Chapman had ever met him?'

Mr Tupps shook his head. 'I met him,' he said. 'Not formally introduced, like, but I seen him a few times. Not at the races. Freshfield Road is too big – it's like Euston Station these days, what with the new stand, and I don't go often. No, I met him scouting the boxers. Up at the church club. I don't think Elsie read the *Express*. She was more one for the proper racing papers. She loved horses. As far as I know she never came across the fellow and, like I said, I only met him a couple of times, myself.'

'Are you a religious man, then, Mr Tupps? If the boxing was at the church hall, I mean?' Vesta held out the bag of sweets to encourage him to keep going.

'Yeah.' The caretaker took a green Jelly Baby and held it up. He bit off the head. 'The church is all I got now. It's the institutions that endure. That's the thing. So I'm here all week and there on Sundays. The war sent you one way or another, didn't it? The Blitz. Where was you when the war was on? Where do you come from, then?'

Vesta wasn't sure how to answer this question. The old man was expecting her to say Jamaica, she supposed, or Barbados. Somewhere black. The truth was she'd been born and brought up in South London but somehow the Blitz had only grazed her childhood. She'd played on the bombsites. She'd known what was going on. There were nights they'd slept in a shelter or even in the Tube but somehow Vesta's mother had always made it into an adventure. When they heard a bomb going off, Mrs Churchill would rock her children in her soft, strong arms and say, 'It's only a thunderstorm. When we go outside, everything will be fine. You'll see.'

Vesta didn't recall being scared. Not once. 'I'm from Bermondsey,' she said, 'I was just a kid during the war. I didn't notice it much.'

Mr Tupps cocked his head. 'I was in the East End, and we was hit hard, what with the docks. South London got it almost as bad. Buildings down and fires all over. You didn't get evacuated then when you was a nipper?'

'No. My mother didn't want us sent away and what with being, well, black . . .' Now she thought about it, of course, her mother had kept her at home. It struck her what an amazing job her mother had done – looking after Vesta and her brothers and never letting them feel intimidated. The class size at school had shrunk till it was only a few black kids and one or two of the poorest white ones, whose parents hovered on the fringes at church or occasionally at the school gate as if they were ashamed. Vesta's father had been stationed in Yorkshire. He had come home every three months for the weekend. Vesta popped a sweet in her mouth and tried to explain to Mr Tupps. 'Black people aren't accepted. Not the same way. We stayed at home.'

Mr Tupps stared at her. 'That's not right, is it? You can't help the colour of your skin.'

'The thing is,' Vesta steered herself back to the reason she had come to see the old man in the middle of the night, 'people didn't seem to care about Mrs Chapman because she was only a cleaning lady. The Superintendent didn't care her. And the woman down at the Pavilion. But I knew you would. And Captain Henshaw did, too – he was upset. He wanted some privacy for her, I expect. He knew she was a goner.'

'Captain Henshaw's a decent man,' said Tupps.

'That's why I came back,' explained Vesta. 'For Elsie. People shouldn't just be cast to one side and forgotten.'

'I cared about her all right, but everyone's gotta die, don't they? Sometimes these things just happen. It's someone's time.' Mr Tupps's tone was earnest.

'Well, I wanted to find out more about her because I care.' Vesta was surprised that she felt so passionate. Tears pricked her eyes. 'And my boss cares, too. I wanted you to know. I wanted someone to tell you. So, if there's anything you can think of, anything that might help, then please say so. Mirabelle thinks Mrs Chapman's death is tied up with Joey Gillingham's murder, somehow.'

Mr Tupps considered this.

'I can't see it, love. I'd like to help. But if Elsie knew the fella, she never said so. You're getting all het up, and that isn't going to help no one. Not Joey Gillingham nor Elsie either. It seems like a different kind of thing, doesn't it? The two of them dying.'

'Did Mr Gillingham ever come here, to the lodge? Do you know if he was a freemason? It's just that that could be the connection, couldn't it?'

Mr Tupps sat bolt upright. His expression hardened. Vesta felt a tingle in her spine. The old man was eyeing her like she was prey.

'I'm a mason myself. That's how I got this job,' he said. 'They've been good to me here. If you're looking to smear the brethren you won't get any help from me. You got to be loyal, aintcha? Elsie didn't know that Gillingham fella – how could she? None of us knew him – not really. You leave the masons out of it, you hear me?'

'I don't understand the big secret.' Vesta couldn't back down now. 'What do you do here? All this brotherhood stuff. Why's it so . . . closed?'

Mr Tupps looked like he might spit at her. 'The masons don't owe you an explanation. We do a bit of work for charity. There's meetings. You don't need to know any more than that. It's private.'

'Why?' Vesta insisted. She couldn't help thinking that Mirabelle would do this differently. It wasn't going as well as she'd hoped. Mirabelle would have told her to stop asking questions and just listen but she couldn't. She had to press him. 'Are you sure Joey Gillingham didn't come along?'

'I never seen him.'

'So, as far as you're concerned, the deaths aren't connected?'

'You're looking for a conspiracy, girlie, and you won't find one here. There's no point in getting hysterical.'

'But the police think it's murder. That's two murders in two days. And if Joey Gillingham was a freemason and Mrs Chapman worked here, and they both bet on the horses, then there's a connection. More than one. Something's going on, Mr Tupps. There has to be. I'm just trying to join the dots, that's all.'

'I can't say what the police think. I know what I think though,' he said sternly.

'What?' Vesta felt breathless.

'I think it's time for you to go. You don't know what you're doing, girlie. A fella's likely to get hit by friendly fire dealing with you. That's what I think. You got no right. No right at all.'

The old man got to his feet. He left his Jelly Baby headless on the table and half his tea untouched.

Vesta's cheeks burned. 'Mirabelle and I have solved several murders,' she squeaked.

Mr Tupps remained unimpressed. He gestured to the girl to get up, and made his way back to the dim hallway, not even looking to check she was following. 'Come on. It's chucking out time. Don't worry about Elsie Chapman. She's in the arms of heaven now. Whatever happened, the police will figure it out. They're doing a post mortem. That'll put your mind at rest, you'll see. There's no value in letting your imagination run riot.'

He held open the front door. Outside a church bell was striking eleven.

Feeling sheepish, Vesta stepped into the doorway and turned to face him. 'Sorry,' she said, 'I just wanted to help. And the police don't always . . .'

Mr Tupps put up his hand and ushered her outside. 'Good night, Miss,' he said with finality. 'You stop looking for trouble and you'll sleep sounder. As if Elsie would be mixed up with some cheap hack.' He closed the door with a bang.

Vesta stepped backwards as the white light above her was extinguished and she was left in the amber gloom. 'Well!' she exclaimed.

Mr Tupps was more imposing than expected. Quite brutal. Mind you, the poor old thing didn't have anything else but his lodge and his church. Perhaps she'd just pushed him too far. In the distance she could hear a gull screeching. They didn't usually make a sound once it was dark and the high-pitched wail hung in the air. Vesta turned back along Queen's Road with her handbag over her arm, arms folded, deep in thought. Home was only ten minutes away on the other side of Old Steine. She wondered if Mrs Agora might still be up. Then, momentarily, she wondered if Mirabelle had figured out any more of the puzzle. Well, she wasn't giving up. Mr Tupps was wrong. She wasn't looking for trouble; she was looking for a solution. She hadn't let her imagination run riot. Instead she'd used her eyes and her ears. Now she just needed to figure out exactly what had happened over that kitchen table tonight. Everything people said was important. Every detail. There had to be something. Perhaps sleeping on it would help.

Chapter 14

Breakfast is the most important meal of the day.

Mirabelle had forgotten to close the curtains, and the bright, early morning light had woken her early. If the night before there had been ghosts lurking in the shadows, there was no place for them now in the sun-drenched bedroom. She watched two boats crossing the horizon like tiny toys.

As she turned away from the long windows she saw, on her bedside table, a tiny drop of malt left in the bottom of her glass. Behind it sat the bottle she had procured from Fred last night. It was almost full. He had not been joking about the strength of the spirit. Mirabelle had choked on her first sip before she added the water. Then the whisky had opened into a smoky, barley-infused delight. She'd sat sniffing it for five minutes before she tasted it. Two glasses had taken almost an hour and had bought her a deep all-encompassing sleep. Now her tongue felt furred and her eyes dry.

She picked up her watch and groaned. It was ten to six. Still clinging to the hinterland of sleep, she thought about the faded splendour of the Royal Pavilion, the secrets of the lodge and the spectre of poor Mrs Chapman's body. She found herself wondering whether the woman had looked older or younger when she was alive than when she lay lifeless on the meeting-room floor. Then she ran through what Fred had said about Joey's notebook and Bill's assessment of the journalist's murder, the involvement of the masons and Ida's motives. Slowly she pulled on the green silk robe that was the only item she had of Jack's wardrobe and padded through to the bath-room where she ran a basin of lukewarm water.

As she bent over, she realised her stomach was growling. She cast her mind over the day before and remembered she hadn't eaten a thing. Back in the bedroom she quickly pulled on a silk summer dress the same colour as the sky and fixed her hair in place with a single pin. She discounted cooking the egg Fred had given her and instead set out briskly into the morning. She turned in the direction of the bus stop. There was somewhere she needed to go.

Mirabelle liked the early buses. For the most part, the passengers climbed aboard alone and sat in silence. She could gaze out of the window in a daze, watching the city before it was properly awake as if she was catching the landmarks unawares, fresh before the day could claim them. As the bus turned away from the front towards Freshfield she checked the view down the hillside behind her. Brighton sparkled in the sunshine, the sea – a precious sapphire – its greatest treasure. As the journey continued she watched housewives scrubbing their doorsteps, and delivery vans and heavily loaded drays unloading at corner shops. A paperboy whistled as he made his rounds. When Mirabelle finally disembarked she headed not only towards breakfast but also in search of information. She felt focused.

The cafeteria at Brighton racecourse was open early whether there was a race that day or not. There were always people who needed sustenance: bookmakers, trainers, jockeys and, occasionally, even owners, who would pop in and out regardless of the season. The bar remained closed unless the public were admitted, but Mrs Fellowes, who ran the café, kept a supply of rum and brandy under the counter and made an excellent bacon roll whether you had coupons or not. There was little money couldn't buy at Brighton racecourse if you had enough of it. I wouldn't be surprised, Mirabelle thought, if Fred and Mrs Fellowes were acquainted.

By the time she had crossed the doorway it was quarter to seven. Two cleaners were mopping the linoleum hallway that ran the length of one of the viewing galleries. She picked her way across the wet floor and opened the swing door. Inside, at a Formica table, three jockeys smoked and drank coffee sharpened with spirits rather than risk not weighing in on the money for the weekend's races. They each had an eye on the table next to them where the notorious Frank Wooldridge, who manned the scales on race day, was eating egg rolls with his grandson Dickie. 'That's my boy,' he said proudly as the kid wiped away the yolk dribbling down his chin.

At three other tables men sat on their own, bookmakers by the look of them, engrossed in their notebooks. Lastly there was a party of four blokes who had clearly been up all night. Unshaven and still drunk, they laughed uproariously while stuffing sausages encased in white bread into their mouths. Mirabelle thought she heard one of them say he'd been at the jazz till the sun rose.

Mirabelle tried not to think of how unhelpful Vesta might be at the office if she'd stayed up till dawn with Charlie. It would do the young couple more good to sit round their kitchen table and discuss Vesta's marital concerns. That was far more important than staying out jamming till all hours. No sooner had the thought formed, than she bit her lip. Honestly, she was turning into a narrow-minded old spinster. It hadn't been that long since she'd stayed up all night dancing with Jack. Not that long at all. Vesta would get round to talking to Charlie in her own sweet time. For now, at least there was breakfast to be had. The smell of frying bacon was undeniably promising. Mirabelle headed towards the gantry where Mrs Fellowes eyed her carefully over the counter.

'There's no racing today, Madam,' said the woman, noisily clearing teacups and avoiding Mirabelle's eye. Mrs Fellowes' hands were like spades and the rest of her was no less industrial. The woman swept the counter surface with a cloth, which she then shoved into the pocket of her blue nylon housecoat. 'The public are not admitted.'

'I'm meeting a friend who works here.' Mirabelle let the lie slip off her tongue. 'I'd like a cup of tea, please, and a bacon roll.' She laid three shillings on the counter. 'Keep the change.'

Mrs Fellowes silently altered her position. Her lips tightened as she picked up the coins. 'I'll bring it over.'

Mirabelle chose a table by the window that overlooked the racetrack. Two horses were thundering round, and a man in a sheepskin coat and a felt hat was timing them with a stopwatch. The jockeys in the cafeteria, she noted, were keeping an eye on this activity, letting out an exasperated sigh or whoop of excitement depending on the performance. She couldn't help thinking that the man in the sheepskin coat must feel rather warm.

At length, Mrs Fellowes padded across the linoleum and delivered Mirabelle's breakfast. Mirabelle sipped the tea and nibbled the bacon roll. It felt good to eat something. She was considering buying a newspaper when one of the men who had been sitting by himself appeared beside the table. He was middle-aged, overweight and his skin was blotchy, a result, Mirabelle guessed, of heavy drinking. He had that look about him. There was a stain on the lapel of his jacket.

'You worked for Ben McGuigan, didn't you?' He tipped his hat.

Mirabelle nodded. Ben had died almost two years before though the firm still bore his name. He'd been well known and popular in Brighton. It was a testament to his character – not every debt collector managed to retain the goodwill of his clients.

'I thought I recognised your face. I heard it was a woman who took over the agency. That's ballsy. It was a terrible business, what happened to poor Ben. Gives the trade a bad name when there's scams. Every fella's got to make his money but there's no need to be greedy, is there?'

'How did you know Ben?' Mirabelle asked.

'I'm Mr Terry,' the man introduced himself, sitting down unbidden and motioning towards Mrs Fellowes for another cup of tea. 'A nice cuppa – can't get going without one,' he said cheerily. 'Sometimes it takes half a dozen.'

Mirabelle crossed her legs and drank her tea. 'It sounds as if you're at home here, Mr Terry.'

The man chuckled. 'Well, yes, you could say that. Mrs F. does a nice breakfast and I like to get going early. I'm a book-maker, see. But you knew that. Any bird that takes over Ben McGuigan's debt collection agency is going to be able to read people, or she isn't going to last five minutes. And it must be a couple of years now. How's tricks?'

'Good, thank you. I'm here on business, in fact. I wonder if you knew Mr Gillingham, the sports writer? Since we're discussing things.'

Terry slurped the tea from his cup and eyed Mirabelle care-fully. 'The dead bloke? Well, you get straight to the point. I can't blame you, love. There's a lot of interest in him at present. That's a shocker even for Brighton, that is.' Terry drew his finger across his throat. 'I mean, a slasher – you just don't expect it. They say the grit always settles at the bottom and Brighton's a tough city, but still.'

'At first I thought Mr Gillingham must've owed someone money.' Mirabelle laid down her cup.

Terry laughed. 'The sod never lost. Hardly never. Luckily he didn't bet with me.'

'Do you only cover the racing?'

Terry pulled a packet of cigarettes from his pocket and lit one. 'Nah, I'm not fussy. I'll give odds on anything. Sport, that is.'

'The boxing, too?'

'Now you're on the money. That junior team from the church youth club – they're wiping the floor with all comers. It's nice to see that, I have to say. I almost don't mind paying out.'

'I saw two of them the other night at the Crown and Anchor,' said Mirabelle. 'They were really good bouts. Extraordinary.'

Terry stared open-mouthed. He held the smoking cigarette in his hand without taking a draw. 'You seen much boxing, then?'

'I used to. In London. Before the war. Only occasionally. There was a ring near Waterloo but it got blitzed.'

'You didn't go in that get-up,' Terry remarked, looking at Mirabelle's dress. The ring had been a working-class venue. Everyone knew that. Mirabelle looked nonchalant. 'It was a jape. I used to sneak over. I liked the crowd. The excitement. It's a different thing in Brighton. Still, I enjoyed the match the other night. I wonder what will happen to the team as they turn of age. Do you think they'll go professional?'

'Yeah. What with them being *extraordinary*.' Terry eyed her. 'So, you was at the Crown and Anchor? Well, well. My trouble is I can't get anyone to bet against the buggers, so we end up closing the book. If you ever want to lay odds against the Brighton junior team, then I'm your man.' He grinned. 'Not that I'd recommend it. Still, everyone comes crashing down sometime. Everyone.'

Mirabelle waited. Terry sat back confidently. He looked dispassionately at the track for a minute and then turned his attention back to the table.

'What is it you want, Mr Terry?' Mirabelle leaned forward. 'Why did you come to sit with me?'

Terry might have blushed had he been twenty years younger but with his ruddy complexion it was hard to tell. As it was, he looked down shyly. 'I came over for Ben's sake, Miss. See, a lady shouldn't be in here on her own. You spot any ladies dining out?'

'I see.' Mirabelle put down her cup. 'So, you're rescuing me? A knight in shining armour?'

'Yeah. I said to myself, that lady's come here for Gillingham. You have, aintcha?'

'What makes you say that?'

'It's obvious. Apart from it being the first thing you mentioned. I got to be honest, I figured who you was and I liked Ben McGuigan. So I came to offer my assistance.'

'And do you have anything to tell me about Mr Gillingham?'

'Like what?'

'Who did Joey lay his bets with, Mr Terry?'

'Why do you want to know?'

'Because Mr Gillingham's sister, Ida, is very upset. Joey laid bets on several races this week and the police have mislaid the slips that she says were on his person when he was killed. As her brother's heir, she's entitled to claim the winnings. She's engaged McGuigan & McGuigan to find the slips and claim the money on her behalf. So, do you know who Joey laid his bets with?'

'I can see what Ben liked in you, Miss. I can see why he took you on.'

Mirabelle sat up. 'Mr Terry, I can ask you anything, can't I?'

'You go ahead, love.'

'And whatever I ask you, you aren't going to answer.'

Terry smiled broadly. 'All right. All right.' He paused for effect. 'Joey laid bets with different fellas. He'll have had a couple of bookies up in London, I'm sure, but down here it was Tony Grillo, the Italian, and Victor Everett. They're both solid blokes. They're both experienced. Tough guys, but then they're bookies, ain't they? It's a tough profession. People try to take the mick so you gotta be solid.'

'And if you're a bookmaker, Mr Terry, and you have a client who never loses, what do you do?'

'Well, you don't cut his throat, if that's what you're asking.'

'Are you sure?'

'Look, you might stop taking the bugger's bets – pardon my French – but you don't cut his throat. A good bookie always makes money and Joey Gillingham always bet with the best. It's simple arithmetic. The world's got us down as crooks. A good bookie'll never back down from an argument over money but really he's a mathematician. If someone lays a quid on one thing, then you cover it by taking bets on another. Me, I'd shorten the odds I offered him and give better odds on the horses he doesn't want to bet on. Then either the guy goes somewhere else where he can get three to one rather than two to one, or at least it's easier to cover the back end. And no one wins all the time. Even Joey Gillingham lost now and then.'

'And Tony Grillo and Victor Everett . . .'

Terry stubbed out his cigarette, which had burned down without him taking a single puff. 'Well, they're not early birds. But you'll catch them later, if you're interested. I wouldn't go so far as to guarantee that neither of them are murderers, but cutting a guy's throat in a barber's chair to avoid a payout? I doubt it.'

Mirabelle patted her lips with a napkin. 'Thanks,' she said. 'I suppose that's what I wanted to know.'

Chapter 15

Charity begins at home and justice begins next door.

Out in the sunshine, looking west along Freshfield Road, Mirabelle checked her watch. It was still early. The warm air felt fresh in contrast to the smoky cafeteria. Thinking that Bill and Vesta wouldn't be in the office for at least another hour, Mirabelle headed for the bus stop. The road was getting busier now. People were on their way to work, and kids, chucked out after breakfast, would soon be heading for school, she thought, as she crossed to the shady side to wait. If Joey's sporting activities were hardly shrouded in mystery, Elsie's were quite another matter. Mirabelle contemplated these as she got onto a bus that was heading away from town and found a seat on the lower deck. The windows were open and there was a pleasant breeze as the vehicle headed away from the centre towards Patcham.

Mirabelle had been here before. She thought of the little village as the last reaches of north Brighton – a jumble of pretty stone houses, some of them half-timbered. The scale and the colours were a contrast to the grand stucco Georgian properties in the centre of town and open fields stretched beyond the last cluster of houses. On instinct, she made for the bakery, which was doing a brisk trade. The bell at the door chimed as customers came and went, punctuating the sound of traffic outside. The shelves were already half-empty and there was laughter from the back room. As she entered, Mirabelle cast her eyes across the remaining coconut fancies.

'Can I help you, love?' A man in a white coat looked over the counter.

'Actually, I'm looking for directions. Elsie Chapman's house?'

The baker smiled. 'She's just off Church Hill. It's a five-minute walk. Turn off at the top and look for a black door with geraniums. Ask anyone when you get up there. She won't be in though. Up with the larks, Elsie. I didn't see her this morning, come to think of it. Maybe she was in a rush.'

'Thanks,' Mirabelle said, deciding not to tell him what had happened. The jungle drums, it seemed, beat faintly in Patcham.

The house, when she got there, was as described – two glossy black tubs of bright pink geraniums sat by the door and a shiny brass plate was engraved with the family name. The road was quiet. Mirabelle paused. She hadn't been sure if there would be anyone at home. From inside, however, there emanated the sound of two women angrily shouting at each other. Whoever they were, they were having a proper scrap. Mirabelle took a deep breath, considered this unexpected turn of events and rapped on the door. Then she stepped back and waited.

The shouting stopped dead. A few seconds later the door opened to reveal a heavily pregnant girl. She was no more than twenty-one, blonde and glowing with robust health. 'Yes?' she said.

'My name is Mirabelle Bevan. I'm terribly sorry to disturb you, but I was with Mrs Chapman yesterday. When she died.'

In the hallway a thin pale girl with dark hair appeared behind the rosy apparition. 'You were with Mummy?' she said.

'Oh, for God's sake, Ellie,' the pregnant woman snapped. 'You're not her baby any more. You're a grown woman. Stop calling her that.'

'She was my mummy,' Ellie objected, 'and I'll call her whatever I want to.'

The pregnant woman glared at Mirabelle. 'Well?' she said, but the other girl pushed forward.

'Honestly, Vi, show some manners. Please, Miss Bevan, come in.'

Mirabelle slipped past Vi and followed Ellie into the front room. Inside, it was sparsely furnished but clean and tidy. There was a vague smell of violets. On the mantelpiece was a framed sepia print of a man in uniform. In another print, the same man was pictured with a strikingly pretty young woman with a wide easy smile. Mrs Chapman had been a stunner. Mirabelle wondered fleetingly if when she was older, people would wonder if she had ever been beautiful. At what age, she pondered, did that spark disappear?

The girls had evidently been going through the contents of a box file at the table: what looked like birth certificates, books of ration coupons and a tatty old bible. Beside it there was an old tea canister, half full of coins: Mrs Chapman's savings, Mirabelle guessed.

'I'd offer you some tea,' Ellie said, 'but my sister and I haven't got ourselves organised yet. We don't have any milk, I'm afraid.'

'Please, it's quite all right,' Mirabelle replied. 'I came to offer my condolences and to see if there was anything I could do to help.'

'How did you know our mother exactly?' Vi pulled up a chair and sat down, motioning to Mirabelle to do the same.

'I didn't know her, really,' Mirabelle admitted. 'I was at the lodge in Queen's Road when she collapsed.'

Ellie's face crumpled as she began to cry. 'I had to identify her body. I was the first here, you see. I came down from London. I can't quite believe it, even now . . . I'm sorry.' She sniffed.

'For goodness' sake, Ellie, pull yourself together. I'm her daughter, too, and I'm not causing a fuss. You're not the little favourite any more.' Vi didn't offer her sister a scrap of comfort. 'It'll all go three ways – not that there's much to split – and there'll be no more trying to make you into a lady, that's for sure. You'd better give up that fancy course of yours and get a proper job. Not so high and mighty now, are you? Not so high and mighty when she's not here to pay for everything.'

Mirabelle shifted uncomfortably as Ellie sobbed and Vi stared into the empty grate of the fireplace, quiet for a moment in her triumph.

Then Vi perked up. 'Bobby will be here later and we can finish up. We'll pay the undertaker for when the police release Ma's body and we'll close up the house and hand back the key and that will be that. It's not much to show for a life, I'll grant you. But then Mum was hardly a society figure. Why she was so keen on you being posh I'll never know.' Here she paused as if she'd only just realised they had a visitor. 'We're waiting for our big brother, Bobby, you see.'

Mirabelle nodded. There was an awkward silence during which it appeared Ellie had shrunk in the face of her sister's tirade. The girl had such thin wrists, Mirabelle noticed, and her eyes were circled with dark shadows. Mirabelle felt tremendously sorry for her. The attack had appeared unprompted. It was always telling to see how people behaved in a crisis. When Mirabelle's parents died she had been only nineteen and she had felt hopelessly alone. She remembered wishing she had someone to share her grief – a sister, a brother, a cousin. Looking at Ellie and Vi she realised having siblings wasn't always the way only children imagined. This, she realised, must be worse than not having a sister at all. She was about to say something to lift the atmosphere when the silence was broken by a knock at the door.

Vi got to her feet. 'Who the blazes is it now?' she said and left the room.

Mirabelle passed Ellie a clean handkerchief from her handbag. 'I'm so sorry,' she said. 'I'm sure your sister doesn't mean it.'

Ellie rolled her eyes. 'No. She does. Every word.' She blew her nose. 'We've never got on. Mummy was good to me. Better than she was to the others. That's the problem.'

'Will you give up your course now?'

'I don't expect so. Mummy paid the fees in advance and I can use whatever I get today to pay for my digs until I've got my secretarial certificate. They say we'll get jobs easily as long as we make the typing speeds. It's only another month or two, and my landlady's a decent sort. I'm sure it will be fine.'

'Your mother would have been proud of you, then.'

The girl smiled gratefully. 'She was proud of me all the time, no matter what. But she said if I could get a job in London it'd be for the best.'

Mirabelle could hardly blame the girl. If her life in Brighton had been peppered with the kind of outburst she'd just witnessed, she'd want to get away, too.

There was movement in the hallway and the muffled sound of the front door closing as Vi returned, leading a tall, smartly dressed man into the room. His hair was slicked back and he ran his hand over it after he removed his hat. His dark eyes were solemn.

'This is my sister, Ellie, and Miss Bevan, an acquaintance of our mother's,' Vi introduced him. 'This is Mr Grillo.'

'Pleased to meet you,' said Mr Grillo. His accent contained only a hint of an Italian past. 'I came when I heard about what happened. Time like this, it's only fair. Your mother was a good client of mine. I'm sorry for your loss.'

'A client?' Ellie asked. 'What do you mean, a client?'

Mirabelle said, 'Mr Grillo is a bookmaker, isn't that right, Mr Grillo? Your mother, as I understand it, had some skill with the horses.'

'You could say that.' Tony Grillo nodded gravely. 'Yeah, that's about right.'

Vi laughed harshly. 'Mum? Really?'

'I heard your mother was a country girl,' said Mirabelle, watching Vi closely.

Ellie joined in enthusiastically. 'That's true. She was born on a sheep farm. She told me stories about it when I was little . . .'

Vi shot her sister a venomous look. 'How charming,' she spat.

'Well, your mother had an eye for the horses all right,' Mr Grillo brought the girls back to the point, 'however she got it. She laid an accumulator bet at the course and now it's come off. She said she wanted the money to go to her youngest.' He reached into his inside pocket. 'Seventy-five quid,' he said, pulling out a sheaf of white fivers.

It was a small fortune. Vi's face lit up. She stepped forward and snatched the money out of Mr Grillo's hand. 'That'll help with the funeral expenses,' she snapped, shoving the banknotes into her apron pocket. 'And Mum's estate will be split fair and square between the three of us, thank you. I've got two kids and one on the way. It's only right.'

Mr Grillo's eyes remained still. 'I'm only telling you what she said. Those were her wishes. It's up to you whether you respect them or not.'

Ellie stood up. 'Well, there's plenty for all of us, isn't there? Seventy-five pounds. It's a lot of money.'

The girl was absolutely decent despite her sister's unpleasantness, Mirabelle noted. It was nice to see.

'It's very kind of you, Mr Grillo, to deliver this money to Mrs Chapman's children.' Mirabelle smiled. 'Do you require some kind of receipt? Or should we look around for Mrs Chapman's betting slip – surely you must need something?'

'It's all right, lady. Elsie's bet with me for years. I couldn't just let it go, could I? Cash makes a difference at times like these.'

Ellie sank down onto a chair and stared, as if she was running through all the times her mother had paid her bills and suddenly understood where the money might have come from. 'It makes a huge difference, Mr Grillo,' she said. 'And we'd never have known. It's very honest of you to pay up like this. Thank you.'

Tony Grillo put on his hat. 'It's my way of paying my respects,' he said and turned to go.

Mirabelle waylaid him. 'Mr Grillo, I wonder if Joey Gillingham laid bets with you, as well?'

Mr Grillo's eyes flickered from Ellie to Vi. The girls had settled now. The money appeared to have quashed Vi's temper. For her part, Ellie sat on the edge of her chair, perfectly composed, waiting to hear Mr Grillo's reply.

'Joey Gillingham? Sure,' he said, 'he bet with me from time to time. Did you know him, Miss . . . ?'

'Miss Bevan. I know his sister. She's concerned that he might have outstanding bets. The police, you see, have mislaid his notebook, and his betting slips were inside. As his heir, Miss Gillingham wants to claim whatever he's due.'

'I'll check my book.'

'You can find me at McGuigan & McGuigan on Brills Lane.'

'Ben's old office?'

Mirabelle nodded. 'I was concerned we would need the slips. Because they're bearer bonds, aren't they? It seemed to me a matter about which someone in your profession might be particularly careful.'

Tony Grillo's eyes momentarily sought the ceiling. 'I'll look into it,' he said as he tipped his hat at the Chapman girls. 'Well, I'd best be off.'

Vi accompanied him to the door and Mirabelle fell into step. He wasn't getting away that easily.

'I wish you the very best,' Mirabelle said to the sisters as she stepped into the sunshine behind Mr Grillo. The door closed behind them.

No shouting came from Mrs Chapman's house. Mirabelle hoped the girls would manage to clear up their mother's affairs without any more fighting. She turned. The street was deserted apart from a sports car parked on the other side of the road. Tony Grillo didn't move. Mirabelle was suddenly aware of her fragility, her slim build compared to the bookmaker's bulk. She composed herself.

'I imagine you don't really need to check your notes to see if Mr Gillingham laid a bet with you. It seems to me a gentleman like you would probably remember if he'd money outstanding. You know every penny you're carrying, don't you, Mr Grillo?'

'Correct.'

'And you don't pay out, I imagine, without a slip. Not ever. Do you?' She smiled.

Tony Grillo nodded and turned his attention towards the car. He pulled the key from his pocket. 'Miss Bevan, I'm not going to tell you why I gave that money to those girls so don't bother asking.'

'Mr Grillo,' Mirabelle held her ground, 'I don't imagine for one moment that the money came from you. Mrs Chapman didn't lay an accumulator, did she? And certainly not one that netted her that much money. Might I ask if you're a freemason, Sir?'

Tony Grillo let out a let out a low chortle, like an engine turning over. 'Oh, I like you,' he said. 'You're fantastic.'

Mirabelle folded her arms. 'Well, are you a member of the freemasons? Do you attend meetings at Queen's Road?'

Tony Grillo crossed the street. He unlocked the car and leaned on the driver's door. Mirabelle noticed that the window was down. The bookmaker might have locked the vehicle but he clearly wasn't afraid anyone might steal it.

'We Italians got our own little club, Miss Bevan. I'm not a freemason. I'm not even sure they take Catholics . . .'

'As I understand it, the brotherhood is entirely non-denominational,' Mirabelle interjected.

Grillo chortled again. 'Is that so?'

'But it was a freemason who paid you to come here today, wasn't it? Might I ask if the gentleman had any distinguishing features? Might I ask if he had only one leg?'

'I can see why Ben liked you.' Tony Grillo slid into the driver's seat, closed the door and started the engine. 'A very astute man. He passed the business to the right person.'

Mirabelle continued to speak through the open window. 'Thank you,' she said, 'that was everything I needed to know.'

As the car pulled away, Mirabelle looked back towards the little house. The money might have been meant for Ellie, she thought, but if by sharing it the girl managed to repair at least some of the relations with her sister, then it would be well spent. Twenty-five pounds was more than enough for her to finish her course and set herself up in London. Silently, Mirabelle wished Ellie well as she turned back towards the main street. Checking her slim gold watch she noted that it was only nine o'clock and already the day had been tremendously eventful. She might be late for work but at least she'd bring news.

Chapter 16

The only good is knowledge.

'So you think Ellie was a love child?' said Vesta with relish an hour later in the office. 'My, that's a bit of gossip all right.'

Bill rolled his eyes in Mirabelle's direction. 'Yes,' he said. 'Don't you see? That's what the money's about. When Elsie Chapman dies, Captain Henshaw sends this payment. It's not charity from the masons. They wouldn't have to hide that by getting Grillo to deliver it and concocting a story about some accumulator bet. And besides, if the lodge was pitching in, surely they'd send money for all the woman's kids. From what Mirabelle said the two girls are chalk and cheese anyway, and Grillo as good as admitted he was acting for Henshaw. No, I'll bet the bequest is personal and Ellie Chapman is Henshaw's kid. I'd lay money on it. Poor bloke. When Elsie died he couldn't admit to having had an affair, but he still wanted to look after the girl. It's decent of him, really'

'Mr Tupps said Captain Henshaw was a decent man. It's only . . .'

'What?' Bill grinned.

'It's just the thought of them being lovers.' Vesta's eyes narrowed. 'They were a bit past it, don't you think? Him with one leg and she looked about ninety with that terrible hairdo.'

'Watch it,' said Bill. 'Mrs Chapman was in her fifties. I'm not so far off myself.'

'Well, Mr Tupps did say she had admirers,' Vesta admitted.

'Oh, she was beautiful.' Mirabelle stood up. 'I saw an old

photograph of her this morning. Besides, Ellie is seventeen or so. So Mrs Chapman would have been in her late thirties when she had the girl. It's not beyond imagining.' She moved towards the half-open window. The breeze was soothing. The air smelled sweet as it wafted up from the stalls on the Promenade, as if it was calling her. Mirabelle tried not to think about Jack and how she might have had children with him. She'd been young enough when Jack died. If they'd married it would have been something she'd hoped for. She tried to focus on the morning's activities and piece together the deduction about Captain Henshaw and Mrs Chapman with the information Vesta had turned up at the lodge the evening before. Mr Tupps was an interesting character and she'd overlooked him. Vesta was coming along, even if she hadn't immediately understood the significance of Tony Grillo handing over a large sum of money.

'It's such a huge secret to keep and they kept it for a long time.' Vesta sounded wistful. She couldn't keep a secret to save her life. 'So do you think he paid Tony Grillo to deliver the money?'

Mirabelle nodded. 'If you wanted someone who'd be a tough nut to crack, you'd likely pick a bookmaker. Grillo was well known. It made sense to choose someone like that. And Elsie Chapman liked the horses. The girls didn't even question it. We're only questioning it because we can see more of the picture. I'm just not sure how it all ties in with the lodge.'

Vesta picked up a pencil and began doodling on the notepad in front of her. 'I don't understand all the secrecy there. Mr Tupps chucked me out last night because he thought I wanted to tar the lodge with some dreadful smear. But they ask for that kind of thing by keeping everything so hidden, don't you think? He was such a nice old bloke and then he went a bit potty.'

Mirabelle tried to crystallise her thoughts. In the war there had been a great deal of secrecy but in those days it had been vital. By comparison the masons' focus on discretion seemed pointless, and by keeping their small secrets they undervalued the things that were really important. Even at Elsie's last breath Henshaw hadn't come clean. If Mrs Chapman was aware he was there, that must have hurt. If she loved him, all she'd have wanted surely was for him to hold her as she died. Wasn't anyone honest any more?

'Do you remember yesterday when Mrs Chapman was on the floor? Henshaw was distressed. I mean, it *was* distressing, but at the time I thought he became so defensive because we were in his stupid meeting room or because he wanted some dignity for Mrs Chapman. It must have been awful for him.' Mirabelle remembered Henshaw's face set in a stern expression as Elsie writhed on the floor.

'It doesn't bear thinking about,' Bill said. 'Watching someone you love die. Still, all this information doesn't turn up what we need. It's all circumstantial, isn't it? It's all conjecture. We don't have any real evidence yet about why either of them died. And that's a big job.'

Mirabelle smiled at Bill's 'policeman' voice. His tone changed periodically when he was giving a professional opinion rather than a personal one.

'Don't knock it. This is good conjecture, Bill,' Vesta insisted. 'It makes sense, don't you think? And the more we know about everyone involved, the clearer we'll see what's been going on. I reckon we're getting somewhere.'

Bill stroked his chin. The women were right. It was a plausible theory. 'Well,' he said, 'it still doesn't tell us who killed the old bird or Gillingham either.'

'No,' admitted Mirabelle. 'We need to know the kind of poison they used on Mrs Chapman before we can get a proper start on her killer. And we might want to find out where she'd been the evening before and that morning, too. Before she came in to work.'

Bill looked at the paperwork on his desk. 'I'd better get on with my calls,' he said reluctantly and made for the door. He didn't want to get too involved with Mirabelle's extra-office activities. But he was still fascinated by them. 'I'll keep an eye out,' he promised. 'And for anything to do with Gillingham. Meantime, don't do anything I wouldn't do,' he said cheerily, grabbing his hat and slamming the door behind him.

Vesta pulled out what remained of her Jelly Babies. She picked out a black one and sucked its feet, offering Mirabelle the bag. 'He's right. It doesn't tell us who killed Mrs Chapman. And we haven't really made the other connection yet.'

'With Gillingham? No,' Mirabelle conceded, waving away the sweets. 'It'll take time, but we're getting there. I'll find out more details from McGregor next time I see him. We just need to keep thinking.'

'So you're going to see him again,' said Vesta. 'For dinner?'

Mirabelle took in a sharp breath. 'Oh, for goodness' sake,' she snapped. 'I'm not interested in that kind of thing. Really I'm not.'

'Well, McGregor is. It's written all over his face. He goes moon-eyed when he sees you. Mr Tupps said love is the most important thing, you know.'

'Mr Tupps said entirely too much,' Mirabelle retorted.

Then she wondered if perhaps the old man had. If the reason for all these murders resided in the lodge, Mr Tupps might be in danger himself. It seemed to be the people on the fringes who were at risk. A journalist and a cleaning lady to start with – how far behind might a caretaker lag? Though Mr Tupps had told Vesta he was a signed-up mason – part of the group – and he certainly appeared to be a loyal employee. She sighed.

The air suddenly felt heavy with secrets. Her stomach twisted with guilt. Perhaps she ought to have a word with the Superintendent. Just to make things clear. But there never seemed an apt moment. There were so many other things on her plate that felt more important. Joey Gillingham's murder and Elsie Chapman's, too. As well as the correspondence that was sitting right in front of her. She mustn't forget that.

'We'd better get down to work,' said Vesta.

'Yes,' Mirabelle agreed. 'Something will turn up. It always does.'

Chapter 17

The human race is governed by its imagination.

By the end of the afternoon a good deal of McGuigan & McGuigan's business had been cleared, but Mirabelle realised she couldn't remember the detail of any of it. She had even gone to the bank and paid in Bill's collection money and all the cheques, but now she found she couldn't recall the actual figure or for that matter the route she'd taken to Barclays. Instead, she kept returning to the mystery of Elsie Chapman's death.

By four o'clock Vesta declared herself ravenous and suggested they pop over to a café in the Lanes for fish pie and mushy peas. Mirabelle agreed. A walk often helped to shift a problem. They had just locked the office door when a shadowy figure came hammering along the corridor.

He was tall and slim, and as he came closer they could see he was immaculately turned out in police trousers and a buttoned-up shirt. The man peered over the women's shoulders at the name on the office door. 'Is Bill Turpin in?' he enquired.

'I'm sorry. Bill's out on a call. Can we help you?' said Mirabelle.

'You must be Charlie's missus.' Belton held out his hand to Vesta.

'Are you Sergeant Belton?' Vesta stepped in. 'Charlie told me about you.' What Charlie had actually said was he'd never seen a dude who looked like he'd been freshly ironed before. 'Did you turn up anything on that notebook?'

Jim Belton looked over his shoulder. 'Hot day,' he said, as he considered whether to trust the women with the news. The ladies weren't quite what he expected – neither of them hard-faced harridans. The older one was as elegant as a model in a magazine. Charlie's wife was – Belton searched for the word – lush. Yes, that was it. She was exotic. Beautiful. He'd not expected this. He took a deep breath and weighed the matter in hand. He'd other things to be getting on with, after all, and they'd see Bill before he would. Besides, from what he'd said before, Bill rated the women.

'Yeah,' he made the decision, 'I asked around. I didn't find what Bill was hoping for, thank goodness. I could do without a police scandal, thank you. No, you tell Bill I reckon the killer took Gillingham's notebook. I've asked in both stations. The book was gone by the time our lads got to the body. The force has got feelers out for it themselves. I'll keep half an eye out and let Bill know if it turns up. The feeling is that the murderer made for London straight after he clipped the poor bloke. We don't have any professional hitmen in Brighton. It's a London thing, thank God.'

'That's very helpful,' said Mirabelle. 'We'll let Bill know. I wonder, though, Sergeant, if you've any idea why Mr Gillingham's body was moved so quickly? It's been on my mind.'

Belton shrugged. 'It was a hot day . . .'

Mirabelle eyed him, waiting. She was a skilled interrogator, Belton thought. She left exactly the kind of space in a conversation that it was tempting to fill and her voice was like a glass of cold beer. Wouldn't that be nice?

'I wouldn't worry about it, love. After all, we've got a killer to track down, and that's far more important. I won't hold you up any longer.' The sergeant turned. 'I've got a break-in to deal with. I just thought I'd pop in while I was passing. You're close to the scene, see.'

'A break-in? Near here?' Vesta enquired as they all trooped downstairs.

'We're just lucky the thieves don't seem to have taken anything,' he said, glad to have something to talk about. 'They must have been disturbed. Broad daylight, too, cheeky beggars. Two kids spotted the door was open. Usually schoolkids cause more trouble than they're worth. But this time the kids were good 'uns and they ran for the beat bobby as soon as they saw something was wrong. The door is usually locked, see. They knew something was up.'

'Well, the owner will be glad you've been so efficient.' Vesta smiled.

Belton looked momentarily confused as they emerged into the sunshine. 'Oh, there's no owner, love. Not as such. There hasn't been anyone living there since the war when they used it as a hospital for the Gurkhas. No, the Royal Pavilion's boarded up. Closed to the public. Bleeding huge it is, too. We're still searching to make sure a sneak thief isn't hiding inside.'

'The Pavilion?' Mirabelle and Vesta said in unison.

'Yeah,' said Belton. 'What of it?'

The path was shady and a policeman was guarding the gate. A crowd of boys kicked a can along the street, jumping and laughing in the bright light, their thin legs a blur as the tin puttered against the paving stones.

'Anyone from the council here yet?' said Belton.

'No, Sir.'

'You want to move them on,' he nodded in the direction of the children.

'They ain't doing no harm, Sarge,' the bobby objected.

Belton glared and the man sighed and lumbered over to send the kids in the direction of the shore.

'Hop it,' he said and the youngest boy scrambled to get hold of the can as the others moaned and tutted, slipping their hands deep in their pockets as they walked away.

'You can't come in. It's a crime scene.' Belton turned to Mirabelle and Vesta. He'd been perturbed when the women fell into step with him. As they'd walked towards the main road he kept thinking they'd bid him good afternoon and turn off in a different direction but they hadn't.

'I'd like to make sure my friend Daphne is all right,' said Mirabelle. 'She works here, you see. She's a restorer for the National Trust. Poor thing must have had a terrible fright.'

Belton loitered at the gate. 'Who?' he said.

'Daphne Marsden,' Mirabelle insisted. 'Vesta and I visited her here only yesterday.'

'It must be her day off. We haven't come across anyone since the report came in. There's a guy coming down from the council at some point but they couldn't really be bothered – I don't think they care what happens in the old place. If there's a woman who knows the building, we'll need to speak to her. Where are her digs?' He removed a notebook from his shirt pocket and licked the tip of his pencil.

'I'm not entirely sure,' Mirabelle dodged the question, 'but Daphne's always here. She's dedicated to saving the Pavilion. She's been working on the restoration of the woodwork day and night.'

'I suppose she'll be able to confirm if there's anything missing. So far we haven't come across anything obvious but it's difficult to tell. The place is so higgledy-piggledy.'

'We could have a look if you like. We were in there yesterday – at least in some of the rooms,' Vesta offered.

'It's police business, ladies.' Belton eyed Mirabelle.

The team from McGuigan & McGuigan had been known to all but take over a case. What had happened last year with that London business had been humiliating. In Belton's opinion, Superintendent McGregor hadn't been strict enough but then this woman clearly had him pussywhipped. Now he'd seen her, the sergeant couldn't entirely blame him.

'You can't just barge in,' he insisted.

'We're offering to help you, Sergeant. That's all.' Mirabelle's tone was measured.

The sergeant had to admit that if the women had seen the place it would be helpful to have their view. 'All right,' he said, making the decision. 'Just till the council turns up.'

Inside, it took a moment for Mirabelle's eyes to adjust to the low light of the vestibule. Vesta shivered. It seemed colder than the day before.

'Careful,' Belton instructed as they turned into the long hallway. 'Well, do you notice anything?'

'There was an ashtray there – a gold one. That's gone,' Vesta said as they approached the foot of the stairs. The blue sofa had been straightened and the spray of white feathers cleaned away. The magazines were also missing. It had been carefully done, Mirabelle thought. She wondered by whom. Belton took a note. *Gold ashtray*, Mirabelle read over his shoulder as they went into the room with the ebony statues.

'This looks the same. I don't think anything's gone. We were upstairs in the Yellow Bow Room, too. The Duke of Clarence's,' said Mirabelle. 'Oh, and the kitchen.'

Vesta looked away. She found it difficult when Mirabelle lied. Sergeant Belton didn't question it. He led the women upstairs into another hallway where everything smelled even more musty. The long carpet had been rolled back, exposing wide wooden floorboards caked with dust.

Two policemen passed them, the beams from their torches catching dust particles in the air. 'There's no one up here, Sarge,' one of them said.

'Close it up,' Belton ordered. 'We're just going to see if Miss Bevan and Mrs Lewis can identify anything that might be missing.'

'That's what Daphne was working on.' Mirabelle gestured

towards the carpet. 'Saving the textiles. Both Daphne and Mrs Chapman, in fact.'

'Mrs Chapman? Wasn't she the victim at the lodge yesterday?' Belton sounded surprised.

'Yes. We were there when she died. That's what we were doing here. We came to tell Daphne what had happened. Mrs Chapman worked here, as well as Queen's Road. Didn't you know?' Belton's grey eyes flickered. It only took a moment but the sergeant was looking at the women in a different way. Mirabelle realised he had moved them onto a mental list headed 'possible suspects'. She couldn't blame him. Being at two separate crime scenes within days was unfortunately not unusual for them.

'This hallway must have been very beautiful in its day,' Vesta mumbled.

Belton stiffened slightly. 'It's along here, isn't it?'

'To the rear,' Mirabelle said confidently. 'It's difficult to remember all the passageways. Ah, yes,' she cooed, as they turned into a bedroom with a curved window that overlooked the garden with Old Steine beyond. A four-poster bed with faded gold-trimmed hangings stood forlornly against one wall. A mahogany dressing table sat by the window some way off. Through a connecting door they could just make out a similar adjacent room. Neither contained a camp bed or any of Daphne Marsden's clothing.

'Not much up here, is there?' said Belton. 'Do you notice anything gone?'

Mirabelle shook her head, catching Vesta's eye.

'Looks like the thieves just ran off then, or if they did get away with something it was small.'

'It's Daphne you need to speak to – she knows the place inside out. I can't see anything different, really. Everything that belongs here seems in place. I'm worried about her, though. She's a reliable sort and, well, in effect, she's missing. Normally there would be a few of her things about the place, and they're gone.'

'What kind of things?'

'She works here. The ashtray, for example. Her overcoat. Notes.' Mirabelle didn't want to betray the girl but at the same time Daphne appeared to have disappeared. She bet the television set would be gone, too, but telling Sergeant Belton about it would have been too much of a giveaway. 'She has lunch here every day,' Mirabelle wound up. 'But I can't see anything of hers – not even a cup and saucer. Do you think she might have been spirited away for some reason?'

Belton considered this. 'That's a bit dramatic, surely,' he said, leading them back through the hallway to the head of the stairs. 'Perhaps she had the day off and took her things home for cleaning. It might be that we're not dealing with a break-in at all. She could've left the door open by mistake when she left. You'll need to leave a description of her. Don't worry though. We'll run her down one way or another.'

'Would you like us to check the kitchen?' Mirabelle asked.

Belton shook his head. 'No, there's nothing in there worth lifting. We'd have noticed. It's all tiles and ironmongery.'

Mirabelle noted that Daphne's Primus stove had probably disappeared along with any supplies. As they returned to the vestibule, the sergeant gestured towards the door and nodded to Vesta. 'Thanks, and give Charlie my best. I might pop in tomorrow and hear him play.'

Vesta grinned. 'He'd like that.'

'In the meantime, I don't want you two ladies going anywhere. All right?'

'What do you mean?'

'Stay in Brighton. We might need you. This friend of yours is the acquaintance of a murder victim. And you're her acquaintance.' Belton's voice was expressionless. It didn't sound like a threat and yet somehow it felt that way. 'If you were at the scene of that poor woman's death yesterday, you're also witnesses. Besides, if this is a break-in it might be tied to the old woman's murder. I'm surprised the policeman in charge didn't instruct you to stay in the vicinity yesterday. We might need to be in touch. Don't leave Brighton. Neither of you.' Belton's voice brooked no question.

Mirabelle couldn't help but feel slightly miffed. McGregor wouldn't give her that kind of order. Of course he would know she was innocent, quite beside the fact that he wouldn't dare.

Sergeant Belton kept an eye on the women as they walked down the pathway.

'Well, either Daphne packed up . . .' Vesta began to postulate.

Mirabelle put her hand on Vesta's arm to stop her talking until they were out of earshot. They were almost at the main road when she considered it safe to continue. 'Packing up would be both odd and suspicious,' she agreed, 'but it looks that way.'

'Well, it's either that or she was taken. But if she was taken, who took her? Absconding is far more likely, and, if so, there's a chance Daphne's the killer. Perhaps she murdered Mrs Chapman and Joey Gillingham. Maybe she panicked and ran off. We might have had a lucky escape yesterday – she had us in there. Alone. We could have been in all kinds of danger.'

Mirabelle couldn't help but laugh. 'Daphne Marsden cut a man's throat? Do you think she might have tied us up and stabbed us with an eighteenth-century fruit knife? Or poisoned the cleaning lady? Honestly, Vesta, I can't see it.'

'Why does everyone think that Mrs Chapman is irrelevant because of her job?'

'You know I don't think that. Come on. Belton isn't going to get very far finding the girl. It would be best if we track her down. We need to get back to the office.' Mirabelle picked up the pace.

Vesta glanced forlornly in the direction of the Lanes and her long-overdue fish pie. 'Can't we just go . . .'

Mirabelle was adamant. 'Don't be ridiculous,' she said.

The women turned down East Street and straight into the doorway of the office building. They ran up the stairs and Mirabelle drew out her key. Vesta had become jumpy in the three minutes it had taken them to get back.

'Do you think it's some kind of dreadful plot?' She was beginning to panic. 'I mean, Daphne might be anywhere. Anyone might have her. Some monster – some absolute beast.'

It ran through the girl's mind that she might have known. Mirabelle had a nose for this kind of thing. The minute she got interested in a case, it was a dead cert there'd be something serious. Vesta had been kidnapped two years before. She'd been released safely, but the man she'd been taken with hadn't been so lucky. Maybe Daphne was tied up somewhere, praying desperately for someone to come and get her.

By contrast Mirabelle remained calm. Her fingers fluttered a little, but that was all. 'You need to work from your last certainty, Vesta. Haven't you learned anything?' she scolded as she reached for the telephone and called the operator. 'Be sensible,' she mouthed as she turned her attention to the voice at the other end of the line. 'Could you put me through to the Headquarters of the National Trust?'

Vesta lingered.

'Don't fuss. It won't help,' Mirabelle whispered sternly with one hand over the mouthpiece. 'Sit down,' she gestured. 'Eat something.'

The girl drew out the last of her Jelly Babies for comfort. One orange and one lime sweet fell onto her palm as she up-ended the bag. She passed the green one to Mirabelle who scrutinised it as if it was a deadly insect.

'Good afternoon,' she said. 'I wonder if I might speak to someone about Daphne Marsden, an employee of yours who has been involved in restoration work at the Royal Pavilion in Brighton? . . . I'm trying to get in touch with her, and I hoped you'd have her contact details.'

At the other end of the wire, the woman's voice was so shrill that Vesta could hear every word. 'What is it in connection with?' the woman squawked.

Mirabelle thought quickly. 'A bereavement. I need to get in touch with Miss Marsden as soon as I can, but she isn't at the Pavilion today. I don't want her to miss the funeral, you see.'

'Hold, please. I'll check the records.'

The telephone clicked. Vesta felt calmer. The situation was in hand. She eyed her friend with pride. Mirabelle really was unflappable. She was tenacious, too – she'd follow every lead right to the end. Vesta wondered where Mirabelle had learned to sit so straight. You could crown the woman with an ostrich feather and it wouldn't so much as flutter.

The lady at the National Trust office returned. 'Hello. I'm afraid I have no Brighton address for Daphne, but you might be able to contact her through her family. I'm looking at the file now. They live, let me see, in Cambridge. This form has been filled out entirely incorrectly,' she tutted, 'but her father is a professor, it seems. I'm sorry – I don't have an address, and really I should – but I'm sure if you phoned the university and asked for him they'd point you in the right direction. Peter Marsden – he's Professor of Architecture at Downing College.'

Mirabelle smiled. 'Thank you.' She put down the phone with a satisfied click. 'There, that's a good start.'

Vesta stared. 'She might not be there.'

Mirabelle looked doubtful. 'She might not,' she admitted, 'but we're a step closer.'

Vesta chewed her Jelly Baby. Mirabelle might be right, and, for that matter, admirable, but sometimes she could also be infuriating. 'What do we do now?' she mumbled. 'Ring them?'

Mirabelle slipped the green Jelly Baby into her mouth and sucked. 'Oh no. We have to go there,' she said slowly.

'Where?'

'Cambridge, of course. When you think about it, it ties in very nicely. Architecture, you see. It's quite masonic – or it can be.'

Vesta decided not to ask. Not just yet.

Mirabelle picked up her handbag. 'Right,' she said, checking her watch and winding it thoughtfully, 'if we catch the next train to London we can make it to Cambridge just as they'll be finishing dinner. We'll have to stay over.'

Vesta got to her feet. 'But Sergeant Belton said we shouldn't leave Brighton.'

Mirabelle's eyes twinkled. 'You stay if you like. I'll be back tomorrow. There's no substitute for meeting people, Vesta – you pick up so much more. If the girl has absconded then her family might have an idea where she's gone, if they aren't sheltering her at home. Most people go home, you see, when they get into trouble. It's only natural.'

Vesta considered the matter. Home for her, she realised, was her little bedsit now, not the brick-built house where she'd grown up. That's how it felt.

'When did we ever listen to a policeman, anyway?' Vesta shrugged her shoulders.

When Mirabelle got in one of these moods it was best to hang onto her coat-tails and hope for the best. She'd leave a message for Charlie with Mrs Agora.

Chapter 18

Above all, be armed.

The women bought pork pies from a stall at Victoria Station before they caught the Tube to King's Cross for the Cambridge train. It felt good to be back in London, if only for a few minutes, thought Mirabelle. The city still clung to the vestiges of Coronation fever that had pulsed through the whole country only a few weeks before, and the streets around Victoria were busy with people heading to and from St James's park. Descending into the Tube to cross town, Vesta stowed the pies in her capacious handbag. Only a few minutes later the women exited King's Cross on Euston Road. They could hear someone playing an old wartime hit on a piano in a nearby pub. A tatty Union Jack was still hoisted from an upstairs window. On the north side of the station women on the game leaned in doorways, smoking and chatting and dressed to the threadbare nines. Several cars were waiting at the traffic lights on the road towards Bloomsbury, their engines a background purr. Mirabelle liked it here. London felt like the biggest and best city in the world. Gritty and glamorous, its streets would always be scarred by the Blitz though now the worst of the city's wounds were slowly closing over.

The women decided to go to the station bar for some sustenance. Inside, Vesta pushed through the crowd and bought two bottles of beer, which she also stowed in her handbag for the second train.

'Something for the journey. That's us all set.' She laughed as they hurried to make their connection.

The carriage rocked like a cradle and the women fell silent, sipping the beer, eating the pies and staring out of the window as the city receded. The down-at-heel trackside houses turned in due course into factories and then fields. As they left town, the train stopped at a series of small stations with glossy green benches and tubs of forget-me-nots, pansies and primroses. Almost at Cambridge the sun began to sink into the fens. In the half-light Mirabelle could just make out Ely Cathedral as she finished her drink.

'We're almost there,' she said. 'It's pretty, isn't it?'

'Did you study here?' Vesta asked.

Mirabelle shook her head. 'Quite the reverse. Oxford.'

Vesta giggled. If anywhere was the opposite of the University of Cambridge it was Southwark Secretarial College where she had taken her shorthand qualification and had learned to type. To Vesta the two august institutions were interchangeable.

'I visited Cambridge now and then in my university days,' Mirabelle reflected. 'I was keen on debating. It was quite competitive.'

Vesta tried to imagine it. For someone who now said so little it was curious to think of her friend banging her fist on a wooden lectern as she argued and difficult to conjure an image of Mirabelle that was younger and more argumentative. What had she worn, Vesta wondered, as she expounded her opinions? How had she done her hair? Mirabelle seemed perpetual – like a statue set in stone, without a past or a future. And now Vesta came to think of it, even in company Mirabelle never really functioned as part of a team. She was always slightly detached. She'd known Mirabelle for two years and still had very little idea about her personal life, even where she'd come from, let alone what she'd done in the mysterious office where she'd worked during World War II.

'I'll bet you were good at debating,' she said.

Mirabelle checked her hat was in place and gently smoothed Vesta's collar where it had twisted. 'We used to stay in rooms at St Catharine's, but there was a nice B&B near the Fitzwilliam Museum. We'll book into that one,' she said decisively. 'I hope it's still there.'

The train pulled in just after nine and Cambridge appeared all but asleep. As the handful of other passengers dispersed, the women slipped into a taxi. Vesta took in the deserted winding streets and shopfronts. Even the pubs appeared only half-open. A dull glow in the windows was the only sign that anyone might be inside. A multitude of bicycles lined both sides of the road. The gold lettering from the university outfitters shimmered in the headlamps, and shop after shop appeared to sell nothing but books and sports equipment. Occasionally a high wall or a closed gate denoted college grounds. Ancient stained-glass windows set into the outer walls looked as if they were lit only by candles, and signs seemed for the benefit of insiders only. 'Reach Library By The Backs' one said, and 'Silence During Evensong', without any indication of the time of the service. The taxi slowed to give way to a white-faced boy in a black academic gown who scuttled across the street without looking left or right.

'Doesn't anyone eat?' Vesta asked, straining to make out a bakery, a restaurant or a grocery – anywhere that might provide food. The evening air was devoid of the smell of cooking.

'Well, there can't be many people about. It's the end of term now. In any case, mostly people dine in college,' Mirabelle remembered.

Cambridge, after all, was smaller than Oxford. The university dominated everything. It wanted its dons on campus not carousing in town. When the locals went out to eat they chose pubs and restaurants on the river with views over the countryside. There wasn't much to do in the city centre apart from buy books and drink beer.

'Tomorrow, if we've time before we go back to Brighton, we can pop into Fitzbillies,' she offered. 'Very good rock buns.'

Satisfied with this, Vesta settled into her seat as the cab turned onto a wide road of Victorian houses and shops. A little way along, the driver pulled up next to a grand gate set into a high brick wall. 'Downing College, ladies,' he announced.

'Quiet night,' said Mirabelle as she handed him their fare.

The driver shrugged. 'I'm off home now. I just live round the corner. Thank you, Miss.'

Vesta rang the bell beside the gate. When the porter arrived he was a cheery fellow in a bowler hat who beamed when Mirabelle mentioned Professor Marsden.

'He'll be glad to see you two.' The fellow winked, eyeing Vesta up and down. 'I can take you over, if you like.'

'Just point us in the right direction, if you don't mind.' Mirabelle scanned the grounds.

The man raised a hand as if he was directing traffic. Downing College was lavishly laid out with wide pathways and long quads between the buildings. It was just starting to get dark. One by one the outside lights were switching on.

'Down the path,' the porter gestured, 'past the chapel and then the library. You'll see it when you get there. It's the third block on the left.'

As the women started down the pathway, the man retreated into his office, removing his bowler hat before he'd even made it through the door.

'Benji, that dog Marsden's got another two up there,' they heard him say, his accent as broad as it was leering. 'Frisky old sod.'

Mirabelle peered over her shoulder. The professor, it might be deduced, was one for the ladies. A veritable Cary Grant.

A beautiful landscape of well-kept lawns and terraced college buildings opened before them. It seemed vast in comparison to the cramped streets they'd seen on the way from the station. Some of the lawns had been laid over to fruit and vegetables. Mirabelle spotted rows of leeks and potatoes as well as raspberry canes and what looked like a plot of green beans and marrows. Downing had evidently done its bit, dug for victory and was still going strong. Somewhere in the distance Mirabelle could hear the contented cluck of chickens as the dusk fell. The college must have its own supply of eggs. Despite generating its own food by turning its quads into farmland, the place still felt grand.

To Mirabelle the feeling of coming off a street into a hidden world was familiar. The last time she'd been in Cambridge she'd visited a pub called St Radegund's. The group had gone there after the debate was over. The pub was far enough away for the students to be able to let down their hair – on King Street, near Jesus College, a fifteen-minute walk from where they were staying. Women hadn't been welcome but the landlord made an exception for her – the only girl on the debating team. Ironic, she remembered thinking, as St Radegund was female. Once the pints had been pulled and gin poured, the doors were locked and the debating teams of both universities got down to unofficial argument jammed against each other in the cramped, smoky room. Coming back into the college afterwards it felt as if the world had disappeared beyond the walls. She remembered feeling sophisticated – 'a female pioneer' her tutor had said. In the morning she'd woken to sunshine and cherry trees scattering petals like confetti across the quad. It had been 1934. It felt like a million years ago.

Now, she took in the surroundings. Downing was a relatively modern college – late Georgian she guessed. The boundary was skirted by a long stretch of high railings that separated the college grounds from those of the institution next door. To the right a classical chapel built of Portland stone loomed out of the balmy half-light. Further along there was a library fronted by a row of columns. Above them symbols were carved beneath a stone apex. It was too dark to make out exactly what they were, but there was a scale of justice in the centre. Was that masonic?

Vesta clutched Mirabelle's arm. 'I've never been anywhere like this before,' she whispered. When Mirabelle had said they were going to a college, Vesta had expected a single building, not this immaculate place that was more like a little town.

At the doorway of the accommodation block the nameplate for the first floor indicated Professor Marsden's rooms.

Mirabelle patted Vesta's hand. 'Keep your eyes open,' she said. 'We need to find out about his daughter, and I expect he'll be smooth as silk.'

Vesta grinned. The college might be intimidating but she was well able to deal with a gentleman's advances. A year with Charlie hadn't dulled her skills with the opposite sex.

'Ready?' Mirabelle checked.

Vesta nodded and Mirabelle knocked. When the door opened, a fug of pipe smoke assailed their senses.

'Professor Marsden?' Mirabelle enquired.

The man who stood on the threshold was portly, grey-haired and wearing a thick brown cardigan despite the warm weather. He was not what either of the women was expecting as he peered towards them owlishly through a pair of dark-rimmed spectacles. Tufts of hair poked out of his ears and his hair was too long to be respectable. Rather than an anti-establishment style statement it seemed far more likely that the professor had simply neglected to trim it. He coughed. 'Yes,' he said. 'Who on earth are you?'

Mirabelle hid her confusion. The porter's comment had hinted at a ladies' man. This individual looked as if someone had knitted him into being. Something about his sartorial disarray was reminiscent of Daphne and her crumpled linen trousers, though the girl's fine features must come from her mother's side.

'I'm Mirabelle Bevan, pleased to meet you, and my friend Vesta Churchill. We're looking for your daughter. Might we come in?'

Professor Marsden appeared bamboozled by this request but he stepped backwards nonetheless, albeit slightly unsteadily. The room was large, fitted with mahogany and packed with books, some of which teetered in piles on the floor. The tables and chairs were strewn with papers and bound manuscripts, many of which lay splayed, face down. Two drawing boards were covered with reams of paper held in place by a combination of paperweights and string. The walls were covered with prints of ancient buildings and black-and-white photographs of what looked like Greek ruins. The windows looked as if they hadn't been opened in decades. The bedroom, which lay through an open door to one side, appeared not one iota more tidy or welcoming than the study.

The professor retreated towards the sideboard. 'Lady visitors are not allowed after curfew,' he said. 'Not even in vacation time. The porter shouldn't have admitted you.'

Mirabelle smiled and made no reply. The combination of the overwhelming smell of pipe smoke and the unexpected appearance of the professor had left her momentarily stunned.

Professor Marsden lifted a decanter in the direction of the women. 'Brandy?'

Vesta shook her head.

'No. Thank you.' Mirabelle recovered herself. 'I wondered if you had heard from Daphne lately?'

The professor poured a drink and took a gulp before he answered. He had been drinking for a while, Mirabelle realised. She told herself this might be a good thing. No matter what they thought, drunks invariably let their guard down. Whether they were angry or sad or uncooperative they always told you more than someone with their stone-cold wits about them.

'Daphne? None of the women in my family speak to me unless they have to,' he spat. 'Not one of them. Daphne included.'

Mirabelle's eyes fell to one of the drawing boards. She'd lead him a little dance, a wander around what she'd like to know. She pointed at the sketch that lay on top of the pile.

'That's the chapel we passed on the other side of the main path. Did you draw it?'

Marsden nodded.

'It's very good.'

'Thank you.'

'I like the carvings on the masonry. I couldn't quite make them out in the evening light. You're a professor of architecture, aren't you?'

Marsden lurched across the room to point out the features with a sudden burst of enthusiasm. 'Symbolism is one of my specialist subjects.' He started to reel off the details of laurel wreaths and snakes. He favoured Latin terms and architectural jargon, Mirabelle noted. Daphne's father was not a man of the people. She nodded as he continued but Vesta's head was cocked to one side – many of the images looked simple but the professor used such complicated terms to describe them and the tone of his voice was set in such a deathly drone that it was difficult to follow what he was saying.

'These are masonic symbols, aren't they?' Vesta cut to the chase when he finally paused.

'Well, what of it?' He sounded angry.

'Are you a brother mason, Professor?' Mirabelle enquired gently.

Marsden crossed his arms. 'That's none of your business.'

'I was only curious.'

'This is something to do with Hilary, isn't it? *She* sent you.'

'Hilary?'

'My wife. You look as if you've something to do with her. Women's Institute through and through. White knickers and crossed legs.' He took a swig of his brandy. 'She's allowed her club but I'm not allowed mine. Isn't that the way?'

Mirabelle shook her head and decided to ignore the implication. With anyone drunk, you had to guide them to where you wanted and then guide them back again when they rambled. And, of course, the comment meant he was a mason, so that was a start.

'No. It's Daphne we're looking for. Your daughter.'

'They're all the same,' he said bitterly.

'I doubt that, Professor.'

'Do you, indeed?'

Mirabelle felt her hackles rise. This man, after all, had left his daughter with an allowance so small it was impossible to live on it. Surely he must realise the girl's job didn't pay a living wage.

'I'd have thought you'd be proud of Daphne,' she said. 'She's following in your footsteps after a fashion. She seems to be doing good work for the National Trust. If it wasn't for her efforts, the Royal Pavilion would be in a far worse state than it is. Surely you approve? She seems a thoroughly decent girl to me.'

Marsden spluttered. 'Daphne? Well, she's obviously pulled the wool over your eyes. My daughter doesn't care about heritage. She doesn't give a fig about our past. She hasn't got the first idea about history and no discrimination about what's really important. That girl is the only thing that Hilary and I agree upon. She's nothing but trouble. My daughter is obsessed with money and possessions, Miss Bevan. A green silk scarf can turn her head. It suits her, of course – matches her eyes and so on – but that's not the point. Money. That's Daphne's real interest in the people around her, and I've no doubt, in her precious Trust, too. It's her only interest in anything. We should never have let the little gold-digger leave home.'

'Gracious. I had no idea. Well, you can't force them to stay, can you? And I can see it's making you terribly cross.' Mirabelle continued to lead him in and out of his argument.

Marsden's demeanour softened at the sign of what he took to be her sympathy. He lit his pipe and sank into a chair beside the fireplace. Then he propped his head in his hand and took another swig of brandy. Mirabelle motioned towards the sofa and Marsden nodded. The women sat.

'How did you meet Daphne?' he asked.

'We had a mutual acquaintance.'

'Look, I haven't seen the girl for months,' the professor said. 'We got together at Christmas for a dreadful week of family celebrations. A dozen people with the same surname, that's all. I don't understand why you're looking for her. What has she done now?'

'We met Daphne in Brighton,' Mirabelle said slowly. 'Both Vesta and I live there. Today we went to visit her and she had simply disappeared. Her digs had been cleared and the door left wide open. She didn't turn up for work at the Pavilion, and that isn't like her. Naturally, we were concerned and when we rang the Trust they gave your name as Daphne's only contact. We came to check she was all right – we thought you'd know where she was. We were worried something might have happened to her.'

'Oh, I shouldn't worry,' Professor Marsden said dismissively. 'She'll have met a man.'

Mirabelle's eyes narrowed. It was disrespectful of him to talk about his daughter this way, drunk or not. Calling the girl a gold-digger was nasty enough, but throwing out the assumption that she'd left town with a man on a whim was quite another. Daphne was a good-looking girl but she hadn't given any sign of being fast. It was the quickest way to discredit someone, she thought, to accuse them of loose living – especially a woman. On principle, Mirabelle never judged the private lives of others. She knew that's what would have happened to her had people known about Jack. They'd have thought she was a home-wrecker. A scarlet woman. And they would have been wrong.

Marsden glanced at his wristwatch. Unlike the rest of his attire it was smart and expensive. A Longines, Mirabelle noticed. He checked it again as surreptitiously as he could. So, he wanted to get rid of them. It was time to press Professor Marsden's buttons.

'I noticed Daphne wasn't keen on the masons when I spoke to her,' she tried. 'What was it she said, Vesta?'

Vesta was transfixed by the books and the pictures. She tore her eyes away from the walls as if she was startled. 'She said they didn't care much about equality.'

'Yes, that was it. She seemed annoyed that the freemasons didn't admit women.'

Marsden's stare was uncompromising. Just for a moment, he looked as if he might erupt in rage, but he controlled himself. 'She's always been jealous of her brothers,' he said. 'Ever since she was little. And she resents me, of course. That goes without saying.'

'So, Daphne's the only girl apart from your wife?'

Marsden gave a half-nod. 'Well, my wife has sisters. But that's not the point. Women don't belong in the masons. It's not that kind of organisation. We don't need women.' He was slurring now. 'We never have. There's a female chapter in London. It was set up by a bunch of dykes. Ridiculous! They're not affiliated at all. Freemasonry is a man's business.'

He checked his watch again.

'Well,' said Mirabelle, getting to her feet, 'it has been very interesting to meet you, Professor.'

Vesta glared. She clearly felt there was more mileage to be had.

'Come along. We have to go,' Mirabelle chivvied her.

'Will you stay overnight in Cambridge, Miss Bevan?' The professor's manner became unexpectedly solicitous now that he knew they were leaving.

'No. There's a late train, I believe.' Mirabelle shook the man's hand. 'If we leave now we'll make it. I'm sure Daphne's fine and she'll be back in a few days. I had no idea about her behaviour. We'd never have come had we known.'

The professor looked relieved. 'I'm sorry that she bothered you,' he said. 'It was kind of you to take the trouble, but, really, there's no point in trying to help Daphne, Miss Bevan. She's a lost cause.' He got to his feet and ushered them to the door. Mirabelle noted that he remained there, making sure they walked down the staircase. As she glanced back, he raised an encouraging hand. The moment the women set foot outside, Mirabelle grasped Vesta's arm.

'Don't look back,' she whispered. She was convinced that the professor would be watching them from his window, checking that they were heading for the gate.

'Well?' said Vesta as they rounded the corner and ground to a halt. 'What was that about?'

'She's obviously been here.'

'Who?'

'Daphne.'

'Really?' Vesta declared. 'After all the I-hate-my-daughter and there's-no-place-for-women-in-the-masons. And that weird stuff everywhere – creepy old pictures and books lying around. He can't actually be reading them all. The old man's mad.'

'It's the green scarf, don't you see? Daphne said her uncle sent it with the television. But if Daphne hadn't seen her father since Christmas, well, he couldn't have known it suited her – he'd never have seen it. So she's been with him in the last few weeks – since the Coronation. He won't have gone to her, let's face it. So, she must have been up here. And I tell you what, I'll wager it was today.'

'Why on earth would Daphne want to see him?' Vesta sounded mystified. 'If he was my father I'd avoid him like the plague.'

'I don't know. But no other woman's going to want to go up there, is she? Think about what the porter said. Marsden's a joke, don't you see? He's a charmless old misogynist. He's had women visitors for the first time in the college's history. Three of us in twenty-four hours. The porter thought it was hilarious, and no wonder.'

Vesta's mouth spread into a grin.

'When they made out he was a catch, I hoped he might be your type,' she started to giggle.

'Don't be ridiculous.'

'You've got to meet a man sometime, Mirabelle. A woman like you needs someone. I thought a brain-box professor might be your type. Though perhaps not that one. Look, maybe someone else told him about the silk scarf and he just knew it would suit Daphne's eyes. If Marsden had a lady visitor today, it could be anyone. Maybe he's cheating on Hilary already,' Vesta whispered. 'Maybe he got lucky. You never know.'

Mirabelle frowned. 'Today? On the very day his daughter goes missing? By chance? A fine specimen like Peter Marsden? No. Daphne's been here. And let's face it, she wouldn't have come if she hadn't had to. The old fellow was watching the time the whole time we were there. He's expecting visitors. Come on, we need to keep an eye on the entrance to his rooms without being spotted. We'll have to swing round the long way. Thank goodness it's almost dark.'

Chapter 19

Wickedness is its own punishment.

Trying to keep the click of their heels on the cobbles to a minimum, the women sneaked into the shadowy entranceway directly opposite Marsden's rooms. The last of the light had faded. It was ten o'clock. All over Cambridge, church bells were striking. Two students parked their bikes and disappeared with a clatter into a building further along. The porter, now wearing an old-fashioned cape, set out on his rounds, checking the library door and making sure the gates in the railings that skirted the campus were locked and chained. Out of habit, Mirabelle timed him. The accommodation blocks, unlit for the most part, were completely silent. A fox stalked elegantly between the rows of potatoes and disappeared through the railings at the other end.

Vesta sighed and wriggled around on the bottom step of the stairway. She rested her chin in her palm. It had perhaps been half an hour but, Vesta thought, it seemed considerably longer.

'This isn't promising,' she complained. 'Nothing's happening.'

'Surveillance is always boring,' Mirabelle replied.

She seemed entirely resigned to sitting here for however long it might take for something to happen. Vesta wondered if Professor Marsden had been simply checking his watch because it was almost time to go to bed.

'What are you hoping for?'

'I'm not sure,' she admitted without taking her eyes off the professor's window. 'We'll have to wait and see.'

A further forty minutes later Vesta yawned heavily once more and wished she'd worn flat shoes. She cocked her head to read the time on the slim gold watch on Mirabelle's wrist. The lights in Marsden's room were still switched on. 'He's just up there drinking himself into a stupor,' she said. 'Sad old man. Don't you think we should head for the B&B?'

'You walk round if you like.'

'Yeah. I won't have any trouble booking in by myself.'

Mirabelle sat down next to her. Last year checking into a London hotel, the receptionist had assumed Vesta was Mirabelle's maid. The memory still made her cheeks burn. It wasn't easy to be black. It wasn't easy, Mirabelle told herself, to be different in any way.

'I'm sorry,' she said. 'Mind you, they're a bit more open-minded here – Oxford and Cambridge are probably better than London. Colleges are accustomed to visitors from overseas.'

'I'm English,' Vesta said petulantly. 'And there's hardly any white people round here, never mind black ones. I'd prefer it if you'd come with me.'

It was a fair point. Whoever ran the B&B wouldn't be a cosmopolitan university professor, and the provincial English landladies of Vesta's experience had usually never seen a coloured person, let alone accommodated one.

Mirabelle stared across the quad. Jack always said information was vital – of course it was – and in this instance there was no other way to get it than to sit things out. There was a strong argument that surveillance had won Britain the war. On that basis alone, she told herself, there were ample reasons to stay. Daphne had been here. Professor Marsden had lied about it and where there was a lie, there was a reason for a lie.

'Sorry,' she said. 'We've come all this way and he's trying to hide Daphne. It only takes a second to miss something important. Hopefully it shouldn't be too much longer. At least it isn't cold tonight.'

That much was true. It was also silent, or near enough. You could almost believe you were in the countryside.

Then, on the evening air the women heard men's voices, indistinct but in conversation some way off. They both perked up. Vesta sprang to her feet. Perhaps here was their evidence. They craned to see two figures, strolling along the path on the other side of the quad. The gentlemen looked like typical academics, Vesta decided. One fellow had a moustache and was wearing a well-tailored three-piece tweed suit. The tone of his voice was low and he gestured emphatically as he walked. Neither of the women could make out what he was saying. The other fellow was dressed in an old-fashioned black outfit that looked as if it might be clerical. Clean-shaven, he was tall and slim, and sported a bowler hat. A bit like Alastair Sim, thought Vesta.

Mirabelle held her breath as the men passed the doorway to the professor's rooms and instead entered the next stairwell. Inside, a moment later, the first-floor curtains were drawn and a dim light seeped over the potato plants.

Vesta sighed with frustration. 'I'm exhausted. You think of stairwells as places you move through,' she said. 'Not for dossing down. I feel like an old tramp.'

Still, she slipped back to the step, leaned her head on the wall and closed her eyes. Back in Brighton Charlie would have got her message by now. He'd sit up with Mrs Agora and then go to bed early, she thought. He was always tired on Wednesdays after the gig on Tuesday night and the long day in the kitchens that followed. Now Vesta imagined she was curled up next to him on their thick soft mattress. They had taken to sleeping naked in the heat, their winter nightwear abandoned and only a thin blue sheet over the top. She liked slipping out of consciousness with Charlie's arms wrapped round her, his smooth skin warm along her back. Some nights she woke up to find she had puckered her lips onto his forearm and was sucking his skin like a hungry baby.

'Sorry,' she'd murmur drowsily. But Charlie didn't mind. He didn't mind anything. Not her flashes of temper, her independent streak or her inability to keep things tidy. With a rush she realised how much she missed him.

'I love Charlie, you know,' she whispered sleepily. 'You mustn't think that I don't.'

'Of course you do,' Mirabelle soothed. 'Perhaps you should say yes to him and stop fretting all the time. Being Mrs Lewis wouldn't be half as horrifying as you're imagining – it might be lovely.'

'Mr Tupps said that institutions are all that matter – all that endures. The masons. The church. Marriage, too, I guess.'

'He might be right,' Mirabelle whispered. She was about to say more – something about how important marriage was and how lucky Vesta and Charlie were to have found each other – when Vesta let out a little snore and she realised the girl had fallen asleep. Mirabelle envied her. Vesta always seemed so relaxed at the heart of her whirlwind. Underneath the disarray and excitable thinking the girl had a great capacity for happiness. Vesta was an alien creature sometimes. She wondered if the girl's mother, a loving but strict woman from South London, might be the reason that domestic life held such terrors for her. The Churchills had been shocked enough at Vesta's behaviour when she took the job at McGuigan & McGuigan, never mind how they'd feel if they knew Vesta and Charlie were sharing digs. So many people seemed to live their lives in reaction to their parents, Mirabelle pondered. If she hadn't been orphaned while she was still at college, perhaps she'd have done the same. It must be difficult for Daphne, she realised, with a father who was so uncaring. Girls needed their fathers and, given she'd gone into restoration, Daphne must feel a connection with her old man, even if it wasn't reciprocated. Perhaps in getting involved with the Trust she had been trying to please him or at the very least show him that she was worthwhile. In return, the professor was almost unbelievably cruel.

Vesta's breathing was even. An owl hooted, far off, the sound carrying on the still night air. At long last, just before midnight Mirabelle noticed someone on the path. She stood up and pressed herself against the wall. She couldn't make out if the figure was male or female but then it passed beneath a light and it was clear that not only was it female, it was Daphne. She was wearing a cream, belted mackintosh with the green silk scarf tied jauntily at her throat. A pair of patent pumps flashed in the lamplight. Mirabelle allowed herself a smile. She'd been right. Persistence always paid off. Daphne turned into her father's stairwell.

Mirabelle was about to lay a hand on Vesta's arm to wake her when something made her hold off. There wasn't any time to explain and Vesta would be dozy. She'd make too much noise. This wouldn't take long.

She intended to sneak up the stairs and listen at the keyhole. Any conversation between Daphne and her father must surely be illuminating. She tiptoed between the plants to avoid sinking into the soil. She was halfway over, at the most exposed point, when she caught sight of a man walking down the main path. Instinctively Mirabelle flung herself to the ground, squashing several plants but hiding herself in the centre of the vegetable patch. She could just see the man loitering in the light from Marsden's windows, staring upwards as if something was on his mind. This close, she recognised him as the porter who had let her in. Eventually the man shrugged his shoulders and continued on his round. Mirabelle pulled herself up. The earth smelled musty and the sap of the plants let out a fresh perfume. The dirt was dry and it would brush off easily.

Thank goodness this was all happening in a warm June, she thought, rather than a soggy November.

With her eyes on the receding figure of the porter, Mirabelle stole to the foot of the stairs and crept upwards. During the war, she told herself, men had visited bars frequented by Nazis all over occupied France and had calmly sat listening to loose talk from SS officers. The best intelligence had come from people who risked their lives. What she was doing was mild by comparison. She tried to calm herself. Still, her heart was pounding and her fingers felt weak as she lingered, leaning in to listen outside the door.

'Of course I haven't brought it with me,' the girl was saying. 'Do you think I'm a complete fool? You're only the broker, Daddy – that's all. They need to pay before they'll get a sniff at it. Those are my terms.'

Mirabelle couldn't hear Marsden's response but she could tell that he was furious. What had he expected Daphne to bring to his rooms in the middle of the night, she wondered. She crouched down, placing herself behind the hinge of the door. If it opened suddenly she could dash up to the next flight and be round the corner in seconds.

'You aren't seriously expecting me to boo-hoo and just give up?' Daphne taunted her father. 'You can shout all you like. Honestly, Daddy. Not such clever old men now, are you – you and your "brothers"? Don't you wish you'd been nicer to me?' The girl sounded as if she was enjoying herself.

'It's a lot of money, Daphne.' The professor's voice was rising, which made it easier to make out. 'Thousands of pounds. You're being far too greedy. It's more than your brother's inheritance, for God's sake.'

Daphne dismissed the objection. 'It's worth every penny and you know it. If Danny isn't clever enough to make his own money, that's his lookout. And it isn't only the cash. Those bastards killed poor Mrs Chapman. You owe me justice as well as money. You're paying the market price, that's all. I'm not looking for any favours. You're used to hiding criminals in your ranks. Well, I won't have a cover-up. Not this time.'

'From what I understand, the woman who died was a criminal.'

Daphne laughed. 'Elsie Chapman? She was no angel, but you killed her, Daddy. Who on earth deserves that?'

'It wasn't me.'

'You know exactly what I mean. You killed her. You people.'

'She wanted five hundred pounds, I heard. She was a blackmailer.'

'She underpriced herself.'

'She threatened to expose the very man she wanted to pay her.'

'So what? I'll bring down the whole organisation if I don't get what I want. I'm only telling the truth, after all.'

'Sometimes, I could strangle you, girl,' spat Marsden.

Daphne laughed again. 'You'll never get what you want that way. I've well and truly covered my back. Your brothers won't like it if you finish me off. I've got it hidden, Daddy, and it'll all come to light if anything happens to me.'

Marsden made a furious huffing noise. 'You're going too far, Daphne.'

'On the contrary. I'm going just far enough,' she insisted. 'You're only annoyed because you thought I'd come home with my tail between my legs and just hand it over. Either that or you thought I wouldn't realise its significance. Well, you're wrong. You've treated me disgracefully for years. This will draw a line under everything. Stick to your end of the deal and I'll stick to mine.'

Through the keyhole Mirabelle saw Daphne adjust her scarf in front of a small mirror by the door. She was fixing her hair when, from behind her in a rush, Professor Marsden caught the girl unawares. He grabbed her roughly and shoved her against a bookshelf.

'You don't know what you're getting into. They're danger-ous people, you little fool,' he growled.

Daphne pulled away. 'Me, too,' she said, turning with a steady gaze. 'I could bring the whole lot into the open. All it would take is a little donation to the British Museum. Or the Royal Scottish Academy. Any institution would do. Or perhaps I'll deliver it straight to a newspaper – one that isn't run by a freemason, of course. And *bam!* There'd be headlines all over the world. But luckily for you, I'd rather have the money and some justice for Elsie. You know how to get in touch with me when you're ready, and you'd better not be a penny short, old man, or I might change my mind.'

Mirabelle sprang to her feet as the door handle moved. She got out of the way just in time. The girl burst into the hall slamming the door shut behind her. Her patent shoes flashed down the steps and onto the paving stones. With one eye on the closed door, Mirabelle followed. Outside, she realised that Daphne must have broken into a run as she rounded the corner. Up ahead, she was already almost at the porter's lodge. She had stood up to her father but it had terrified her. It was admirable really that she held her nerve and that she was set on bringing Mrs Chapman's murderer to justice. As admir-able, Mirabelle told herself, as a blackmailer could ever be. So, the masons killed Mrs Chapman over whatever it was that Daphne had got her hands on. That made sense. Mirabelle kept her eyes on the figure of the girl up ahead but she was moving too quickly. Daphne disappeared through the unlocked gate.

Mirabelle stopped suddenly. Over her shoulder she noticed the professor's light was now the only one switched on in the quad. Like a vague pulse from above, she heard the low tenor of male voices in discussion. The noise was coming from Marsden's rooms. With Daphne gone, Mirabelle turned and crept back upstairs. It was odd. She had watched the entrance all night. No one else had gone in. She'd seen no telephone in the rooms. Was the drunken old sot talking to himself in a rage?

Back at the keyhole, she caught a flash of tweed, brown with a stripe of red through it, as the man with the moustache who had crossed the quad earlier took a seat by the fire. The men's voices were low and she had to strain to make out what they were saying. Daphne had shouted at her father and he had shouted back, but the tenor of a more normal conversation was difficult to make out. The fellow in black followed his friend silently across the room and sat down. Mirabelle put two and two together. There must be a connecting door with the rooms in the next stair.

Mirabelle shifted her position against the door, ready to listen, but her ankle turned and her gasp of pain echoed up the stairwell. Inside, the man in the tweed suit sprang to his feet. She hurriedly backed up the stairs and round the corner, ignoring the pain, with her heart pounding as the door opened below her.

'I didn't hear anything.' Marsden's voice was muted.

The man in tweed sniffed. 'Perfume,' he commented. 'Though I can hardly make it out over your damn pipe smoke, Marsden.'

His accent was Scottish, Mirabelle noted, deep and gravelly, the vowels more drawn out than those of Superintendent McGregor's soft Edinburgh accent.

'It'll be Daphne's,' said Marsden.

The man in tweed hovered. 'You're sure?'

'I don't make a habit of sniffing my daughter, but as she just left it would seem logical.'

Marsden and the man in black resumed their conversation. Mirabelle heard the man in tweed go down a few stairs. He must be checking outside.

'She's determined on justice for her friend.' The professor's voice sailed up the hallway. 'That ghastly cleaning lady who was killed. Poisoned.'

'Who did it?' The man in black was also Scottish, but his accent was softer.

'Damned if I know,' Marsden replied. 'It doesn't really matter, does it? Daphne appears to have been fond of her. She's convinced it was us.'

'Poison? That's a woman's way to murder,' said the man in black, his voice dripping with contempt.

'Who knows what the Brighton lodge has been up to?' Marsden said.

The pair fell silent. The man in tweed returned to the landing. Mirabelle couldn't tell exactly where he was but she held her breath. She glanced upwards. There was another floor but now he was in the hallway he'd hear her if she climbed the stairs.

From inside the room Marsden's guest continued speaking. 'Well, the money's the easy part. If the girl understood what she had or, indeed, who she was really dealing with, she'd realise we'd have paid more. As for the rest of it, Laidlaw, you'll need to find out what the hell has been going on. They're a bunch of amateurs down there. Killing off old ladies.'

'Aye,' the man paused in the doorway, 'I'll get to the bottom of it, and once I'm at the bottom I'll dig us out. Someone's got to do the dirty work.'

'Good man.' The fellow in the chair sounded enthusiastic. 'Laidlaw here is good at doing whatever it takes. Never afraid of a stramash, eh, Laidlaw?'

'No.'

'And afterwards . . .' said Marsden.

'You'll write us a history, Peter. The history we want,' the second man said firmly. 'And you'll be paid handsomely for it. You're a respected academic after all, as well as a respected brother. Don't worry.'

'I don't want money,' the professor insisted. 'I want further in. Further up.'

'That's all anyone ever wants,' the man in tweed said from the hallway, his voice sarcastic.

'You'll have earned it.' The voice from inside the room was clearly in charge. 'Come back in and close the door, Laidlaw,' he instructed. 'There's no one out there.'

The footsteps sounded and the door closed. Mirabelle edged back down the stairs but as she bent towards the keyhole the men were preparing to leave. She scarcely managed to catch a glimpse of Professor Marsden. He wore a sober look that appeared quite uncharacteristic. The man in tweed was making for the door with his friend close behind him.

Mirabelle backed out of sight again just in time. The men emerged into the stairwell and said their gruff goodnights. Then the door swung closed and she crept downwards, following the Scotsmen at a distance as they walked in silence towards the front gate. The air outside smelled clean by comparison to the hallway, which was drenched in Marsden's pipe tobacco. The man in tweed moved with a jaunty gait but the other one – the master – was as gangly as a teenager, though his hair was grey. Ahead of her, they passed through the gate and disappeared onto the shadowy road beyond. Mirabelle heard an engine pulling up. A car had been waiting. She'd like to get the number plate, she thought, but as she made it to the porter's lodge the now familiar red face of the man on duty dodged out of the doorway and blocked her way.

'Evening, Miss.'

Mirabelle nodded, trying to move round the man's figure so as not to lose sight of her mark.

'Would you like me to find you a cab? It's very late.'

Outside, the two men were getting into a black vehicle a little way along the street. She couldn't see the driver or make out the number plate. She needed Vesta – the girl knew more about cars. The vehicle pulled off, its engine echoing in the silence.

'Those gentlemen . . .'

'Visitors,' said the porter.

'When did they arrive?'

'Before I was on duty.'

That was a lie. 'Have they come here before?'

'You ask a lot of questions, Miss. College business is considered private at Downing. Some might find that kind of enquiry rude.'

Mirabelle didn't back down. She tried to move around the porter but he dodged her.

'I can call a taxi but it'll take a while,' he offered.

'I'm fine, thank you.' She turned back. The car was gone now and she'd best fetch Vesta.

'Oh no, you don't.' The porter nipped round and blocked her path in the other direction. 'I'm afraid there are no ladies allowed on campus at this time of night.' The man took her arm firmly and led her into his office. 'You'll have to wait here,' he said. 'I'll get you a car. Come this way, please.'

'I don't want a car,' Mirabelle insisted, but before she could free herself from his grip she found she had been steered efficiently into a room beyond the reception desk. The porter talked all the while – blustering on about history and tradition and rules. Cambridge was as curious a place as Oxford, she thought, as she turned towards the threshold to push her way back out, but the man was too quick. The door slammed shut in her face. Mirabelle reached for the handle but she couldn't move it.

There was an eerie silence. Then the porter spoke. 'We don't like snoops at Downing. Those fellows have a right to their privacy.'

'They're on the square, you mean,' snapped Mirabelle. 'And so are you.'

'You'd best cool off, Miss. Stop fretting. I'll let you out at the end of my shift.'

'But you can't lock me in here . . . that's kidnapping,' Mirabelle shouted.

There was no reply. She tried once more to turn the handle but he'd locked it. She realised there was no keyhole on the inside. The only light came from a lamp that cast a low glow, but the room stretched well beyond it. In front of her there was a grille and further on a small flight of stone stairs and a line of racks – the college wine cellar, she realised, with a chill running up the back of her neck. There wasn't a window in sight and the cellar itself must cover an acre, Mirabelle thought. She could be here for a very long time.

Chapter 20

Suspicion is a heavy armour.

At the bottom of the stairs Mirabelle clicked on a light and made out wine bottles that were stacked carefully in stamped wooden boxes. Glancing up and down, she read the names on the sides. Saint Honoré. Haut Médoc. The first bottles were the latest arrivals. Young wines from the Langue- doc and Burgundy from 1949 and 1950 and several cases of Saint-Émilion from the year before had clearly just been deliv- ered and were piled at the front.

'Let me out!' she called, feeling slightly claustrophobic. She didn't expect a reply. The porter wouldn't be back till dawn, assuming he was working a nightshift and stayed true to his word. She shuddered and moved further into the cellar. It quickly became apparent that the college had laid down pre- war vintages and was still drinking them. Creeping along the aisles was like walking back in time. Had she drunk some of these wines when she was at college? Had she shared any of these grand vintages with Jack when they had dined occasion- ally at Claridge's or Café de Paris?

Mirabelle turned her mind to what she'd heard outside Professor Marsden's rooms. The men had left intending to quieten Elsie's murderer. She ran through the parts of their discussion she had managed to catch – Elsie had tried to black- mail someone at the lodge in Brighton. Most likely the blackmail attempt had concerned the object that Daphne was now holding over her father. In any case, Daphne seemed sure that the men she was dealing with had done for Elsie. But neither of the Scotsmen nor Professor Marsden knew who had perpetrated the murder. Mirabelle wondered what on earth Daphne was selling. It was something important enough to bring these men to Downing College in the middle of the night. Something so important that they'd kill for it.

Mirabelle shivered as she recalled the threat she'd heard the man make in the hallway. 'I'll get to the bottom of it,' he had said. What he meant, surely, was that he'd go to Brighton and find out who had poisoned Elsie and punish them. Something niggled in Mirabelle's mind. This information changed matters. If Elsie wanted to get money in exchange for a masonic object she surely would have gone to her erstwhile lover. That gave Captain Henshaw a motive for her murder. He had to be the chief suspect. That being the case, the captain was potentially in danger. Mirabelle sank onto a stone ledge. She didn't buy Henshaw as a murderer. She'd seen him as he'd watched Elsie's life being snuffed out. No. There was something she was missing – a crucial piece of the jigsaw. What on earth was it? Still, whether he was guilty or not, as the obvious suspect Henshaw was in terrible danger.

The cellar stretched a long way under the paths she'd walked down earlier. So, Mirabelle reasoned, if she wanted to get out, the first job was to check the ceiling. There was an outside chance there was a drain in the paving, which, even if it didn't open into the cellar directly, might still be accessed as a means of escape. This proved fruitless. The low ceiling stretched unbroken by any kind of hatch. The racks were mired in thick dust and as she made her way between them, sight of the doorway receded. As a precaution, Mirabelle began to mark the stands on the right-hand corner, fingering an 'X' in the cobwebs, so she could find her way back. Towards the rear and by her reckoning as far along the quad as the library, the last few columns were reserved solely for brandy, port and whisky. Inspecting these and realising she could do with a pick-me-up, she selected a bottle of Speyside marked '1914'. The year she was born. Mirabelle didn't recognise the name of the distillery but she decided to break the seal. There was no soda – the entire contents of Downing's cellar were alcoholic. With a shrug she took a slug from the bottle and then coughed as it took her breath away. The whisky was much too strong to drink neat. It stung the inside of her mouth but the taste revived her. She replaced the bottle and made her mark in the dust.

Here, however, she stopped. The side of this particular rack was nowhere near as filthy as the others. With her curiosity piqued, Mirabelle peered along the row. From halfway up, the boxes containing bottled whisky turned into casks stacked on top of one another. At the bottom were sherry casks, far too heavy for her to move, but two thirds of the way up were three layers of blood tubs – smaller barrels and more manoeuvrable. The pile reached the low ceiling.

Mirabelle decided to investigate. Like the rack on the corner, the casks were devoid of the thick layer of dust that had settled everywhere else. Upon examination she realised they had been in place for some time. At the bottom, one had a lading notice pasted to its side showing it had been delivered to Downing in 1921. Mirabelle looked up quizzically and decided to scale the pile. The barrels formed a roughly constructed but stable stairway, and even in heels it didn't take her long. At the top, crouching, she removed the two uppermost barrels and realised why the dust had been disturbed. Above the blood tubs, the ceiling plaster had been stripped away. There was a cavity covered by three wide floorboards cut to fit the space. Reaching up, Mirabelle dislodged one with a hefty push and looked through the hatch into a moonlit room. Lined with bookshelves, its dimensions were similar to those of Marsden's study, but it was tidy and smelled of lavender. Mirabelle pulled a second floorboard out of the way. Some clever student, she thought, had tunnelled into the cellar and found a method of hiding their tracks. They could take as much wine as they liked as long as they were careful.

It would be easy to haul herself through. First, though, she nipped back into the cellar and removed two bottles of the 1914 Speyside, choosing from the back of the box. Then she scaled the casks, pulled herself through the hole and carefully replaced the last barrel to obscure the exit from easy view.

Through the window she could see she had come up into the accommodation block next to where the professor lived. The lights in his room had now been extinguished. She checked the time – just after one – and cursed herself for wasting time. She opened the window as far as the sash would allow and clambered out, checking to make sure that she wasn't in sight of the porter's lodge. The porter made his rounds on the hour. She must be careful. She had to get both herself and Vesta out safely.

The evening air was fresh and it felt good to be free. But, as she looked into the stairwell where she had left Vesta. Her heart skipped a beat. The girl wasn't there.

'Vesta,' she hissed.

Silence.

'Vesta,' she tried again a little louder.

Mirabelle climbed a little way up the stairs. The girl was nowhere to be seen. She tried to guess what Vesta would have done when she had woken up on the step alone. Clearly, she'd try to find Mirabelle. That would entail sneaking up to Professor Marsden's rooms after which, finding no joy, she would most likely cross to the lodge and ask the porter if he'd seen her. Of course she would. The college, after all, only had one obvious entry and exit point. Mirabelle sighed. There was nothing for it. Vesta could be in trouble. Still, she assured herself, she could always nip back into the wine cellar if the porter had locked the girl in there, too. Now she knew how to break out, it would be a piece of cake.

Mirabelle sneaked towards the porter's office. From the shadows outside she could see the man sitting at his desk. Keeping close to the brick wall and staying low she stopped beneath the window and looked tentatively over the sill. She almost laughed out loud. Vesta was ensconced on a leather chair, sipping a cup of tea on one side of the desk while the porter sipped his on the other. A packet of peppermint creams lay open between them. What a cosy scene! Vesta, Mirabelle noticed, was giggling and clearly charming the old porter.

Mirabelle had seen Vesta do this before. When she worked at Halley Insurance down the hall, the girl had cast the same spell over every man who walked through the door. This had resulted in her having nary a Friday night to herself, in her pre-Charlie days. She could coax a fellow into practically anything – tea and peppermint creams would have been easy. Well, she did better than me, thought Mirabelle and smiled. At least the porter hadn't incarcerated the poor girl. Now to catch her attention. Mirabelle knew that the younger a person was, the wider their peripheral vision, and women had far better awareness at the fringes than men. Positioning herself carefully out of the porter's line of sight but well within Vesta's scope, she put up her hand and waved frantically. Even in the dark surely Vesta would see the movement. Nothing. Mirabelle tried again. Vesta put down her teacup and cocked her head to one side as the porter regaled her with stories. When he stopped speaking Vesta said, 'Well, I can't imagine what's happened to my friend.'

Mirabelle bit her lip with frustration. It was better if the girl stayed off that topic of conversation for it could only lead to the wine cellar. She waved again. Vesta's eyesight was clearly deficient. The girl should go to an optician when they got home. There were some very attractive spectacles available these days.

Mirabelle changed tack. She looked for a good-sized stone and then, staying out of sight, she pitched the object at one of the library windows, scuttling back into the shadows as it found its mark. Satisfyingly, the sound rang out. This had the desired effect. Inside, a chair scraped back, the door opened and the porter looked out. He disappeared for a moment, and more distinctly this time Mirabelle heard him say, 'I'd best do my rounds, love. Wait here and I'll be back shortly. Don't worry, your chum's probably just gone off. When I get back, we'll sort out that lift, shall we?'

Vesta murmured, making a sound that suggested her mouth was full. Mirabelle held her breath. The man took a torch and clumped across the paving stones to investigate the noise. She waited until he was a good few yards away before she sneaked towards the door. Putting her fingers to her lips as she entered, she managed to get Vesta to suppress the inevitable squeal.

'We have to get out of here,' she whispered. 'Come on.'

She pulled the girl out of the lodge door and towards the gate but realised quickly that the porter had locked it. 'Dash it,' she said, scrambling in her bag for her lock picks as she checked over her shoulder. This would take extra time. The light of the porter's torch was still visible proceeding down the pathway in the other direction, but he'd be back soon. His rounds, she recalled, lasted only eight minutes. There wasn't long.

'Don't worry,' said Vesta. She ran back into the little office and leaned across the man's desk. She lifted a peppermint cream with one hand and drew out an iron ring of keys with the other. 'Pretty careless of him,' she said as she strolled back outside.

'Thanks.' Mirabelle snatched the ring and searched its contents for the key to the gate while still keeping one eye on the path. It gave a satisfying jangle as she found the right one and turned it in the lock. The women slipped onto the deserted street, locking the gate behind them.

Mirabelle dropped the keyring into the gutter. 'This way,' she said.

Vesta stared at it. 'I could put the keys back, if you like,' she offered. 'It'd save him the trouble.'

The girl had no idea what had happened. Mirabelle grabbed Vesta's arm to pull her along the road. 'This way he'll have to spend time looking for the spare set. He won't be able to follow us as quickly.'

Vesta stood firm. 'Well,' her eyes were accusing, 'what happened to you? They're never going to let us into the B&B this late. Where on earth are we going to sleep?'

Mirabelle looked up and down the street. 'That odious little man locked me in the wine cellar.'

Vesta giggled. 'Sid?'

'Yes.' Mirabelle was not amused. 'Sid. While you were sleeping, Professor Marsden had visitors. Daphne first of all, and then two men. Masons, I think. The men who crossed the quad and went into the building next door – do you remember? Daphne's blackmailing them. She's found something at the Pavilion. Something they want. Elsie Chapman was killed because of it. She tried to blackmail them, too, on her own. The puzzler is that these men don't know who killed the woman but they're heading for Brighton to find out, and when they get there there's going to be trouble.'

'Why didn't you wake me up?' Vesta was furious. 'You're always leaving me out. You can't do that, Mirabelle.'

Mirabelle stopped for a moment. The girl was right, of course. 'I'm sorry,' she said. 'Really, I am. But you were fast asleep and we haven't got time to argue now. We have to get back. Superintendent McGregor has to be informed and I think he should take Captain Henshaw into custody. Logically, the poor man will be their chief suspect. These men felt dangerous. If not Henshaw, then someone's going to get hurt. I'm sure of it. McGregor needs to know.'

Vesta checked her watch as Mirabelle processed this information. 'Now? Brighton? It's the middle of the night.'

'Yes. We're going to have to find the driver. He went this way, didn't he?'

'What driver?'

'The cab driver. Remember? The one who brought us here.'

'Couldn't we just find a phonebox and call the police station? I'm sure we could get a message to McGregor. It'd be easier.'

Mirabelle turned. 'You want to phone a police station and tell whoever is on the desk that some masons may be planning a murder? Given what Bill said about the number of masons on the force?'

Vesta hesitated.

Mirabelle gripped the girl's arm more tightly. 'We have to look for the cab now,' she said. 'We can talk about it on the way if you like, but we have to get going. McGregor's our best chance of dealing with this, honestly.'

Vesta relented. 'All right,' she said. 'Well, the car was quite new. An Austin FX3.'

Vesta's old job at Halley Insurance had some advantages. She could name any car that graced England's roads.

'Come on.' Mirabelle smiled. 'It's got to be around here somewhere. He said he lived round the corner.'

They trawled the side streets of terraced brick houses that surrounded the college. There were hardly any parked cars. Cambridge was a town of bicycles and punts, after all.

'What's close by to someone in a vehicle isn't necessarily close for a pedestrian,' Mirabelle said ruefully.

'Do you think Sid will come after us?' Vesta glanced behind.

Mirabelle shook her head. 'I hope not. It'll take him a while to get out, don't you think? There must be a spare set of keys but even so . . .'

By the time they found the cab it was almost two in the

morning. The Austin was parked in front of a two-up two-down a good half-mile from the college. Mirabelle strode to the door. She pulled back the brass knocker and rapped several times. A thin woman in a white nightdress appeared in the upstairs window of the house next door and glared down at them. Mirabelle gave the knocker one more try. At last, from inside, they heard muffled voices and the sound of someone trudging downstairs. The front door opened to reveal the driver who'd picked them up at the station. He was wearing a pair of striped pyjamas. His hair was standing on end.

'Yes?' the man said, annoyed and sleepy.

Behind him at the top of the stairs Mirabelle could see a woman pulling a pink dressing gown around her shoulders. 'Cyril, what the hell is going on? It's the middle of the night. Oh, sweet Jesus!' She caught sight of Vesta. 'What's a darkie doing here? What've you been up to?'

'I'm so sorry to trouble you,' Mirabelle interrupted. 'You picked us up at the station earlier. We need a car to take us out of town. It's an emergency, I'm afraid, and we don't know anyone else in Cambridge to drive us.'

'Out of town? Where?'

'Brighton.'

'Cyril?' shouted the woman.

'I'm seeing to it,' the man growled back at her. 'Brighton? You've got to be joking. That's over two hours away. Maybe three even. It's the middle of the night. What kind of emergency?'

'It's very important. Police business.'

The man looked dubious. 'Well, get the coppers to take you then.'

'The policemen we need are in Brighton. We desperately need your help, Sir. Neither of us knows anyone here and we have to leave immediately. I can pay.' Mirabelle reached into her bag. In the lining she kept a slim wad of emergency cash. Now she pulled out two five-pound notes and unfolded them.

The man scratched his head and looked longingly at the money. 'It's a lot of petrol. Cash or no cash. Who do you think you are? The queen or something? My tank's half-empty. Why don't you just hop the train? The first one's half four. It'll take you straight to London.'

'That's more than two hours away. Every minute counts. It's important we get back. Please.'

'The train's quicker.'

'Not if we leave now . . .'

'I can't magic it up, love. I can't help you if I ain't got the juice.'

Mirabelle would not give up. 'Have you got enough to get us there?'

'Yeah, but I've got to get back, don't I?'

'I'll pay for a full tank to get you home again.'

The driver leaned against the door jamb and rubbed his eyes. 'Nah,' he said, without taking his eyes off the banknotes. 'It's the middle of the night. Tell you what, though, there'll be a milk train from Victoria. I could take you to London and you could pick it up good and early. There's plenty goods trains leave first thing.'

'How long will it take us to get there?' Mirabelle checked.

'A bit more than an hour, I reckon. An hour and a half?'

Mirabelle nodded. It was a good deal quicker than waiting for the train, given they'd have to cross town from King's Cross to Victoria. 'All right.' She held out her hand and the man shook it. She handed over one note. 'I'll give you the rest when we get there.' Then she paused. 'Oh,' she added, pulling out a bottle of the 1914 Speyside. 'I'll throw in one of these if you get us there inside ninety minutes. Do you like Scotch?'

This was one of Jack's tricks in the field. Soldiers would give you their loyalty regardless but civilians were trickier. If you were unsure of someone, he said, once you've done a deal, always give them something extra they aren't expecting if they do what they said they'd do. If you can get people to like you and still not think you're a pushover, you'll get more out of them in the long run.

The cabbie grinned. 'You're on,' he said. 'I'll just get dressed.'

Chapter 21

A journey is the best medicine.

The sun was rising as they arrived in London. Vesta had as good as passed out on the back seat after they got going. She managed to sleep most of the way to Victoria while Mirabelle watched the flat countryside slip past the car windows in the moonlight. Cyril had driven in silence and Mirabelle had time to consider what she'd heard in Marsden's rooms. What was it, she wondered, that Daphne had found in the Pavilion that was so important? And if the men she'd overheard hadn't killed Elsie Chapman, had they murdered Joey Gillingham, or was that someone else? The connection between the murders still wasn't clear. Mirabelle had imagined the masons worked like a spy network, with fluid communication between their different chapters – a well-oiled machine. But it seemed not. It was obvious from the men's conversation that one lodge had little idea what the other was up to. For all its reputation, it wasn't much of a deadly secret club. Not a patch on the Secret Intelligence Service.

Considering this, she realised it made it more difficult to anticipate what was happening. Inefficiency was erratic. If you knew what somebody wanted, you knew how they were likely to behave. In the old days there had been only two sides: you were either with the Allies or against them. The game was to outwit the other party: everyone's concerns were clear and their moves relatively easy to anticipate. In this situation, however, everyone was in it for their own interests: Elsie had tried to get money out of the masons, one of whom was her lover; Daphne was hell bent on revenge on her father. And heaven knew how Joey Gillingham fitted in. It was an untidy jumble that was only loosely interconnected. Everything seemed too personal.

She resisted the urge to drink some whisky and glanced enviously at Vesta, stretched across the leather seat. She used to be the one who fell asleep while Jack stayed up thinking things through. Mirabelle imagined how it would feel if he was here now and she could simply let go and not have to be the one who was holding everything together. Had Fred been right, she wondered. Would Jack be shocked at her inability to get over his death? Would he tell her to move on and find someone else to love? She didn't want to think about it.

In the lemon-tinted early morning light at Victoria the women waved off the cab driver who was delighted with his bottle of whisky. 'Just made it,' he beamed.

The train was almost empty and the women had a compartment to themselves.

'Well,' said Vesta as they pulled out of the station, 'everyone seems to have forgotten about Joey Gillingham. It's strange – we don't even know what the poor fella looked like. I can't see him in my mind's eye.'

Mirabelle thought back to Bill's description of Ida. It's always the women who are left, she thought. Ida and Ellie, clearing up what was left of their loved ones' lives.

'He probably looked like his sister. Fair hair and pale skin – that's what Bill said. What's on my mind is that Henshaw is in a tricky position. I wonder how much he knows about what else is going on? The first thing we need to do is get him taken into custody and then McGregor can untangle it all. These men all have different priorities, but whatever Daphne has laid her hand on is very valuable, and that makes it dangerous. McGregor will need to be on top of his game, that's for sure.'

Vesta's eyebrow arched. It was the first time she'd ever heard Mirabelle defer to the Superintendent. 'It didn't seem like Henshaw murdered Elsie to me.'

'No. I agree. But he did have a motive,' Mirabelle reasoned. 'And the men we saw won't take long to figure that out. They certainly didn't kill her. Not by what they said. So, they're going to take a long hard look and track down whoever might have done it. Henshaw first, and then anyone else they reckon might be a suspect. There's a lot at stake.'

The early morning air was chilly in Brighton, and the women shuddered as they walked up the platform just before six o'clock. Porters were unloading boxes and trunks from the freight cars. In a solemn procession a coffin was picked up by two men driving a hearse. The porters doffed their caps in respect as it passed. Consequently, the women didn't notice the uniformed policeman striding in their direction.

'Miss Bevan?'

'Ah, yes,' said Mirabelle, who, Vesta noted, managed to sound as if she expected him.

'I thought it was you, Ma'am. If you don't mind, you and Miss Churchill are to accompany me to the station.'

'Did Detective Superintendent McGregor send you, Constable?'

Perhaps the Superintendent was further ahead than she expected. Perhaps he already knew at least some of what had been going on. The constable did not reply. He simply motioned them towards a black police car that was parked under the canopy at the front of the station.

'This way.'

'We can walk, thank you,' said Vesta sweetly. 'It's a lovely day and it isn't far to Bartholomew Square.'

The constable thought for a moment. 'I think it might be a matter of more urgency,' he said, opening the car door. The women obediently slipped into the back seat. The car pulled off, heading towards the sea. It sailed past the usual turn-off to the left.

'Excuse me,' said Mirabelle. 'But I think you've missed the turning. Bartholomew Square is back up the hill.'

'It's not Bartholomew Square today, Ma'am.'

'But Detective Superintendent McGregor doesn't work in Wellington Road.'

The man cleared his throat. 'It's not McGregor who's asked for you.'

This prospect was mystifying. 'Well, who has?' Mirabelle enquired.

The man said nothing.

'Ah,' she said, realising.

'What is it?' Vesta asked. 'Who's asked to see us?'

'Belton.' She tapped the man on the shoulder. 'He's had you keeping an eye out for us, hasn't he? Is that it? You've been watching the railway and bus stations.'

The man kept his gaze fixed on the road. Mirabelle momentarily considered bolting. She put a hand to the door handle but realised it was locked. Besides, she couldn't leave Vesta alone. Not again.

'I have to speak to Detective Superintendent McGregor.' Her voice was officious, schoolmarmish. 'Please. We have to go to Bartholomew Square straight away. You can take me to Belton afterwards if you like, but I need to speak to McGregor, or at the very least Sergeant Simmons. Mr Belton only wants to tick us off for leaving town, but I have information that is genuinely important. McGregor needs it.'

The man didn't respond.

Vesta slipped forwards in her seat. 'Look, it won't do any harm if you take us to Bartholomew Square first, and it might do a lot of good. What's your name, anyway?'

The man ignored her. 'We're almost there,' he said, rounding a corner smoothly. 'You can't go off like that, ignoring police orders. You can't just waltz out of town when you've been explicitly told not to. It's a serious matter, Miss.'

'It's a free country,' said Mirabelle.

'Where did you go?'

'Cambridge, if you must know. It's hardly a criminal bolthole.'

The constable parked beside the station and switched off the engine. 'If you're on a report you've got to stick to it,' he said. 'Otherwise it's just anarchy. This is England, you know.' He got out and opened the car door, standing as if at attention.

'We'd better face the music, I suppose,' said Vesta.

Mirabelle remained frosty. As she slipped out of the car she refused to even look at the fellow. She checked her watch – perhaps if they simply took a dressing down they'd be able to get to McGregor without too much delay.

Inside the police station, Belton was at the front desk. The large clock on the wall behind him clicked towards six.

'Ah,' he said. 'There you are, ladies. I was getting worried. We've been looking for you for some time.'

'They came off the London train, Sarge,' the constable said. 'Miss Bevan says she's been in Cambridge.'

'Cambridge, is it?'

Mirabelle drew herself up to her full five feet five inches.

'Sergeant Belton, I need to speak urgently with Detective Superintendent McGregor. I have some information relating to a murder case which is of life and death importance.'

'Which murder case, Miss?'

'I'm not at liberty to say.'

'Where were you yesterday evening between eleven o'clock and approximately one a.m., Miss?'

'I told you. Cambridge,' Mirabelle replied. 'Look, Sergeant . . .'

Belton didn't let her get further. Instead he loomed over the desk.

'I saw you in Brighton at not long past four o'clock. I asked you not to leave, Miss Bevan, but it seems not more than an hour later you did just that.' He checked his watch and totted up the hours she'd been away. 'Can you prove you went to Cambridge?'

'Why on earth would I require to prove such a thing? Sergeant, we're wasting valuable minutes. A man's life is at risk. Perhaps I haven't made myself clear.'

'Which man?' Belton asked. 'If there's someone at risk, you can tell me. I'm a policeman, Miss Bevan.'

Mirabelle paused. 'Are you also a freemason, Sergeant Belton?'

'Oh, for heaven's sake. What has that got to do with it? Ma'am, you are obstructing my inquiries and frankly that question only serves to make me more suspicious of what you've been up to. Constable, would you please escort these ladies to the cells? We'll need to question them more closely in due course.'

Both Mirabelle and Vesta burst into a chorus of objection.

Vesta suddenly felt terrified. It was only the year before that her friend Lindon had died in police custody in London. In adding her voice to Mirabelle's she injected a tone of panic to the proceedings. It had no effect. Belton overruled them both.

'The Detective Superintendent is engaged on a murder inquiry, Miss, at Bartholomew Square. As are we at this station. You're wasting police time with these histrionics. Once you've calmed down and answered my questions satisfactorily, I might get in touch with McGregor. But we have a policy of first things first here.'

'This is unconscionable,' Mirabelle objected once more but it was hopeless.

The burly constable bundled the women through the door and along the corridor that led to the cells. Wellington Road did not have separate facilities for female prisoners and she knew the cells downstairs were particularly grim.

'Will you put us together, please?' Vesta implored.

The constable did not reply. He just kept pushing them along the stairwell. Vesta gripped Mirabelle's hand. Her nails cut into the soft flesh of Mirabelle's palm and tears welled in her eyes.

'Are you charging us?' said Mirabelle. 'You can't detain us like this if you're not charging us with anything, surely?'

The constable's glance betrayed his lack of concern.

Mirabelle made her decision. 'All right,' she acquiesced. She'd play his game if she had to. Vesta was clearly terrified. 'There's a cab driver who can vouch we were in Cambridge.'

The man stopped. 'What's his name?'

'Cyril Fanshawe. And I have an address,' said Mirabelle.

'And the information you have for McGregor?'

Mirabelle shook her head.

The man laid his hand firmly on Vesta's shoulder and pushed her towards a cell.

'Mirabelle,' Vesta squealed.

Mirabelle interposed her body as best she could. She held up her hands in a gesture of surrender. 'All right. All right. I fear a man called Captain Henshaw may be in danger.'

The constable laughed loudly. 'You can say that again. None of that is going to get you off, you know. You're going to have to tell us everything.'

'But it's true,' Vesta exclaimed.

'I take it you haven't read the paper?' The constable was genuinely unimpressed. He smiled a broad unpleasant grin and twisted his hands together as if he was wringing out a wet cloth. 'Henshaw topped himself. He jumped off the roof of his house. Last night. Hear that sound?' He put a mocking hand to his ear. 'That's the sound of his poor wife trying to hush it up, poor soul.'

'But he can't be dead,' said Mirabelle earnestly. She cursed herself silently. She'd been too slow. They'd got to him more quickly than she'd expected.

The constable continued. Now he'd started he was eager to tell the story. 'The wife was out playing canasta and found him on the lawn when she came home. Poor bloke shattered his gammy leg and all. The coroner's insisting we pick up every splinter. There'd be nothing worse, would there, if you was his missus and there were bits of your dead husband on the grass. We've got a team up there now.'

'When did Henshaw jump? Do you know the exact time?' said Mirabelle.

'While you were in Cambridge, Madam,' he said sarcastically. 'Some time in the early hours. Why do you think Belton was trying to ascertain your whereabouts? Let's put you in this cell together. It's bigger. The sergeant will get to you in an hour or two. You're helping the police with their inquiries, that's all. I ain't taking your possessions or nothing.'

'If you'd just let me use the telephone,' Mirabelle tried to cut in, but the door was already closing and if the constable replied she couldn't make out what he said, only the sound of his measured footsteps receding down the corridor.

As Mirabelle turned, Vesta sank into the corner of the dingy cell. She covered her face with her hands and started to cry.

Chapter 22

The law is reason free from passion.

At his desk at Bartholomew Square, almost two hours later, Superintendent McGregor sipped his tea. He'd been there since early doors. The Gillingham case was going nowhere, but Henshaw's suicide had kept McGregor up late, staring at Elsie Chapman's file. The connection between Mrs Chapman and Joey Gillingham was tenuous but the dead woman's connection to Henshaw was easier to define. Like the team at McGuigan and McGuigan, he had deduced a long-term affair and an illegitimate child. Still, it seemed, somehow, too cut and dried for his liking.

The night before, when he finally went home, sleep had evaded him so he got up, dressed in the half-light of dawn and dragged himself back into the station where he sat at his desk trying to piece things together. He'd come to the conclusion that too many pieces of this puzzle were missing and the pieces he had, though they certainly tied up into a nice neat parcel, somehow felt unsatisfying. He was missing too many motives and far too much background information. To say that the masons were secretive was an understatement and, for that matter, discretion was a byword for anyone who might know anything useful at the track. With Henshaw's suicide, the case was panning out to look depressingly domestic, though if he could figure out how Joey Gillingham fitted in that might change. McGregor's instinct told him that all three deaths were interconnected, but none of the evidence seemed to point that way. Except for Mirabelle's convictions, and they counted for something. Increasingly these days he found himself wondering what Mirabelle would think.

McGregor read Gillingham's file one more time. When he stayed in Brighton, Gillingham had roomed in a small boarding house on Tillstone Street that was convenient for the racetrack and the boxing club. The proprietor had no connection to Elsie Chapman, the racecourse or the boxing and by his own account was not a mason.

'I follow the football,' the man had said, trying to be helpful.

'What's on the slate today, Sir?' Robinson asked cheerily as he breezed into the office at nine.

McGregor looked up. The fact that Henshaw had died on Wellington Road's patch was obviously set to make things difficult. The fact that the old man was a mason was going to make it even more so. Perhaps, McGregor reasoned, Robinson might be able to help with that, though whether he intended to or not was another matter. He decided to apply some pressure.

'Sit down.' McGregor motioned towards the vacant chair on the opposite side of his desk.

Robinson looked perplexed. The Superintendent was not in the habit of inviting him to the table. He bobbed nervously. 'Sir,' he said, putting a hand on the back of the chair.

'Sit,' barked McGregor.

Robinson looked at the desk as if it might be booby-trapped. He glanced at the door, hoping for rescue. None came, so he sat down, crossed his legs and then uncrossed them.

'You heard what happened last night?' McGregor checked.

Robinson nodded. 'It ties it all up, doesn't it?' The inspector sounded positively cheery, or hopeful at least. 'Elsie Chapman, I mean. It sounds like old Henshaw took her death hard. So, that's that.'

McGregor put his hand to his chin. His eyes flashed. 'No, Robinson, it's not. It's far too tidy is what it is. You knew Captain Henshaw, I assume?'

'Yes, but . . .'

'Good. Did you know about this affair of his? When he was alive.'

'No, Sir.' Robinson's voice was flat. 'Of course not.'

'Did Captain Henshaw seem the type to you?'

'The type?'

'Suicide risk? Murderer?'

Robinson's eyes sought out his shoes. 'No, Sir. Not exactly.'

'He was some kind of office holder, wasn't he?'

'I couldn't possibly say, Sir.'

McGregor leaned over the desk. He realised his accent made it easier to sound threatening. The English, at heart, were nervous of the Scots. He suppressed a smile. A lad from Davidson's Mains was considered soft at home but exported to England he became a hard man. McGregor wondered what the inspector would make of a real Scottish tough nut, should he ever come across one. In the meantime, he thought, he'd have to do. He kept his voice steady and low. 'I swear to God, Robinson, if this membership of yours impairs my investigation I'll have you demoted. Masons or no masons. I'm not asking what the poor bugger did in this little club of yours, I'm asking about his status, that's all. Now, Brother Henshaw – some kind of office holder? Long term?'

Robinson nodded slowly.

'Organisational skills?'

Robinson nodded again.

'A logical sort, who saw things through?'

Another nod.

'Not the kind of fellow then who might kill his lover in order to avoid exposure one day – presumably to save embarrassing his wife and his order – and then, less than twenty-four hours later, expose the whole damn affair anyway by jumping off his own roof?'

There was a sharp rap on the office door and Sergeant Simmons' face appeared.

'They've turned up a suicide note,' he said. 'I thought you'd want to know.'

Robinson looked smug.

'What did it say?' McGregor's voice had an edge.

Simmons shrugged.

'It came in the first post to the Chief of Police over at Wellington Road. Turns out he and Henshaw were friends. Well, I suppose they were both in the brotherhood.'

'I want to read it.'

A glimmer of a smile passed across Robinson's face. At Wellington Road there were no senior officers who didn't regularly attend meetings at Queen's Road. Simmons sucked in a long breath. His concerns were more organisational. The two police stations were separate jurisdictions.

'It might be tricky. I don't know if they'll release you the evidence. You know the way things stand.'

'If we're looking into Mrs Chapman's death, the two cases are contingent on each other. We'll need to work with Wellington Road, or try to. It's a bloody circus, this.' McGregor snapped shut Joey Gillingham's file and stood up. He reached for his hat.

'Come on, Robinson,' he said. 'Everyone's busy. The quickest way to cut through the red tape is to go over there.'

Robinson looked round as if the Superintendent might have been speaking to someone else.

'Well, look lively,' McGregor chivvied him as he strode out of the office. He was enjoying baiting the poor man. 'I need you to drive.'

Motoring through the sun-dappled streets McGregor could hardly believe there had been three murders in two days here –

or at least that's what there had been if he was right. Brighton looked picture-postcard pretty. He wound down the window and took a deep breath.

The station desk was manned by a young constable.

'I'm looking for Sergeant Belton, son.' McGregor flashed his warrant card. The lad could not have been much more than nineteen years of age and fresh out of National Service if his haircut was anything to go by.

'Yes, Sir.'

McGregor breezed past him with Robinson lagging behind. They were halfway up the hallway that led to the detectives' offices before Belton caught up with him.

'Morning, Sergeant. I think you've got something for me,' said McGregor.

Belton looked as if he had been caught off guard. 'How on earth did you know?' He sounded genuinely mystified.

McGregor grinned. 'Actually, I don't know nearly enough yet. But if we're going to get to the bottom of this we need to work together. I can't be doing with all this cloak-and-dagger nonsense, whatever the damned jurisdiction.'

'We were going to ring you.' Belton sounded wounded. 'I just thought that giving them a fright would make a lesson of it. That woman rides roughshod over the rules. She's only been here for three hours and she's already tried everything. How did you find out?' Belton let out a defeated sigh. 'I'll get one of the lads to take you down, Sir.'

'Down?'

'To the cells. Miss Bevan might be your lady friend, but that doesn't put her beyond the law.'

'Mirabelle?' McGregor made an abrupt about-turn, his mind veering off all thought of Captain Henshaw's suicide note. 'What the blazes has she done now?'

'I told her not to leave Brighton. Yesterday she was at the

scene of a break-in. And between that and being up at the lodge when the second murder took place . . . She left town almost immediately after I told her not to. She's a woman who needs a firm hand, Sir, if you don't mind me saying.'

McGregor laughed. 'You're a braver man than I am, Sergeant. She's been asking for me?'

Belton nodded.

Downstairs the constable unlocked the door. Inside the cell there was the familiar oily smell of incarceration that the scent of the women hadn't quite cancelled out. Vesta jumped to her feet. Mirabelle was standing underneath the small window. She looked particularly pale, he noticed. She nodded curtly. Robinson put his head round the door and grinned widely. McGregor waved him off.

'We'll talk down here,' he said. 'Robinson, see if you can turn up that note, will you? I'll be up in a minute.'

McGregor left the cell door half-open. He waited, listening to make sure they were alone. He motioned for the women to sit on the bench and took his place on the other side of the tiny room. It looked as if the graffiti on the wall behind Mirabelle was emanating from her head like a storm of angry thoughts.

'We have to stop meeting like this.' McGregor couldn't help himself.

Vesta grinned. She was relieved to see him. 'The sergeant told us not to leave town,' she said. 'But we were onto something.'

'Onto something?'

'Yes.' Vesta took a deep breath and was clearly about to tell McGregor everything.

Mirabelle put up her hand to silence the girl. 'Thanks for coming,' she said.

McGregor shrugged. 'Least I could do,' he replied, his eyes in no way betraying that he was at Wellington Road on another matter entirely.

'There are two things.' Mirabelle got straight to the point. 'First, Henshaw's death. And second, what exactly did Mrs Chapman die of?'

McGregor took off his hat and ran his hand through his hair. She was quite a woman and, now he came to consider it, somewhat rude. 'Normally I ask the questions,' he said.

Mirabelle stared. 'It's quicker this way,' she said flatly.

McGregor nodded curtly. In this, he had to admit, she was probably right.

'All right, have it your way. But then you have to tell me what I want to know.'

'Of course.'

'Henshaw jumped some time in the early hours this morning, according to the pathologist. Eleven till one is the range they're quoting. His body was found by his wife. She had been out playing cards. Of course, whether he jumped at all is another matter. I've sent Robinson to turn up the suicide note. It arrived this morning in the post. Current thinking is that Henshaw killed Mrs Chapman because she threatened to expose their love affair, but having done so he was consumed by guilt. I have my doubts. Henshaw, as I understand it, lost his leg at Gallipoli. During the recent war he worked in Armaments – costings and the like. He volunteered. My sense of him is that he was a resilient chap. Straightforward enough apart from this affair with Mrs Chapman. He may have loved the old dear, but if he was tough enough to kill her – if – then I guess he'd be tough enough to see it through. Which means I just don't buy it as suicide. Quite apart from anything else, if he was to make the last post, he'd have to have put the letter in the box well before he topped himself. Hours before, in fact. That's unusual. I've never heard the like.

'Which brings me to Mrs Chapman . . . The coroner's report is in. He rushed it through. A favour for the brethren, I expect. The old woman's stomach contained a slice of toast

196

with honey (no butter), three cups of tea (milk and a good deal of sugar) and the contents of several laburnum pods. The last of these, obviously, killed her. Laburnum's readily available, so it's not much of a clue. There must be at least a hundred trees scattered round Brighton and its environs, all in full bloom at the moment with plenty of pods ready for the picking.'

'That's the pretty tree at the Royal Pavilion, isn't it?' Vesta cut in. 'The yellow one?'

Mirabelle took in this information slowly. 'There,' she said. 'That proves it. Elsie was definitely murdered. And I think Henshaw was, too.'

McGregor looked confused. 'I don't suppose you know who did it?'

Mirabelle shook her head. 'Not yet. I had a suspect in mind but the timing doesn't make sense. Especially considering this suicide note. Whoever did it, though, my suspect will be delighted. Henshaw was troublesome for them and if he hadn't been killed already he was definitely in their frame. There's been a lot at stake, you see. More than we originally reckoned.'

'Who's your suspect?'

'Well, there's more than one. They're not from Brighton. Masons. This whole freemasonry lark is strange. None of them seems to know what the others are doing. It's another lodge – a different crowd entirely from the lot at Queen's Road. I haven't quite figured it out yet. But two of them, anyway, are definitely from Scotland.'

McGregor crossed his arms. 'Mirabelle, you know I'm going to have to warn you off. Three people are dead. None of us knows yet who did it, but whoever they are, they're extremely dangerous. Look where you've ended up. If I get you out of here will you please go back to Brills Lane? Honestly, I'm half-tempted to leave you inside. I don't want anything to happen to you.'

There was silence.

Then Vesta piped up. 'I'll make sure Mirabelle doesn't get

involved. I've had enough. You're right, Superintendent. We shouldn't be poking our noses into this. We're sorry. Aren't we, Mirabelle? Really, we are.'

McGregor glanced at Miss Bevan. Her demeanour was cool. She got to her feet, slipping her handbag over her forearm as if it was a shield.

'I don't want you to get hurt, Mirabelle. Or God forbid, end up dead.'

Mirabelle looked McGregor straight in the eye before glancing at her watch. 'We're late for work,' she said. 'And, of course, I'd be obliged if you'd release us. Not that we're under arrest, I hasten to add.'

'And you'll stay in your office?' the Superintendent checked.

Mirabelle nodded curtly. 'I can't wait to get there,' she assured him.

Chapter 23

Friendship is a partnership.

'He's right, you know,' Vesta insisted as the women left the station. 'Anything could have happened to us.'

Mirabelle didn't respond.

Vesta stopped to pick up a half-pint of milk for the office. 'Bill won't have remembered,' she said with a smile, 'and in this heat milk goes off so quickly that yesterday's is bound to have turned by now.'

Mirabelle cast her a stony glance that did not deter the girl from linking her arm through her friend's as they continued down the hill.

' "We shouldn't be poking our noses into this." Really, Vesta,' Mirabelle scolded, mimicking the tone of the girl's apology.

'But he's right,' Vesta repeated. 'You know he is. And we're out now, aren't we?'

By the time they turned into Brills Lane it was almost eleven o'clock and it was a relief to get out of the sun.

'There you are,' Bill said as they walked in. 'I think the weather's putting people off business. There's not been a soul over the door all morning. You seen this?' He lifted the paper to show them a short article about Captain Henshaw's death. 'It doesn't say why he did it,' he added.

Panther looked up as the women removed their summer jackets. He let his head fall back on his paws and slowly wagged his tail.

'It's the heat,' Bill explained. 'Neither of us can really get going.'

Mirabelle sank into her seat. She felt exhausted and, worse, unwanted. No one seemed to care what she thought about Captain Henshaw, Joey Gillingham or Elsie Chapman. McGregor wanted to work it out for himself, and as far as he was concerned she was an irritation. Vesta had already given up. She felt angry. The details rushed through her mind but she couldn't grasp them, and for once she wasn't sure what to do next. With no clear pathway presenting itself she leafed half-heartedly through the paperwork in front of her. Bill was right. It had been a quiet week.

Vesta put a strong cup of tea on her desk with an apologetic smile. 'Are you all right?'

Mirabelle sipped the tea. She rubbed her tired, dry eyes.

'You could go home,' Vesta suggested. 'Why don't you have a lie down? You haven't slept a wink all night. Bill and I can manage things here.'

Mirabelle thought about closing her bedroom curtains and curling up on the mattress. It was an attractive proposition. She felt as if she'd wasted her time and run off on a wild goose chase. If no one cared, where was the harm in taking it easy? She might as well get some sleep. For once she didn't want to be in the office. 'Perhaps,' she said.

Vesta fetched Mirabelle's jacket from the stand. 'Here,' she offered. 'You'll feel better once you've had a snooze. We'll see you tomorrow. Leave everything to me.'

Mirabelle folded the garment over her arm and picked up her handbag. 'All right,' she said.

Outside on the pavement she kept to the shadows. Instead of heading to the front and walking along the shore, she went up East Street and past Bartholomew Square. Somehow the sea seemed too bright. It would be better to head along the maze of streets towards Hove. She passed the turn-off for Fred's place without a second glance. Within half a mile she was on the long straight road out of town. Women were shopping, shopkeepers were tending their displays and children were hanging around the bakery. Things were normal. This was what her life ought to be like, she reflected. Grocery shopping and cups of tea. Why did she find herself drawn to these horrible cases? It was none of her business. She hadn't even managed to save Henshaw.

She bought a copy of the local paper and then, heading towards The Lawns, she withdrew her key, almost starting at the sight of the coin on her key ring, a memento of her very first case. Things had seemed easier even only those few years ago. Inside, she slipped off her shoes and turned over the first few pages of the afternoon edition. In the Deaths column Mrs Chapman's funeral was announced – at All Saints on Saturday afternoon. Mirabelle closed the paper and decided to blank out the world by drawing the curtains. Fully clothed she lay down on the bed. The outside world disappeared.

As her breathing slowed, she slipped into unconsciousness trying not to think of poor Ellie Chapman, all alone in the world, or Mrs Henshaw, frantically trying to reconcile her husband's suicide with the man she had lived with for forty years, or Ida Gillingham, sorting out her brother's clothes. Vesta had given up on them all and maybe she was right. As her thoughts eased out with the tide, the warm light filtering through the curtains faded even further and Mirabelle didn't so much as dream.

Chapter 24

Curiosity killed the cat.

Vesta finished work at half past five. Charlie was playing later, but she didn't want to wait for hours in a smoky pub. The humdrum routine of the office had provided more than enough of a steady rhythm and lots of time to think. After lunch Bill had gone on his calls, and she'd been left alone with insufficient paperwork and a nagging sense of guilt. Mirabelle had looked deflated when she'd been packed off. In the two years Vesta had known her friend and partner she'd never seen her look so dejected. Some women distracted themselves from their troubles by knitting or cleaning or playing music or dancing. Nothing perked up Vesta like a biscuit. She didn't hide it. But for Mirabelle these thorny cases she was drawn to were the only things that took her out of herself. They made her feel alive. Mirabelle didn't appear to feel fear. Vesta felt ashamed of herself. If she'd been old enough to understand what was going on, she'd never have made it through the war. Now she was out of immediate danger her mind returned to the thorny issue of Mrs Chapman's death and her curiosity was aroused. Had McGregor succeeded in tracking down what had really been going on, she wondered as she locked the office door.

On East Street she emerged into the sunshine and picked up a paper from the news-stand. Leafing through it, she realised there was nothing that might offer a clue to whatever police action was underway. It was far too soon for that. The evening stretched ahead of her. Neither option of how to spend it – sitting listening to Charlie drum or chatting to Mrs Agora – seemed satisfactory. Looking left and right Vesta made the snap decision to walk up to Queen's Road. She'd call on Mr Tupps. The caretaker had been cross the last time she'd seen him but she was sure he'd have got over it by now. She'd pushed the old man's buttons all right. It'd be interesting to see how he was taking the latest death. Captain Henshaw had been his boss – he was sure to have an opinion – and grieving, he might like some company.

Vesta dodged through the busy side streets. Everyone was on their way home from work. Navvies from the nearby building site were heading for the front. Men in suits slipped into the Black Lion or the Cricketers for a pint or two before going home. As she turned onto Queen's Road several gentlemen were walking up the hill towards the station. Vesta took a seat on a low wall opposite the lodge. One after another at least a dozen men slipped through the building's front door carrying small suitcases. There must be a meeting tonight. She grinned at the idea of them wearing little aprons. Really, it was quite the most ridiculous thing!

In the balmy evening air she began to daydream, running one scenario after another. It was for this reason that she jumped as someone laid a hand on her shoulder.

'Hello,' Mr Tupps said cheerily. 'What are you doing here?'

'Just thinking.' Vesta smiled.

'I thought I warned you off that, young lady,' he said with a grin. 'What's on your mind?'

Vesta shrugged. 'Perhaps I play things too safe. That's what I'm wondering. Do you know if they've found the murderer yet?'

Mr Tupps let out a low whistle. 'It's a bad business,' he said. 'But a man's sins will find him out. If he has sinned, that is. If there is a murderer still at large.'

'There has to be,' Vesta insisted.

'What makes you so sure?'

Vesta considered this, thinking out loud. 'The blackmail,' she said. 'This girl I know has found something. And men from outside your lodge have got involved. That's what the murders are really about. Whatever she's found is valuable, you see. That's the crux of everything. I talked Mirabelle out of looking into it, but the more I think about it, the more I realise we're the only people who will be able to make all the connections. Mirabelle likes this kind of thing. Sometimes I think she needs it.'

Mr Tupps narrowed his eyes. 'You want to discredit Queen's Road – that's what you're after.'

Vesta shook her head. 'No, you're wrong,' she insisted. 'Mirabelle reckons the masons are too inefficient to have done all of this. There's something else at play. These other fellas are from a Scottish lodge. They're the ones to watch. You'd best be careful, Mr Tupps. Truly.'

Across the road another man entered the lodge with a small bag under his arm.

'What is it that you do in there?' Vesta laughed, her mind moving on. 'There's a dozen men gone in at least, just as I've been sitting here, and every one of them looked shifty.'

Mr Tupps nodded towards the building. 'I'll let you have a peek, if you like. You'll be disappointed though. It's only fellas chatting to each other. A few prayers. That's all. Do you want to take a look? I won't let you in the meeting room, of course, but I could get you into the reception room. You can't help being curious. I can see that. Perhaps if you have a look you'll realise it's all on the square.'

'Do they really wear aprons?'

Tupps nodded. 'Of course,' he said. 'They're badges of office. You mustn't make a sound or you'll get me into trouble.'

Vesta looked round.

'Afterwards you can come down to the kitchen and I'll make you a cuppa.'

'All right,' she said. She wasn't going to miss this opportunity.

They crossed the road together and Mr Tupps opened the door. There was a murmur of conversation from the meeting room to the rear. He ushered her through a door on the opposite side of the hallway.

'Quick. In,' he said. 'And keep quiet.'

Vesta suppressed a giggle. And then she felt his hands. One curled around her face and the other manoeuvred her shoulders. As Mr Tupps bundled her into the room she bit hard into his flesh but the old man was strong and he just kept going. What was he doing? Vesta struggled as he opened a door in the wall and pushed her down a set of stairs. 'No!' she shouted but his hand was over her mouth. She managed to squeal – not quite a scream. Down the stairs it was pitch black. Her eyes couldn't adjust.

'Help!' she shouted. 'Help!'

She desperately tried to fight him off. She could feel her blood pumping as she lashed out. Once she almost got away and made it in a scramble as far as the foot of the stairs, but he grabbed her by the hair and pulled her back.

'No, no, my lovely,' he growled. His voice sounded different in the darkness. He wasn't old here and he wasn't wise. He produced rope from somewhere and bound Vesta's hands behind her back. She remembered too late that she ought to flex her wrists as he did so to make it impossible to tie the knot tightly. She'd learned all these things but she wasn't quick enough to put them into practice. Kicking out hard she at least landed a few blows before he tackled her and brought her to the ground, working on her legs with the ropes.

'You hurt me and my Charlie'll kill you.'

Mr Tupps laughed harshly. 'You ain't going to see your Charlie again, girlie. Don't worry about that.'

'I knew it. I knew there was something wrong. All you masons are evil.' Vesta's temper was rising. At least it distracted her from feeling afraid.

'Oh, not all of us. The lower orders don't know about this place, dearie. Most of the men upstairs – you know the ones, with their little bags, coming in for their meeting – never rise above the third degree. No one looks at the caretaker, do they? But he runs the place, do you see? He's the man in charge here. It's only the upper echelons who get to take part in the real fun downstairs. Just a few of us. Men with the nerve to take action when things get tough.'

'You killed Elsie, didn't you?'

'I had to. She was blackmailing poor Henshaw. She was confusing him. Women'll do that, you see. I put a stop to it.'

'And he couldn't live without her.'

Mr Tupps chortled. 'No, he could have. But he went to pieces. You've got to be loyal to the brotherhood above everything else, see. That's what you swear to. I couldn't have him blundering about making accusations. It was as if he just stopped caring about the lodge.'

'You killed him!'

'Yes, and if Mr Laidlaw gives me the order I'll kill you, too. He's in charge now he's here.'

But before Vesta could scream or even reply Mr Tupps stuffed a piece of material into her mouth to gag her. She panicked, scared that she wouldn't be able to breathe. Then Mr Tupps rolled her across the floor as if she was a barrel of beer, and no matter how hard she struggled it had no effect. The floor was hard and cold. He propped her up to tie her in place against a post of some kind – she couldn't see what. I'm going to fight him, she swore to herself. Right to my last breath. She pulled at the tight ropes with her heart hammering. Nothing shifted. She counted to ten and as she brought her panic under control she realised he'd gone. She took a deep breath and then another. She waited. It was so dark. It was silent. And no one but Mr Tupps knew she was here.

And then she heard the sound. It was breathing. Not Tupps, she thought. No, not him. This had a different rhythm. She tried to speak. Tried to scream. The sound that came from her mouth was negligible. Even the low whimper in her throat was barely audible. She kicked blindly as far into the darkness as she could without touching anything. But there was breathing. Someone or something was down here with her.

Chapter 25

Every good act is charity.

Later that night . . .

The hammering on the door woke Mirabelle with a start. Groggily she got up. She peeked through the curtains. The sky was dark beyond the pane of glass. She stumbled to her feet and glanced at the bedside clock – five past three. There was a moment of confusion as she realised she had slept the whole day through and into the night. It must be Friday morning.

She padded barefoot to the front door. Slipping the catch she opened up. Sergeant Simmons and a younger man stood on her doorstep. She could see the strain on the older man's face in the harsh light. The younger one looked unruffled. He was still at an age when staying up all night was an excitement rather than a hardship. As she stood back to let them enter, Mirabelle recognised the boy. He was the young constable from Wellington Road. Both men were in uniform.

'What is it?' she asked.

'Is he here, Miss Bevan?' There was an edge of urgency to Simmons' voice.

'Who?'

Simmons caught the constable's eye. 'Superintendent McGregor,' he said. 'We can't find him anywhere.'

'Why on earth would he be here? It's three o'clock in the morning.'

The constable's steady gaze made it plain the kind of woman he considered her to be. There was, Mirabelle realised, no point in arguing. She had long understood that men thought of women the way they wanted to. There was no way out of that.

'I haven't seen him since yesterday morning,' she said. 'At Wellington Road.'

Simmons' eyes betrayed his disappointment. 'I can't think of anywhere else. Mayhew and I have tried everywhere. He's missing.'

'What were his last known movements?' Mirabelle was familiar with the drill.

'Wellington Road nick, as you say. He talked to Belton about the case.'

'Did he get sight of Captain Henshaw's suicide note?'

Mayhew nodded.

'Typed?'

The boy nodded again.

'He'd done that at the lodge?'

'Yes, Ma'am,' Simmons confirmed. 'He used the machine in his office. They checked, and it was an exact match. He must've written it earlier in the day.'

'What did the note say?'

The constable cast his eyes towards Simmons to check if it was all right to speak. The sergeant gave him the go-ahead with a curt nod and Mayhew formed the words slowly. 'Just that the old fellow had done in the cleaning lady. They had an affair for years and she wanted him to recognise their child. It was a girl, I think. Then he couldn't take what he'd done.'

'That's not what I meant. What did the note say exactly?' Mirabelle pushed him. 'The actual words.'

'He said he loved the woman. I remember that. I thought that can't have been nice for his wife. He said he was overcome with guilt and that he knew he was going to hell but he couldn't take living any more. Nothing unusual for a suicide note.'

Mirabelle's mind darted. 'Thank you, Constable. That's very interesting,' she said. 'And did the postmark tally?'

'Yes. He posted it near his house in time for the last pick-up. He knew what he was going to do. The chief got it the next morning.'

'Well?' said Simmons. 'Does that help? Do you know where McGregor is, Miss Bevan?'

Mirabelle shook her head. 'Not exactly,' she admitted, 'but I'd start at the lodge. That's where he must have been heading, you see. It's the only place that makes sense – the linchpin of it all. It wasn't suicide, you know. It couldn't have been.'

'I've already checked the lodge,' said Simmons. 'I went over when I first realised I didn't know where he was. A call came in and I couldn't track him down. Anyway, the bloke hadn't seen him. The Superintendent ain't been anywhere I'd have expected. Tell you the truth, I'm worried. He's been missing a long time.'

'How many hours?'

Simmons checked his watch. 'Must be close on fifteen now. He left the station at Wellington Road on foot just before midday and there's been no sign of him since. I tried the victims' homes, the lodge, the racetrack, his usual haunts – everywhere I could think of. He hasn't been home either.'

'He was with Robinson at Wellington Road. Doesn't he have any idea?'

'He sent the inspector off – asked him to make a couple of enquiries.'

'About Elsie Chapman's estate? Checking out the daughter? That side of things?'

Simmons nodded.

It was as she thought. 'Neither you nor Mayhew are masons, are you?'

Mayhew examined his feet.

'No,' Simmons admitted. 'That's why I recruited the constable for this. I haven't filed a missing person's report or started a full-scale manhunt. I wasn't sure if making it official was a good idea. I was hoping Mayhew and I could turn up the Superintendent on our own.'

'You didn't think to use one of the female constables? I mean, they'd definitely not be part of the brotherhood.'

Simmons shook his head. 'Something like this, Miss, begging your pardon, but a murder inquiry – the ladies wouldn't be up for it.'

Mirabelle sighed inwardly. Simmons was a good sergeant but he had no understanding. If she wanted to prevent further bloodshed she'd have to get on with things herself. And she decided on balance she'd do better alone. Vesta had made it clear that she wasn't interested and as for involving Simmons, well, the way in was definitely through a woman. Bringing the sergeant in on the game would only put the poor girl's back up.

'I'm sorry I can't help you, gentlemen,' she said. 'All I can tell you is that if I was looking for McGregor I'd focus on the masonic lodge. I hope he turns up.'

The streets were deserted and washed with pale moonlight as Mirabelle hit King's Road. She had quickly pulled on a black dress and flat shoes, and had brought with her a large handbag into which she had tucked several necessities. She felt for the torch in her pocket – she had got into the habit of carrying it during the blackout in London but it had been years since she'd used it. Thankfully the batteries had not worn down. She moved now with a sense of purpose. The lights were out in every building on the way into town and not a single car passed her. It didn't take long to get as far as the pier and head up to the Royal Pavilion. An old-fashioned car was parked alone on North Street – a racing-green Chambers with a soft top. Mirabelle could just make out a road map with a stylish pair of women's sunglasses folded on top of it on the passenger seat.

Apart from that there was no evidence of anybody's presence in the palace. Mirabelle smiled. She'd been right.

Effortlessly she picked the lock on the gate and made a circuit of the building and the grounds. As she passed the laburnum tree, Mirabelle shuddered. The only way inside, she figured, would be through the rear window that wasn't completely boarded up. With the aerial gone, it was easy to jemmy the plasterboard open. Behind it was an oriental casement and Mirabelle slipped it loose of its catch, hauled herself over the sill and landed inside with a soft bump. She flicked the torch over her new surroundings. Above her, a crystal chandelier glinted in the torchlight.

'Daphne,' she called.

There was no reply but then the building was vast. Her voice felt as if it had been swallowed by the dark empty space. Mirabelle made her way into the pink-wallpapered hall. The blue sofa lay as the police had left it, all signs of occupation removed. Daphne usually slept upstairs so Mirabelle decided to try there. Her footsteps didn't make a sound on the carpeted staircase. She noticed that the light from the torch was wavering a little and she steeled herself.

'Daphne,' she called again. 'It's Mirabelle Bevan.'

Nothing.

On one side of the palace the shutters were closed. With no aspect to the world outside it made the rooms seem particularly eerie. A mahogany dresser loomed out of the darkness as she rounded a corner and she let out an involuntary squawk. Getting hold of her emotions, she carried on into the Yellow Bow Rooms. The bed was immaculate. There was no one in the place – not a soul. The Pavilion was the logical place for the girl to retreat. Where on earth was she? It was far safer for her to hand over whatever it was that the masons held in such high esteem in Brighton rather than somewhere in London or Cambridge. Besides, the car parked outside couldn't belong to anyone else. Mirabelle decided to go back downstairs. She had just reached the bottom of the staircase when her whole body was arrested in motion. She was jerked backwards and pulled against the wall. She shouted, 'Get off me!' as strong arms grabbed her from behind and the torch fell from her grip.

Then the wooden panel, against which she had been forced, sprang away and she tumbled into what appeared to be a large cupboard. She gulped in the musty air. Then her training kicked in. As the person behind scooped up the torch and tried to push her forward, Mirabelle used the momentum to tip her attacker's body over her shoulder. With her assailant on the ground, she stamped hard on the wrist, and the torch went flying. She grabbed it and shone the light directly onto her attacker.

'Where the hell did you learn to do that?' yelled Daphne.

Mirabelle's heart was hammering and she felt nauseous. It was difficult to overcome an assailant from behind.

'Never mind. You gave me an awful fright. Why on earth did you grab me like that?'

'I wasn't sure who it was. It's pitch black in here. And, in any case, you're the intruder. You broke in.'

Daphne got to her feet and passed Mirabelle a flask of water. It was the sort of canvas container used by hill-walkers. Mirabelle took a sip and looked around. They weren't in a cupboard; they were in a corridor. Mirabelle wondered if there was something in her stars about hidden cavities and confined spaces – wine cellars, police cells and secret passages.

'Are you all right?'

'Yes.' Daphne smiled weakly. 'I have brothers. Three of them. It's probably just a bruise.' She rubbed her wrist.

Mirabelle looked around.

'Servants' quarters,' the girl said. 'I moved everything out of the main Pavilion to make it look like I'd gone for good. But like an idiot I left the front door open. I was in a rush. The police didn't find my things though, did they? No one ever thinks of this part of the palace. The grooms used it to sneak women up to the bedrooms.'

Mirabelle had a fleeting image of the side gate of Buckingham Palace with its discreet guard station and proximity to the anonymous streets of Pimlico. That sort of thing doubtless still went on. Then she pulled her attention back to the situation in hand.

'I should have garaged the car, shouldn't I?' Daphne was thinking things through.

'Do they know what you drive? Might they guess you're here?'

'Well, you did.'

'Yes, but I knew you were here to start with. I mean, I knew you were living here, and, if you don't mind me saying, I knew you had nowhere else to go.'

Daphne took back the water flask. 'Well,' she said, 'I might have stayed with friends.'

'Most of your friends would probably have a mason in the house. A father, a brother or an uncle. A butler or a footman, perhaps. That would be risky, wouldn't it? You were right. This is far safer. Where did you get that old car, anyway? It looks fifty years old if it's a day.'

The girl pursed her lips. 'It belongs to my aunt,' she said. 'She was the first woman in her county to get a licence but she can't drive it any more. She gave it to me earlier this year. It's my getaway vehicle.'

'Good. That's positive thinking. You're expecting to get away.'

Daphne pulled a packet of Camels from her pocket and lit a cigarette without offering one to Mirabelle. 'Of course I'm going to get away. Off into the sunset. The sunset in the south of France, I expect. At least for a while. What I want to know is what on earth you're doing here.'

'I came to help.'

'Oh no, you don't. You think you're going to get in on the action, do you? You think you can just waltz in here . . .'

'No. Nothing like that. Though I admit I'm curious about what you've uncovered that has them so excited.'

Daphne took a deep draw of her cigarette. The girl's eyes shone in the light from the glowing tip. The smoke hung in the dank air for a few seconds before she spoke. 'I don't know what it is that makes you think I'll treat you like my long-lost mother and spill my guts. Who the hell do you think you are?'

'You know who I am. And there are a lot of reasons you should trust me.' Mirabelle kept her tone even. Daphne was getting angry and it was best not to inflame the situation. 'The main thing that should concern you is that I know more about what's going on than you do by some margin.'

'Ha!' Daphne's voice was scornful. 'I doubt that.'

'For a start,' Mirabelle continued, 'after you left your father's rooms last night he met with two men, one of whom said that if you knew who you were dealing with and what you had, you'd ask for more money. Also, there appears to be more than one secret society – or at least more than one lodge. The men your father is dealing with appear to be very senior.'

'You were at Downing? Yesterday?'

Mirabelle nodded. 'I didn't know you were going to be there, to be honest. But you'd gone missing and I was concerned. I tracked down your father.'

'Jesus!'

'Lucky I did, as it turns out. Your father, by the way, is one of the least caring parents I think I've ever come across.'

'Did you eavesdrop on my meeting with Daddy? Is that what you're saying?'

'Yes,' Mirabelle admitted.

'A real little snoop, aren't you?'

'I expect snoop is a word mostly used by people who don't get important information from people who are engaged in snooping. People who recognise its importance call it intelligence gathering.'

The girl laughed. Then she stopped. 'Tell me, by any chance, were these men Scottish?'

Mirabelle nodded.

'Hmmm.' Daphne leaned against the wall. 'Well, that's a turn-up for the books.'

'What?'

'It doesn't matter. The masons are habitually pragmatic – wherever they come from. I just hadn't reckoned on Dad having such good contacts. Oh well. Money, in the long run, is probably cheaper than most of the alternatives available to them. I knew they'd pay up one way or another.'

'I think you have chosen to play a game with highly dangerous men and you aren't only asking for money, are you? That's why I came. Quite enough people have ended up dead this week, Daphne. I'm worried about you and I expect you could use someone to watch your back.'

'And you're offering to do that, are you? And yet you aren't in it for a cut?'

'I have a gentleman friend who is missing.'

'You thought I was missing.'

'You were. And I found you.'

'Who's this friend of yours?'

'A policeman.'

'From round here?'

Mirabelle nodded.

'A Brighton policeman?' she said contemptuously. 'You know what they're like. He's probably up at the lodge right this moment with his trouser leg rolled up.'

Mirabelle shook her head. 'No. He's not a mason, though I expect you might be right about his whereabouts. Is that where you're meeting them to make the swap? Queen's Road?'

Daphne hesitated for a moment, sizing up this impressive woman who seemed so very well informed. 'All right,' she said slowly. 'I'll tell you. They've taken a suite at the Grand. I insisted on meeting somewhere public and Daddy hates hotels. The old skinflint always says they're a rip-off. So I insisted on the biggest hotel in town and the most expensive room. It's a penthouse suite. It's petty, I know, but it will annoy him. I wouldn't step inside a lodge if they paid me. They can do whatever they want in there. I'm not an idiot, you know. So, that's the plan. A swap at the hotel and afterwards I'll get into the car, drive along the coast and pick up the boat train at Portsmouth to spend the summer in France. I thought it best to get out of the way while they did whatever they were going to do once they'd got what they wanted. I don't want them focusing on me. Daddy is smart, of course, but he's easily distracted. Out of sight, out of mind. By the time I get home the whole thing will be done and dusted. And I can get back to work and stop having to live here, with any luck. I'm going to take a flat somewhere down on the front.'

'What is it that your father and his friends want so very badly? What did you find?'

Daphne pursed her lips.

'If I'm going to help you, then I need to know,' Mirabelle pushed.

'It was under the floorboards.' The girl curled her shoulders as if she didn't like admitting the secret. 'Here. Mrs Chapman rolled up the carpet and there was a loose board with a document case hidden underneath. It was in one of the downstairs rooms – the one George IV used as a bedroom when he got too fat to climb the stairs. He was a Grand Master, you know, at the Grand Lodge in London.'

'What was in the box?'

'Letters. The ink was faded and the writing was difficult to read. Thick parchment. Old. Mrs Chapman didn't understand.

She just handed the papers to me. Honestly, she'd have used them to light a fire. Poor old thing.'

'What did they say – these letters?'

'They were about the history of the masons. Nothing too exciting for most people, though I got excited, of course. That was my mistake. If I hadn't come clean and told her how important they were she'd still be alive. I was trying to be decent, if you can believe that. I wanted to cut her in. I said I could probably get her a couple of hundred pounds but she wanted more. I wish she'd come back to me and just said, but she went to one of the masons at the lodge, and when he refused to pay she got in touch with that journalist.'

'Joey Gillingham?'

'Yes.'

Mirabelle's mind buzzed as the story fell into place. Of course. That was the connection between the two murder victims. Not the racecourse, or the masons, but this information that the old woman wanted to sell and the journalist wanted to buy. Some kind of scoop.

'And Gillingham asked around,' Mirabelle theorised. 'The masons in Brighton might or might not have heard what he was up to, but these other fellows definitely did. You were already dealing with them and they didn't want a journalist sniffing around. But he knew. So someone killed him.'

'I think that was Daddy's friends. Something he said to me on the telephone made me think it must have been. The masons down here are pretty provincial – and a murder like that . . .'

'Oh no,' Mirabelle interrupted, 'I don't agree. The masons in Brighton definitely aren't averse to murder, though these friends of your father's are more professional. If anything there's more real violence here. The whole thing has been a terrible mix-up of circumstances. So what happened? After Gillingham was killed how did Elsie take it?'

Daphne looked at the floorboards as if she was a naughty child who had been berated by her nanny. 'She was furious. It was as if someone had stolen money from her – money she already had. I tried to calm her down. She thought the killer was her contact at the Brighton lodge and she wanted to confront him. I told her she'd have to go away for a bit. I said that I'd pay her the sum she asked but that she had to let me deal with everything. I thought she was in danger. At the least she was a loose cannon. But I reckoned I could handle it.'

'She didn't want to go?'

'No. She said not to be foolish. That she'd keep her man at Queen's Road in check. She wasn't scared of him. That was a mistake as it turned out.'

Mirabelle shook her head but she didn't explain about Henshaw. She wanted to hear the story from Daphne's point of view. 'You must have been terrified when Vesta and I turned up on Tuesday and told you the old woman was dead.'

'I was sick after you left,' Daphne admitted. 'I vomited in a chamber pot. Then I cleared away my things and left. I sent Daddy a telegram from London to say it was time to wind up the deal and that I was coming to see him. Then, well, you heard everything. I told him I want the money and I want justice. I mean, killing that journalist was one thing – awful – but poor Mrs Chapman. I'm determined to get them to hand over her killer. I mean, how dare they? Though that won't be necessary now. I see the creep did himself in. Did you read the paper? Poor Elsie.'

'No, no. Henshaw wasn't the one who killed her. He'd never have done that. He loved Elsie. He'd loved her for years. She was quite right to trust him, even if he wouldn't succumb to her blackmail attempt. Listen, Daphne, let me come with you to the hotel and I'll make sure that Elsie's killer is brought to justice – the real killer. Besides, you might need help. There's no harm in having someone in reserve – someone they don't know about.'

The girl had a lot of guts, Mirabelle thought. She had taken on her father and his friends, and she hadn't shown even a glimmer of fear when she'd heard about Elsie's death the other day. Mind you, she was rather keen on the money. That was interesting. Most people, with this number of bodies piling up, would have fled by now. Instead, Daphne had simply demanded justice along with her menaces.

Daphne stubbed out her cigarette. 'All right. You can come if you like, but I'm not giving you a penny.'

'Don't worry. I'm in it for the glory,' said Mirabelle.

Chapter 26

Well begun is half done.

Dawn was only just breaking as the women crept out of the Pavilion and down the dewy garden path. High above them, seagulls circled in the brightening sky. It was going to be a scorcher. Mirabelle led Daphne across North Street and convinced her not to bring the old car to the hotel.

'You can pick it up later,' she promised. 'It's too conspicuous. The main thing is to attract as little attention as possible. To succeed we may need to disappear.'

Daphne agreed. Miss Bevan seemed remarkably competent. If the girl was honest, she found the older woman's confident manner comforting. 'Have you done this sort of thing before?' she asked.

'A blackmail attempt? Don't be ridiculous.'

'It's not exactly blackmail,' Daphne objected. 'I mean, it's more theft, I expect, or money with menaces.'

Mirabelle shot the girl a look. Things, it seemed, were never ideal. She didn't approve of what Daphne had done. If the girl had simply handed over the letters to the Trust (which, after all, was the rightful place for them) three murders would never have taken place. Still, Mirabelle wanted to look after the kid. Daphne hadn't meant to get into this kind of mess. She had only been trying to lay claim to something she thought should have been hers – a decent inheritance and, Mirabelle supposed, a sense of revenge at having been excluded. Having a father like Professor Marsden must have been awful, and, besides, the girl couldn't have foreseen the murders. Whatever was in the letters was clearly so incendiary who knew what might have happened even if the Trust had become involved? History was paramount to organisations like the freemasons. Recriminations about Daphne's behaviour now would be futile. Seller of secrets or not, of everyone involved the girl seemed by far the nicest. It was best to get on.

Silently Mirabelle turned down one street after another with Daphne following obediently until the women rounded the corner onto a tiny lane.

'What on earth's along here?' Daphne stopped at the point where the pavement simply ran out.

'There's something I need to pick up.'

'There's nothing up there, is there?'

'Wait here if you like,' said Mirabelle.

Daphne decided to follow. She put her hand on the older woman's arm. A smile creased Mirabelle's face.

At the green front door they stopped and Mirabelle knocked loudly. There was no reply. She knocked again. Then she rapped on the dusty windowpane. From inside there was a sound of furniture being moved. A corner of the filthy curtain twitched, and then a few seconds later the door was unbolted.

Fred had pulled a dressing gown around the white vest and shorts in which he had evidently slept. He was unshaven. 'Miss Bevan,' he said, 'you're up early. Everything all right?' He stood back to allow the women to enter. 'Something I can help you with?'

Mirabelle took a deep breath. 'I'm afraid my friend and I have found ourselves in a tricky situation.'

'I'm sorry to hear that.' Fred's tone was absolutely sincere. 'What can I do to help?'

Mirabelle paused. She didn't really want to say the words. 'I think I need a gun.'

Mirabelle felt Daphne tense.

'Look,' the girl said, 'I'm not sure that's a good idea, Miss Bevan. It's illegal, and I mean, Daddy . . .'

Mirabelle's stare stopped the girl in her tracks.

'The kid might have a point,' said Fred. 'Are you sure? A gun is a different kind of illegal from an extra egg here and there, Miss Bevan.'

Mirabelle considered the situation. She didn't relish making the decision. Two years before, she had become embroiled in a fight that resulted in her shooting a young man dead with his own weapon. The court had cleared her of any wrongdoing and the man had almost certainly intended to kidnap and kill her, but it had been traumatic. Now she ran through the scenario that lay ahead at the Grand one more time. The two men she'd seen in Professor Marsden's rooms, the cold-blooded nature of the three murders and the fact that both she and Daphne were of a slim build, neither of them much over eight stones in weight, made up her mind.

'It's only a precaution. I hope we won't need to use the thing,' she said. 'It's insurance.'

'All right.' Fred's tone became businesslike. 'If you're sure, I can probably get something. It'll cost you, mind. Come back in a couple of hours.'

'I need it now, Fred.' Mirabelle slipped her hand into her bag. She drew out the remaining bottle of 1914 malt that she had taken from the wine cellar.

Fred sucked air through his teeth, almost as if he was in pain. He took the bottle to the window and examined the label. 'Is this on the level? Where did you get it?' he asked.

'You tell me where you pick up your supplies and I'll tell you where I pick up mine.'

Fred grinned. 'Fair enough. Will a service revolver do? I've got a Webley or an Enfield. If you want a Victory model I can probably get one before lunchtime.'

'I'll take the Enfield.' Mirabelle sounded more decisive than she felt. Jack had an Enfield in his service days. The gun had a smaller calibre than the Webley but at least it was familiar.

'Right.' Fred put out his hand and Mirabelle shook it. 'And you'll want some ammunition, I expect.' He disappeared into the back room. 'That'll be extra but I won't charge you much.'

Mirabelle reached into her bag again and took out a ten-bob note. 'This should cover it,' she whispered to Daphne.

Daphne's eyes fell to the counter where a small pile of American stockings were on display.

'Those are excellent,' Mirabelle said. 'But I don't think we should focus on them just now.'

Two minutes later, the women were back outside. Daphne didn't speak, only eyed Mirabelle's bag suspiciously as if wondering what else she might have in there. Fred had given them a small box of .38 calibre bullets. 'That should be enough, shouldn't it?' he'd said cheerily and loaded a round for good measure. Daphne had felt like backing out of the door. But she'd held her ground. Now safely outside, she felt anxious. The sight of the gun had scared her. Carrying round a bundle of old letters was one thing, a loaded weapon was quite another.

'Come along,' said Mirabelle, taking Daphne by the arm as she turned left at the end of the lane and headed towards King's Road.

Just before they came to the hotel Mirabelle guided them across to the other side of the street. The women leaned against the rail in front of the sea. No one was yet down on the shore. Off to the west, the pier was still closed, stretching over the still water. It was deserted, still too early for the hordes of candyfloss sellers, the click-click girls with their cameras, the bathers and picnickers. On the other side of the road, the hotel loomed upwards into the blue sky.

Daphne checked her watch. 'I said I'd meet them at half past eight,' she said. 'We're far too early. We could just stand here, I suppose. It's a glorious day.'

Mirabelle pulled the strap of her handbag over her shoulder. 'Don't be silly,' she said as she led the way back across the road. 'We've work to do.'

Daphne expected to walk up to the hotel's grand front entrance and she was forced to swerve as Mirabelle strode confidently past it and up the side of the hotel. A semi-circular service road skirted the rear. The delivery bays were closed and locked. The smell of baking bread wafted across their path and a small chimney belched steam into the air.

'This way,' Mirabelle directed.

Two of the back doors were open – one to the laundry, by the smell of soap and lavender coming from it, and the other to the kitchens. Mirabelle stepped into the second and Daphne followed.

'What are we doing?' the girl whispered.

'Just what you did at the Pavilion,' Mirabelle said. 'You were quite right. No one looks at the servants' area.'

Inside, the corridor split off into several directions. Mirabelle followed her nose towards the smell of baking and was only stopped when a young lad dressed in kitchen whites, with a huge basket of carrots in his arms, walked briskly out of a room.

'Oi,' he said, manoeuvring the basket onto his hip and removing a lit cigarette from his mouth. 'What are you doing here?'

'Health and hygiene,' Mirabelle said without flinching. 'Sussex County Council. I'm looking for a fellow called Charles Lewis.'

'Is that the nignog?' the boy sneered.

'The pastry chef,' Mirabelle corrected him.

Unperturbed, the kid gestured down the corridor. 'He's in there,' he said delightedly. 'Is he in trouble then?'

'On the contrary, we're here to commend Mr Lewis,' Mirabelle said. 'He has by far the highest success rate in the county – hygienically speaking. We shall be awarding him the Sussex gold medal.'

Daphne cast Mirabelle a baffled look.

'When we've done that, of course, we'll undertake a full inspection. Sous chefs are a particular interest of mine. Off you go.'

The boy put the cigarette back in his mouth and fled to scrub the carrots.

In the side kitchen, along the corridor the boy had pointed out, Charlie was piping pastry onto a tray. He didn't look up as Mirabelle knocked on the door jamb.

'Just put it there.' He waved at a marble counter. 'I'll need them in a minute.'

'Will here do?' said Mirabelle.

Charlie raised his eyes. 'Mirabelle! What are you doing here?' Then his voice dropped. 'Is it Vesta? I ain't been home yet. A late night session and then an early shift, you know. Is she all right?'

'She's fine. It's nothing like that. This is Miss Marsden. Daphne. We need your help, Charlie. We need to use the service stairs.'

'Is this going to get me into trouble?' Charlie grinned. 'Give me a second. I just need to finish these éclairs and I'll be all yours.'

The service areas of the Grand Hotel were not as extensive as those at the Pavilion but they included a service lift as well as back stairs. With his éclairs in the oven, Charlie obligingly checked the catering book and confirmed that three gentlemen were booked into one of the penthouse suites under the name of Smith and had ordered an alarm call and morning tea at quarter past eight.

'Eight fifteen, eh? Lazy devils!' Charlie laughed. 'They're the lucky ones, eh? I've been up since, well, yesterday morning.'

'I don't know how you manage,' said Mirabelle with a smile.

'It's the music, Ma'am. Well, if you want to see these fellas you've got a while to wait. Come back down to the kitchen and let me make you some breakfast.'

This, it transpired, comprised strong coffee and warm pastries on a makeshift table in one of the pantries. There was even a small bowl of fresh strawberries. Mirabelle ate slowly, relishing the flavour.

'England's finest,' Charlie declared. 'We ain't got berries like these back home.'

Left alone while Charlie went off to tend to his ovens, Mirabelle sipped the coffee and dabbed her lips with a thick white linen napkin while Daphne took the last strawberry from the bowl. The pastries were delicious. Once she had finished, Mirabelle turned her attention to the matters in hand. She folded her napkin and sat back in her seat, looking at Daphne curiously.

'What do the letters say?' she asked.

'It's so lame – that's the ridiculous thing.'

'It can't be that lame if they've killed all these people to keep it secret.'

'That's the masons for you, isn't it? Drama after drama over something symbolic.'

Mirabelle folded her hands in her lap. 'Well?'

'Do you know the Grand Lodge in London? In Holborn?'

'Yes. Next to the Connaught Rooms.' The building had been renovated between the wars. They'd hoped it would be a monument to peace before 1939 came along. 'It's the oldest lodge in the country, isn't it? The one the king attended?'

Daphne leaned in. 'That's the thing,' she whispered. 'It's ironic, really. I mean, it's not the oldest. That's what becomes clear in the letters and that's what they're interested in. The letters are from a nineteenth-century earl who wrote to George IV. He mentions the real lodge, the *first* lodge – another order that was up and running before the Grand

Lodge. Of course, it's more ancient and more secret. More senior. More everything.'

'And London doesn't want the story to get out?' Mirabelle picked up her cup and took a sip.

'That's what I thought,' Daphne kept her voice low, 'until you mentioned the men my father was meeting. It hadn't occurred to me that the order might still be going. But now it looks as if it is. It's in Scotland, you see. In Ayrshire somewhere. Somehow Daddy has got in touch with them – or them with him. Which is all to the good, really. As you said, they've got more money.'

Mirabelle put down her cup. 'I understand you're in this for the cash, Daphne, but the rule is to stay realistic in these situations. Greed only gets people hurt, and you've already set the terms of your deal. These men – if they are who you think they are – have killed people to defend their history. To keep their order's provenance secret. I'd be wary of pressing them. They seem keen on guarding their ground. God knows why.'

Daphne's face became earnest. 'History is all we have left now. We won the war and lost India and Palestine, and, well, look at us, losing the peace. This country is in tatters. I can't blame them for caring about the past.'

Mirabelle decided not to comment. Britain had fought its way through the war, and the country would get through the peace, too. People were resilient. Better days were already here and there would be more ahead. Her optimism momentarily surprised her. 'So, what do you know about these men? About this Scottish lodge?'

Daphne finished her coffee. She cast her eyes around the pantry as if behind the sacks of potatoes someone might be listening. 'It was pro-Stuart. George was a Hanoverian king. I assumed he'd rubbed out the order – got rid of it, I mean. I'd seen mentions of it here and there before, but no definite proof that it existed. The Hanoverians were not keen on dissent and it was only a hundred years since James Stuart attempted the coup that scared George's great-great-grandfather into reprisals. It was only a few decades since Bonnie Prince Charlie and his troops made it as far as Derby. A potent Jacobite force north of the border was a real threat. The monarchy was afraid of the Scots. When I found the letters I assumed King George had destroyed the order. It seems, though, they escaped George's retribution and they've been keeping their heads down all this time. They've survived by being more secret than anyone else.'

Mirabelle checked her watch as the girl continued.

'Early brotherhoods are fascinating. They're based on knightly principles. Warriors, I think, maybe even Crusaders at the beginning. They were the gatekeepers. The defenders of relics. And, well, there are stories of treasure, of course.' She popped a strawberry into her mouth. 'Not like the masons – they're just boy scouts behind closed doors.'

'And they're definitely Scottish?'

'Yes. At least that's where the letters were written. Perhaps King George didn't have time to do anything about it before he died. The letters have lain there for more than a hundred years. Maybe no one knew about them other than the king himself.'

'We better go upstairs,' Mirabelle said decisively. 'I'd like to have a look at the lie of the land.'

Chapter 27

We die only once and for such a long time.

Charlie ushered the women into the service lift. 'The penthouses have a dining room,' he explained. 'No one was booked to eat there yesterday or today so it's empty at the moment. The fancy rooms are quiet most of the time. It's only now and then the Grand cashes in on them.'

Upstairs, at the end of a wide corridor was a double doorway. Charlie produced the key and let them inside. The room was lovely though it wasn't on the seaward side of the building. The roofs of Brighton stretched up the hill beyond the glass. There was a faint smell of cigars and furniture polish.

'Mostly it's occupied at night,' Charlie explained as he ushered the women inside and closed the door with a quiet click. 'Private parties.'

The view over Brighton might be prettier in the dark, Mirabelle thought. The thing that held the attention was the sky, blue and streaked here and there with a trail of fluffy cloud. The window was framed by blue chintz curtains and dominated by a long mahogany table with two silver candelabra placed at the centre. To one side a chiffonier was stacked with porcelain, cutlery, crystal and silverware monographed with the Grand's logo. Mirabelle noticed that in addition to the door they'd come in there were three other exits.

Charlie followed her eyes. 'That one is the dining kitchen. It's small – for reheating or cooking to order. Most of the food comes up from downstairs in the lift. The other two doors open directly into the suites, and if I'm not mistaken,' he started towards the one on the other side of the room, 'your fellas are in here.'

Mirabelle looked perturbed.

'Don't worry, the doors are locked unless the dining room is booked. But I thought you could have a peek. Like the advance guard.' Charlie put his eye to the keyhole. He turned around. 'They're up,' he whispered, checking his watch. 'They won't be needing that alarm call.'

'Thank you, Charlie. We'll be fine now. They'll be missing you downstairs.'

'OK. If you need me, there's a direct line to the service kitchen. I'll keep an eye on it. And if you want to come down, get into the service lift and press B1. It'll bring you out in the kitchen, right next to where you came in. Oh, and here's the key to the interconnecting door.' He pressed it into Mirabelle's hand. 'In case you need it. It works on all the doors in here – the rooms on this side can be opened into one big suite with dining facilities if need be, so the locks are the same.'

'Thanks.'

'You sure you don't want anything else? I can stick round if you like.'

'No. It's probably best if you go now. I don't want to get you into trouble.'

Charlie hovered. 'OK, Mirabelle. But just to fill you in, there's no one else up here. There's six large suites on this floor and only one of them taken last night. You're on your own.'

'Thanks for not asking too many questions.'

When the door closed behind Charlie, Mirabelle put her eye to the keyhole. On the other side there was a sitting room full of ornate French furniture. In one corner there was a bar. The man in the tweed three-piece suit whom she had last seen in Professor Marsden's rooms was pouring himself what looked like a whisky. He added a dash of soda and then took the glass to the window and sipped it as he took in the view. It was early to be drinking.

'Let me see.' Daphne jostled Mirabelle's shoulder.

The girl bent to get a look. 'Is that him? The Scottish chap? With the moustache?'

Mirabelle stared at the dining-room window and then at the wall to the left of it. The man was twenty feet away at most. 'We have to be very quiet,' she whispered. 'Yes, that's Laidlaw.'

'Oh,' Daphne whispered, 'now Daddy's come in. He must have just woken up. I think he's slept in his clothes. He's coming out of one of the bedrooms. Lazy beast. It's almost time for us to arrive.'

'I'm sure he's come along to keep things in hand. Or, more specifically, you.'

'In hand? I don't think that will be necessary,' Daphne objected. 'It should be quick, shouldn't it? Easy?'

'In an ideal world.'

'Today's the day, then,' said Professor Marsden jovially to Laidlaw, who raised his glass without turning round.

They still had fifteen minutes. The telephone sounded next door and the professor went to answer it. The alarm call, Mirabelle realised, wasn't to wake up the men, it was to ensure they were ready when Daphne arrived.

'Where's the other one?' Mirabelle thought out loud. Charlie had said there were three of them.

She bent down again to see if she could make out any sign of him. Before she could establish anything, there was a knock on the door and Laidlaw went to answer it. A waiter with a silver tray came into the suite and laid out a teapot and cups. Professor Marsden, Mirabelle noted, put copious amounts of sugar into his tea – three lumps at least. If he had been trying to keep up with his friend he probably had a hangover. Three men had booked in, and now there were three cups. Where was the third man? Had someone else joined Professor

Marsden and Laidlaw in the suite? If so, why hadn't he come out when the alarm call sounded and the tea arrived?

'Well,' she stood up, 'there's no point shilly-shallying. We're early but we might as well get on with it. Are you ready?'

Daphne passed a hand over her hair. She walked to the window, looked out and then turned with a wide grin. 'Let's,' she said. 'The early bird catches the worm and all that . . .'

In the hallway the women paused. Mirabelle brushed a hand over her skirt. She wouldn't have worn black for this, had she known. She didn't like wearing the colour at all. Widow's weeds – a grim reminder. She took a deep breath and motioned Daphne towards the door. The girl checked the small pouch of papers in her handbag, then nodded and rapped hard. In an instant the handle moved and the door opened.

Laidlaw stood in the doorway. 'Good morning,' he said. 'You're prompt. You must be Miss Marsden?'

'Yes. And this is my friend, Miss Bevan,' Daphne introduced Mirabelle.

Neither Mirabelle nor Laidlaw held out their hand.

'This lady shouldn't be here,' he said bluntly, blocking their entry to the suite. 'Our business is with you alone, Miss Marsden, and confidentiality is very important. We stressed that, I believe, when the arrangements were made.'

'Then it would seem sensible not to discuss matters in the hallway, would it not?' Daphne kept her cool.

The man considered this for a moment and then stood back to let them enter. Mirabelle, after all, could not be magicked away now she was here.

'Good morning, Daddy,' Daphne said brightly as she strode into the suite.

Professor Marsden let out a grunt and gulped his tea. He did not acknowledge Mirabelle.

'What do I call you?' Daphne asked the Scotsman as she sat down, seemingly completely at ease, in an armchair opposite her father.

Mirabelle was impressed. She hovered behind the girl with one hand on the chair's chintz covering.

The Scotsman looked them up and down. 'Laidlaw,' he said.

'Well, Mr Laidlaw, shall we get started?'

'Not quite yet. Who exactly is your friend?' He pointed at Mirabelle, crossing to the bar and pouring himself another drink without offering anyone else.

'I'm Mirabelle Bevan. I'm just an acquaintance, Mr Laidlaw. Professor Marsden can vouch for that. A family friend, you might say.'

The professor bared his teeth and squinted across the low coffee table. He clearly hadn't told Laidlaw about Mirabelle's visit to his rooms. 'She's Daphne's friend,' he said. 'She was looking for the girl the other day. I hadn't set eyes on her before that.'

The Scotsman downed his whisky. 'Well, she's here now.'

'Yes,' Mirabelle smiled, 'I am. At Daphne's invitation.'

The girl nodded. She passed a hand through her hair as if this was a delightful cocktail party and she was enjoying the company.

'So,' said Mirabelle, 'shall we get down to business?'

'Do you have it?' Laidlaw glowered in Daphne's direction.

'Do you have the money?' Daphne inclined her head.

Laidlaw drew a small leather suitcase from behind the sofa and laid it on the table. Daphne went to open the catch, but he blocked her move with his arm. 'Oh no, you don't. Show me the letters first.'

Daphne removed the neatly parcelled sheaf from her hand-bag and put it on the table. 'There.'

'The way it works, Miss Marsden, is that neither of us removes the goods from the table until they have been inspected and we are agreed. Do you understand?'

Daphne agreed. Laidlaw moved his arm out of the way and she clicked open the case. Mirabelle caught sight of stack upon stack of banknotes. The girl must have netted thousands. Daphne took in a deep breath and her face relaxed. Her summer on the French Riviera was secure. On the other side of the low table, Mr Laidlaw donned a pair of spectacles and opened the letters one by one. He cast an eye over the wide, arching script, pushing each paper along to Daphne's father. After a minute or two Professor Marsden nodded and Laidlaw refolded the thick scripts.

'It appears we have a deal,' Laidlaw stated.

Daphne got up. 'Well, business is easy, isn't it, when both parties know what they want? However, we weren't treating only over the money, were we? There is also the matter of my friend Mrs Chapman – you were to hand over her killer to the police. Miss Bevan here is of the opinion that the man who it is thought committed suicide after killing her is not the murderer. We need to clear that up before we're done.'

Laidlaw paused. He eyed Mirabelle as if she was a curiosity. 'Miss Bevan is correct. I don't want you to worry, Miss Marsden. This is a disciplinary matter and your concerns have been seen to. In fact, I've seen to it personally,' he said with a smile. 'Will you take my word on it? The man who killed your friend has been punished.'

Daphne hesitated. 'Why on earth should I take your word? And I don't want you to punish him, whoever he is. I want you to hand him over to the police. That's real justice, not just a rap on the knuckles.'

It passed across Mirabelle's mind that this man wouldn't restrict himself to a rap on the knuckles if his temper was let loose.

Laidlaw frowned. 'I tell you what – I have a proposition for you that will ensure you aren't worried any more about who killed your friend.'

'What is it?' Daphne asked.

'It'll close the deal, you'll see.'

Mirabelle tensed. Something was off here. Mr Laidlaw seemed to be enjoying himself – quietly, earnestly even, but enjoying himself nonetheless. There was an underlying relish in his tone.

'It'll be a nice tidy affair.' Mr Laidlaw got up as if he was about to fetch something. He stood behind Professor Marsden so that Daphne had to squint to see him against the light from the window. 'I suspect you like things tidy, don't you, Miss Marsden? You look like the kind of woman who prefers it when things work out just so?'

'Absolutely,' Professor Marsden agreed. 'She's tirelessly exacting.'

'Accuracy of that nature is costly in so many ways. And now it'll cost you.' Mr Laidlaw's voice had become almost sing-song.

'It seems to me our business is almost concluded, Mr Laidlaw.' Daphne's tone was clipped. 'I'm only seeking assurance that justice will be done and I've requested that since the beginning. This isn't a game, and I can't imagine what you're trying to say.'

'Imagine this,' the Scotsman said ominously.

He drew his arm around Professor Marsden's throat, almost casually, and then began to throttle him with great force. The professor's eyes betrayed his complete surprise. He spluttered and his skin flushed. He hit Laidlaw's forearm repeatedly and then rose in his chair, trying to ease the pressure on his windpipe. None of which was any help.

Daphne jumped to her feet.

Laidlaw's voice remained calm, his tone even. 'Your father's life will cost you, young lady. What would you say was a fair amount? In such matters it's traditional to call it evens. And as for any idea of justice . . . You're not so worried about that any more, are you?'

'You won't kill him. I don't believe you.' Daphne clutched the thick leather handle of the little suitcase without removing it from the table.

Laidlaw laughed. It sounded like a train rumbling. 'That's entirely up to you,' he said, tightening his grip so that a gurgling sound came from the professor.

'This is ridiculous!' Daphne shouted. 'Stop it!'

Laidlaw looked as if he was quite at ease. 'I can make it take any time I like. Strangle a man with your hands and your grip gets tired. But use the crook of your arm like this and it can go on for a very long time. Just enough air . . . and yet not quite enough.'

He loosened his grip as if to illustrate the point. Professor Marsden slumped into the cushions though his neck remained firmly held in place. He tried to say something but he couldn't get it out. His lips were covered in spittle and he hadn't the strength to form the words. He wheezed horribly as he gulped at the air. His fingers grasped at the Scotsman's elbow, trying to insert a barrier between Laidlaw's arm and his bruised neck.

'P-p-please,' he spluttered, his eyes on Daphne.

Laidlaw tightened his grip again. The man was all muscle. The professor's back arched as if he was having a seizure. 'You see,' the Scotsman said slowly, as if this was a conversation over a point of theory at dinner, 'you probably thought I brought your father because, well, who knows what you thought? There's no love lost, is there? Not between a silly little girl and her daddy. Oh so clever, but not quite clever enough. Desperate to be part of the club. Jesus, I despise masons. They think they choose their calling but what they don't realise is that you have to be chosen. Their little club means nothing. Are you really prepared to see him die, Miss Marsden? Here, right in front of you? Your daddy. Your dear daddy? Killed over the matter of a few thousand pounds that isn't even yours by right? I don't think you want to live with that. Push the suitcase across the table, there's a good girl.'

Daphne's eyes hardened. She turned as if to go, touching Mirabelle's arm lightly and casting her eyes on the handbag in which she knew the gun was secreted. But Mirabelle's senses were tingling. There was more going on here, she was sure of it, and she didn't want to show her hand too soon. There were three men in the suite. She looked round as the professor made another gurgling sound. She couldn't quite believe Laidlaw would really kill him.

'Mirabelle!' Daphne pawed at the handbag's catch.

Mirabelle shook her head and drew it away. The gun would raise the stakes. It was a last resort. 'Give back the money,' she hissed. 'Do as he says.'

Daphne turned in fury. 'No,' she spat. 'I don't care if you kill him. I'm not giving it up.'

Laidlaw tightened his grip with renewed effort. The professor tried to scream but no sound came out of his mouth. His face was contorted now, puce – so grotesque and desperate he looked like a different man. A dying one.

'Daddy, Daddy, Daddy,' Laidlaw said, like a little boy taunting a little girl in a playground. His eyes were vicious. He wasn't going to back down.

Daphne released the handle of the case. 'All right. All right. Keep the stupid money,' she said as she pushed it over. 'For God's sake, Mirabelle, why didn't you . . .'

But her words were cut short as Laidlaw let go the professor's neck, long enough for Professor Marsden to relax very slightly and for Daphne to think she would have the opportunity for recrimination. Then the big Scotsman pounced. There was a loud, horrifying click and Daphne screamed as her father fell sideways. There was no question he was dead. It happened so quickly, Mirabelle thought. This man was insane. There would be no reasoning with him. All of a sudden she realised that he had never had any intention of the professor surviving the deal. He had been playing with Daphne and now he'd turn on her. He didn't intend the girl to leave this room, and nor by association did he intend Mirabelle to get out either.

'You haven't a clue, lassie,' Laidlaw spat. 'You have no idea who you're dealing with.'

'You . . . you . . . said you'd let go of him,' Daphne stammered. 'You said.'

Laidlaw sneered. 'You said. You said. And you turned out to be a Daddy's girl. What a crying shame. I was curious. You must be disappointed in yourself. All your grand ideas and independent talk came to nothing, didn't it?' He stood up and straightened his cuffs. 'You can never tell how people are going to react when the chips are down. Especially women. You lasted longer than I expected, I'll give you that. But I was always going to kill him. No one can know, you see. That's the thing. You didn't really think we'd cut you in and cut him in and, oh, your friend as well, and everyone walks away knowing? We haven't survived all this time by pussyfooting around.'

He reached into his pocket and pulled out a flick knife. Mirabelle acted quickly this time. She pulled out the gun, aiming carefully. 'Stop right there,' she said firmly.

Laidlaw raised his eyebrows but he didn't move. 'I didn't expect that,' he said without putting down the blade. 'Miss Bevan, it seems you're an enterprising woman.'

Daphne grabbed the suitcase.

'Leave that,' Mirabelle directed her. 'Go and check the other rooms. There should be three men here. Someone hasn't come out yet. Concentrate, Daphne.'

Daphne put down the suitcase reluctantly and slipped past her father's body, deliberately turning her face away. She opened the bedroom door. 'No one in here.'

Laidlaw addressed Mirabelle. 'So English,' he said in his lilting accent.

'I thought that someone from an ancient order would be more,' Mirabelle grasped for the word, 'dignified.'

Laidlaw grinned. 'Did you now? Well, you got that wrong. Where I come from, guns are considered too easy. We keep our secrets, and when we kill people we like to do it hands-on – the way of the ancients. I'm going to be very hands-on with you, Miss Bevan.'

'I don't intend to kill you,' said Mirabelle. 'If you come any closer I'll shoot you in the leg. Call it soft if you like, a bullet in the leg is painful enough.'

Laidlaw grinned widely. 'I'm beginning to like you,' he said.

Daphne disappeared into the second bedroom. 'There's no one in here either,' she called.

'But if you think a bullet in the knee will stop me, you've another think coming, woman,' Laidlaw growled before launching himself at Mirabelle. Without hesitation, she let off a shot. Daphne screamed and rushed back into the room. Laidlaw stumbled but kept coming towards Mirabelle. She let off a second bullet, this time into his thigh. He roared, cutting at the air with his knife. She was only six inches out of his reach and everything was moving too quickly. She reached out and slammed the man's arm as hard as she could, hoping he'd drop the weapon.

'I don't want to kill you. Put that down.'

Laidlaw paused for a moment and then lunged. Mirabelle fired a third bullet and as the man went down he grabbed hold of her ankle. She fell and the gun dropped from her hand, spinning out of reach towards the door. Laidlaw still wouldn't stop. He pulled himself up, crawling on top of her, hauling his body into position, reaching out to grab the weapon. She could sense the whisky on his breath and the weight of him pressing down.

'Was it you who killed Gillingham?' she said, trying to fight him off. 'Was it you who slit his throat?'

He gurgled. It was, she realised, the sound of him laughing. She could feel his blood wet on her legs as he slid upwards. 'You're some woman. You'd never think it to look at you.'

He let the gun be, instead drawing his blade and placing it on her jugular.

Mirabelle felt the cold metal sting. I'm going to die, she thought. She'd hoped for it before, in an abstract way, but now the moment was here she found herself regretting the sunny day she'd never enjoy and her morning cup of tea with Vesta. She suddenly wanted to be in the office at Brills Lane. 'Did you kill Joey Gillingham?' she said.

'Aye.' Laidlaw pushed his face close to hers. 'I killed him. Truth is, I enjoyed it. I always enjoy it. No one ever notices. Wear an old suit and keep your mouth shut, and you look just like everyone else, eh? Stay calm and don't look back. You're all soft down here, the lot of you. Where I come from we fight for everything we've got.'

'And Henshaw?'

He shook his head. 'Naw. The lodge did that one. I would have killed him though. He deserved to die. He was set to sell out his brothers over that woman. You never fake a suicide. Bloody amateurs. They just make more work, someone has to clean up after them, and all the buggers want is further in, further up.' Laidlaw slumped, seeming heavier now, as if his sins were weighing him down. She could feel his breath warm on her neck and when she looked up, he was staring into her eyes. 'Nice perfume,' he murmured.

Mirabelle had to stop herself from squirming or trying to kick. It wasn't going to help. Laidlaw smiled. Somewhere he'd found a reserve of energy. He pressed his lips to her mouth and kissed her hard. Mirabelle bit him. She tasted blood.

'Jesus!' he shouted, pulling back, ready to slash.

I hope Vesta marries Charlie, Mirabelle thought, trying to ignore the word that came into her mind. Goodbye.

And then the shot rang out. It sounded as if it came from far away though it couldn't have. No marksman could be that accurate, let alone a girl who'd never used a gun before.

Laidlaw's head swung to one side, or that's how it seemed. Then his body weight suddenly doubled. Mirabelle tried to take a breath. He was half on and half off her. The side of his head was gone but she didn't dare look. Above, Daphne seemed ten feet tall. The gun was in her hand and she was shaking violently.

'That's four shots,' said Mirabelle as she crawled from underneath Laidlaw and scrambled to her feet. 'Someone must have heard them. If nothing else, one of the guests will ring reception and someone will come up.'

There was a smear of blood on her leg and a spray on her fingers. Daphne started to sob uncontrollably. 'Oh God,' she said. 'I should never have done this. I didn't know they really existed. I mean, I'd read about the Scottish order . . . It didn't occur to me that they'd come looking. I thought Daddy's lodge would deal with it – Uncle Johnny and his friends in Holborn. I didn't think he'd end up dead. This is all my fault.'

'What do you mean?' said Mirabelle. The girl wasn't making any sense. Her eyes flicked across the room to the bundle of letters.

'I wrote them. I wrote the stupid things. I found paper from the period – the real thing – and I made my own ink. I left them where I knew Mrs Chapman would find them so the discovery would look more genuine. I did it to get money. It wasn't fair, you see. It wasn't fair. And now Daddy's dead and we're both going to hang.'

Mirabelle's mind was racing. 'It was all a con,' she said as it fell into place. 'But then they weren't going to pay you, anyway.' She grappled with the catch on the suitcase and opened it. With frantic fingers she felt underneath the notes on the top. Sure enough, the case contained about two hundred pounds and a lot of blank paper. That was how things were after the war. Everything was empty. People expected something for nothing and none of it was real. Mirabelle looked at Professor

Marsden's body and Daphne who had sunk to her knees with tears streaming down her face. What a stupid, pointless waste.

Jack always said that you could never tell anything about an agent until their life was threatened. You could train people. You could equip them. You'd think they'd act one way or another. But until they were on active service you never knew what they'd actually do when they got into a tight spot.

Mirabelle's outrage quickly dissipated as she realised she had to get Daphne out of the room now. They had to get away.

She left the girl heaving for breath on the carpet and checked the last bedroom. Her chest felt constricted and she was struggling to breathe. Did they have McGregor in there? She opened the door. Inside, tied to a chair, a man sat slumped. The third man. She bent down to see his face.

'Mr Tupps,' she said out loud. 'Thank God.' She immediately felt guilty. He was dead, of course. She tried to restrain the rush of relief. A dead body should never be good news, she chastised herself, but at least there was still a chance the Superintendent was alive. She grabbed the chair and manoeuvred it into the sitting room, removing the rope that was holding Mr Tupps in place so that he flopped onto the carpet. Then she wiped the gun meticulously and put it into the old man's hand so at first glance it would appear that he had shot Laidlaw. It was the best she could do. It would take the police a while to figure out the sequence of events.

'Who's that?' Daphne asked.

'I think he's the man who killed Elsie. He's the man to whom Laidlaw dished out your justice, Daphne.' The girl looked as if she might be sick. Mirabelle continued. 'He thought he was being loyal to his lodge – protecting it – when he got rid of Elsie and then Captain Henshaw. Then Laidlaw came along and pulled rank on him.'

Mirabelle grabbed the fake letters and arranged them in the grate so that the flame would catch. She picked up the heavy lighter from the table and twisted it open to drip some fluid onto the thick paper.

'What are you doing?'

'I'm getting us out of here,' Mirabelle said, turning the lighter round and setting the papers alight. Then, she fed the fire with the rope that had held Mr Tupps in place. Next she looked Daphne over. 'You'll do,' she said. 'As for me,' she scrabbled inside her handbag, found a handkerchief and cleaned Laidlaw's blood off her leg and her hand, throwing the stained handkerchief onto the fire. It was blazing now.

'Well. Come on,' she said, picking up the suitcase.

'I don't want the money any more,' mumbled Daphne forlornly.

Mirabelle grabbed the girl by the fingers. 'Come on,' she repeated, pulling the key from her pocket just as the hammering started on the door. 'Getting caught won't help anyone.'

'Is everything all right in there?' a voice shouted. 'This is hotel security. Open up.'

Cool as a cucumber, Mirabelle unlocked the door to the dining room. Checking behind her only once, she dragged Daphne like a reluctant toddler out of the room.

'Daddy,' the girl mouthed.

'You can't do him any good now,' said Mirabelle.

Then the women slipped away, locking the door behind them. They crossed the dining room and cut through the second suite, which brought them to the public corridor, around a corner. They could hear banging on the door of Laidlaw's room and raised voices. Then silence as the security guards must have used the skeleton key. Mirabelle led the way downstairs to the next floor, into the service lift and pressed B1 as Charlie had told her. In the kitchens they walked silently out of the back door and into the sunshine. It didn't feel as if it could possibly still be early morning, but around them Brighton was oblivious to what had happened in the last few minutes in the penthouse suite at the Grand. For most people the day was just starting. Church bells chimed nine o'clock further up the hill.

Daphne was pale and shaking.

'Come on,' Mirabelle chivvied her. 'We need to go to my office. Then I have to find my friend, the policeman.'

'Is he still missing?' It was as if the girl was drunk and couldn't quite grasp what was going on.

'Yes,' said Mirabelle, 'but I think I know where he might be.'

Daphne put up her hand to stop Mirabelle from speaking. Then the girl leaned over and vomited onto the pavement. 'Things always go to my stomach,' she said. 'That's what my mother says.' She started to sob again, realising that her mother was newly widowed and she was fatherless. She looked up. Somewhere on the upper floors, Professor Marsden's body was being poked and prodded. The police were being called. The men were putting out the fire Mirabelle had set and wondering what had been burned. 'The irony is, I get a thousand pounds a year in Daddy's will. I didn't mean it to go this way,' she said earnestly. 'You have to believe me. Really, I didn't. We didn't get on but . . .'

'No one meant it to go this way,' said Mirabelle sharply. 'Laidlaw thought he'd be the one walking away. But if we turn ourselves in, you'll be charged with fraud and perhaps manslaughter. Part of me thinks you should be charged. Part of me thinks I should be charged, for that matter. At the least I'm an accessory. If I had used the gun earlier perhaps I might have saved your father and we'd have two dead bodies up there rather than three. I suspect, though, once we'd gone into the room we didn't have many choices. But now we do. I'm choosing to find McGregor and I'm taking you out of here to thank you because you saved my life.'

Daphne was babbling. 'They couldn't lock me up for killing him. Not after what he did to Daddy. Not after what he was about to do to you.'

'I know. I know.' Mirabelle put an arm around the girl's shoulder. 'Come on, dear. Do you think you can walk?'

Daphne nodded. 'What if they come back? More of them? What about that?'

'That's why I burned the letters. The police will find the paper in the grate and the lodge will hear of it. They'll think their secret is safe. It's their history they're interested in, not you or me. And if, well, just about every man we know is anything to go by, they won't come to the conclusion that you killed Laidlaw. They'll think it had to be a man – someone from Mr Tupps' lodge, I expect, or the man who was with Laidlaw in Cambridge. But, now we need to get to Brills Lane. And, Daphne, don't tell anyone that you wrote the letters. Ever. That has to stay secret. We're the last people who know. If they find out they'll kill you. They'll come back. And I wouldn't blame them.'

Chapter 28

Our antagonist is our helper.

B ill took one look at the state of Mirabelle and Daphne and dropped the pencil with which he was making notes in the cash ledger. 'Miss Bevan,' he said, 'what on earth's happened?'

Mirabelle guided Daphne into a chair on the other side of the table and then straightened her clothes and flexed her ankles in the unaccustomed low heels. 'I need your help, Bill,' she said.

Bill looked quizzical. He switched on the kettle. It was something to do.

'Before you make the tea, would you ring the Grand and leave Charlie a message, please?'

'Charlie?' he said. 'What's Charlie got to do with anything?'

'Tell him that you just received the two parcels that he saw to earlier. And thank him. I don't want him worrying.'

Realising that no further explanation would be forthcoming, Bill reached for the handset and began to dial. Mirabelle emptied the suitcase of the money, slipping the notes into the inside pocket of her handbag. 'Don't worry,' she reassured Daphne. 'I'll bring the cash back if I don't need it. I'm going to ditch the suitcase.'

When Bill finished speaking to the hotel receptionist, Mirabelle turned the phone around and dialled the station at Bartholomew Square. 'Sergeant Simmons, please.'

Bill raised his eyebrows and then, taking pity on Daphne, started to make the tea.

'Sergeant, it's Mirabelle Bevan here. I wondered if you had found Superintendent McGregor? . . . I see . . . No. I was concerned, that's all . . . Twice? Really. What did they say? . . . Thanks so much,' said Mirabelle. 'I won't detain you any longer.' Taking a deep breath, she looked around as if noticing the office properly for the first time since she entered. 'Where's Vesta?'

'I don't know.' Bill shrugged his shoulders. 'Do you want a cup?'

Mirabelle shook her head. 'Have you seen her this morning?'

'No,' said Bill. 'I assumed she was with you.'

Mirabelle checked her watch. She picked up her bag. One thing at a time, she told herself.

'Daphne's had a terrible shock and in an hour or two she'll need to ring her mother. Do you understand, Daphne? You remember what I said?'

Daphne nodded. Bill fiddled with the milk bottle with his back turned.

'Bill used to be a policeman. He'll look after you. And don't worry. He's definitely not in the masons. Don't put him in a difficult position,' Mirabelle whispered into the girl's ear. Then she turned to go.

'Bill, you need to look after her. Just till I get back,' she instructed.

'But where are you going?' Daphne asked plaintively.

'Never you mind that. Bill, you make sure this girl is kept safely here for the time being. She's in a state of shock'

'Right-o,' Bill said. 'Leave it to me.'

Daphne was wide-eyed. 'Really? You're not in the brother-hood?' she asked. 'But you were on the force?'

'I don't hold with the lodge.' Bill handed the girl a steaming cup of tea. 'Can I get you some sugar in that?'

*

Outside, the air felt fresh and warm. Mirabelle walked towards the sea front. A police car with its bell blaring passed her on East Street, coming from Bartholomew Square and turning in the direction of the Grand. Mirabelle caught a glimpse of Detective Inspector Robinson. At the bottom of the street she turned left and strode in the opposite direction to the hotel. The pier was only just opening for business and a small crowd of holidaymakers was hovering around the entrance. She slipped inside as the gate swung open and walked briskly past the stalls, taking in the smell of candyfloss. A little boy ran past her towards the helter-skelter. The sound of organ music echoed along the deserted pier.

At the end, Mirabelle paused. She could see the Grand from here. The police car had parked at the entrance alongside two others. A policeman was standing at the hotel door, his uniform austere alongside the gold brocade of the doorman's jacket. From here, the men looked like tiny toys. It seemed too peaceful for what was going on inside. Mirabelle loosened the catch on the suitcase. It was bound to wash up on the beach, she thought, but there would be no fingerprints and it would be impossible to establish a connection with the atrocity that had just taken place. Letting go, she watched the case open as it splashed into the water and the fake banknotes, scattered and sodden, floated off. Soon the police would start looking for the fourth person who had been in the suite. They would assume it was a man.

Turning to the exit, Mirabelle glanced up Old Steine. The city was a blur of white stucco punctuated by dark grey roof slates. She felt nauseous. She made herself take a deep breath. A man behind the coconut shy asked her if she was feeling all right. Mirabelle held up her hand, hoping he wouldn't try to help her further. A little way along, she sat on a deckchair. Somewhere further up a woman was singing 'Greensleeves' with her little girl. Mirabelle looked up. McGregor was somewhere in the mass of buildings beyond her sight – maybe only his body. And Vesta was missing. She took a moment to think. It was all about the suicide note – the one Henshaw had written, or rather the one he hadn't.

McGregor must have realised the note wasn't genuine. It couldn't have been. What was it the boy with Simmons had said when they woke her? It had struck her immediately as being out of place. People didn't lie in suicide notes. Not in her experience and Henshaw had said himself only a few days ago that he didn't believe in heaven or hell. That phrase begged the question of who had written and planted the letter. McGregor might have been suspicious of Tupps already and this would have given him something to question the old caretaker about. He'd have gone straight to the lodge.

Mirabelle tried to remember the old man. She'd only met him at the door on Tuesday morning – it seemed now as if it was months ago. Mr Tupps had been stocky, and now she came to think of it, he looked as if he could handle himself. He hadn't seemed like a killer, but he'd poisoned Elsie Chapman already that day to protect the honour of his lodge. She wondered if he'd thought poisoning her was the kindest way. When it came to Henshaw he hadn't been so kind, but then Henshaw's objections to Elsie's murder were more of a betrayal. Hadn't Mr Tupps told Vesta that it was important to be loyal? For a moment she contrasted the old man with Laidlaw. It was difficult to decide who was the more ruthless. Mirabelle wondered where Vesta had got to. It would all come out in the end. That's what Jack used to say. Mirabelle only hoped that she wasn't too late.

She pulled herself to her feet and flagged a cab at the pier gates. 'Queen's Road, please,' she said and slipped into the back. It wasn't far.

The driver turned the car in a wide arc and turned up the hill. 'On holiday?' The man tried to make conversation but Mirabelle pretended not to hear. She rolled down the window and let the warm breeze caress her skin. As the car turned the corner she said, 'Just let me out here, please.'

Once the driver had gone, Mirabelle walked to the lodge's front door. She pressed the bell. No answer. She tried again. Still nothing. She twisted the knob, but the door was locked. And she couldn't attempt to pick the lock in broad daylight. She began to mull over the possibilities. The street was long and there were few breaks in the frontage but to one side there was a turn-off. Mirabelle decided to investigate. She turned the corner of Church Street and discovered Crown Gardens – a lane that ran along the rear of the buildings.

Checking over her shoulder as she stalked along the alley Mirabelle found a foothold and climbed over the back wall of the lodge in one smooth movement. She dropped lightly to her feet and looked around. The garden was only a small yard with some creepers, foxgloves, belladonna and a small laburnum tree growing by the back wall. Of course. All these plants were poisonous. She peered at a cluster of small white flowers growing to one side. Was that hemlock? She wasn't sure. The thought sent a shiver up her spine.

Mirabelle tried the back door. It was locked and bolted. Set into the Victorian wooden panels there was a large square of stained glass. Mirabelle found a stone and gave the pane a thump. The glass didn't so much shatter as turn to powder, and she had to chip away at it before there was a big enough hole to clamber through. She hauled herself into the kitchen and brushed down her skirt.

This had been the old caretaker's domain and he'd left it ship-shape. A rinsed teapot was on the draining board but it was the only sign of occupation. The place was silent, too. With no meetings until the afternoon and both Captain Henshaw and Mr Tupps dead, the brotherhood would have to make alternative arrangements to look after the property during the day. Mirabelle glanced into the pantry but the shelves betrayed only a tea caddy, an almost empty bag of sugar and some silverware. Behind her, the tap dripped, a plump drop of water splashed onto the enamel and Mirabelle jumped.

Simmons had come here – twice he said when he spoke to her on the telephone. Once there had been no one. The next time he had met Mr Tupps who had assured him Superintendent McGregor hadn't been in the lodge since Mrs Chapman's body had been removed. The sergeant had asked to look around but he hadn't been able to find any evidence in the only room where Tupps would grant him admission – the reception chamber upstairs. Did he have a warrant and was he looking for something in particular, Mr Tupps had enquired. If the sergeant wanted to send someone else – perhaps someone from the fraternity – they'd be able to look round properly, the old man had insisted. Simmons had not pursued the matter back at the station.

'When it's twenty-four hours, I'll log it officially. Then the masons can get involved,' he'd said.

That was still a few hours away, and Mirabelle was here. She'd need to start from the bottom – the servants' quarters again. Methodically she checked the whole of the lower floor – store cupboards, pantries and even a laundry, which was so pristine she doubted anything had actually been washed there. To the front, there was a coal cellar that ran under the pavement outside and, disappointingly, contained only coal. The first floor was familiar and empty – the reception and meeting rooms she had seen the other day. Mirabelle climbed upwards. There was a library with long windows that looked down onto the street.

'McGregor,' she called quietly. 'Are you here?'

Then, as she turned to make her way up to the next floor she noticed something from the vantage point of the staircase. It was only a detail, but she had left the door to the library open, and from where she stood she realised that the wall was in the wrong place. It was too far forward, even accounting for the books. Mirabelle ran downstairs and opened the door to the room below the library. She stood back. There was no question it was out here as well, and by a good three feet. She ran back upstairs, skipping the library floor and going to the top of the house. Here, the wall was exactly where it should be. Over two floors there was a cavity.

Mirabelle stood in front of the wall of mahogany bookshelves. If she were a mason, where would she locate a secret door? A book that was important? There must be hundreds here. She cast her eyes around, scanning the shelves for something – a small lever or a button perhaps. There was nothing. She got down on her hands and knees and peered at the place where the bookcases joined the floor, hoping to feel a breeze or see a tiny gap that might mark a secret entrance. Then looking up, she found it. At the top of the bookcases there was a pattern, carved in wood and repeated all the way round – little gable steps going up and down. A sign.

Mirabelle grabbed the librarian's ladder, which was on castors. She pulled until it came to a stop about two thirds of the way down the cases and then she climbed, reading the titles as she rose. The freemasons were sworn to secrecy, but they must have books they thought were important. And that would be the key. Sure enough, on one of the upper shelves she noticed one entitled *Freemasonry and Symbolism: Freedom of the Mind*. Below the title and tooled in gold there was the same up-and-down symbol as ran along the top of the bookcases. She reached towards the book and pulled. It scarcely moved. She waited and pulled it again, realising it was held in place somehow and wouldn't move from the shelf. Nothing. Changing tack, Mirabelle tried pushing it. Bingo! There was the sound of machinery, an automatic latch moving, and to her left the bookshelves opened inwards like a door. With her heart pounding, she felt in her pocket for the torch and passed the beam of light over the cavity that she had unearthed. Inside, there was a staircase that led downwards. Mirabelle stepped off the ladder and onto the stairs. She couldn't see how far they went or where they led.

'McGregor,' she called, reaching for her old torch, 'are you down there?'

There was a distinct thump.

The door swung closed behind her. Mirabelle felt anxious but she continued downwards. She must be at the level of the library floor, she thought, as she carried on through the downstairs ceiling and beyond. The stairs were steep and her fitted skirt restricted her movement. The light of the torch betrayed nothing but exposed brickwork and the stone staircase.

'McGregor,' she called again.

There was another thump. He was down here, somewhere.

At the basement level of the building the stairs turned into a corridor.

'I'm coming,' Mirabelle called with more confidence.

She must be at the back of the house by now but the corridor continued into what seemed to be a cavern. She directed the torchlight into the absolute darkness but the beam didn't reach very far. Of course, she thought, the back of the building was on a slope. The lodge had taken advantage of it to create a hidden cavity here, like an air raid shelter, but judging by the stairs and the entrance in the library, they had done the work long before the Luftwaffe's raids made underground hiding places common. She flashed the torch slowly across the floor, as far as the light would reach. To her left there were two other tunnels leading away from the end of the garden. She supposed these might bring one out away from Queen's Road, on Windsor Street perhaps. As the light twitched into the darkness, there was another thump to the right, and then another. She felt a wave of relief. He was trying to attract her attention. Mirabelle followed the sound and almost tripped over him.

Superintendent McGregor was tied to an iron post that was

254

set into the ground. He had been gagged. With trembling fingers, she put the torch on the floor. Then she bent down and loosened a knot to free his mouth. The piece of fabric opened in her hand. It was part of a dishcloth.

'Mirabelle,' McGregor's words came out garbled, 'he said he was coming back soon. Tupps. The caretaker. I don't know how long he's been. But we have to get away.'

Mirabelle smiled. 'He's not coming back,' she said firmly, starting to loosen the rope that tied McGregor's hands. 'Don't worry.'

He stank of stale sweat. The smell of desperation and abandonment. He'd need fluid. That would be the main thing. He was shaken of course, but that was normal. What had the masons built this place for, she wondered. Was it an escape route? A hiding place? As she fumbled to untie the Superintendent the torch toppled and the light fell on the wall behind McGregor's frame. Mirabelle stifled a scream. There were niches built into the rough brickwork. One was filled with human skulls, balanced precariously on top of one another as in a catacomb. Composing herself, she flicked the light of the torch further along, her fingers shaking as strange objects appeared out of the darkness – brass candlesticks, dusty dark glass bottles labelled in Greek, jars filled with . . .

'Oh,' Mirabelle gasped as she made out what looked like medical samples suspended in viscous fluid. There was a hand with six fingers in one of the smaller containers and the wide face of a Chinese man with a shaven head, who, when she looked closer, had no ears.

'We have to help Vesta.' McGregor was regaining control of his voice. He put his hand on the torch and lowered it. His skin was cold.

'Vesta?' said Mirabelle. She followed the line of light. And there she was. Over to one side, Vesta sat in the dark. She was bound and gagged like McGregor. She looked terrified.

'Good Lord!' Mirabelle ran to the girl and pulled off the cloth that covered her mouth. Her fingers moved frantically. Finding McGregor was one thing, but poor Vesta had been down here all along, too.

'What on earth have they been doing here?' She turned to McGregor, her voice tremulous as her fingers unravelled the knots.

McGregor was trying to stand up. 'God knows,' he said. 'I've been staring at these things for hours, trying to make them out. It's a chamber of bloody horrors.'

Mirabelle sensed him smile in the darkness.

'The main thing now is to get out,' he said. 'We need to focus on that. How did you get in?'

'The library.'

'He took me through the coal cellar, I think. I was woozy though.' The Superintendent rubbed his wrists and then untied his ankles.

Mirabelle could feel Vesta's whole body shaking. As the girl's hands were freed she flung her arms around Mirabelle, tears streaming down her face.

'You're all right now,' Mirabelle said. 'And you were right, Vesta. It was too dangerous. Far too dangerous. We should never have got involved.' She stroked the girl's hair. 'I'm so sorry,' she soothed. 'There, there.'

McGregor moved the torch slowly to one side and spotlit another niche, which housed several stuffed and mounted birds of prey. At the end, there was a pile of very ancient books. Lettering in faded gold read *Olde Magicke*.

'Magic? Superstitious nonsense, if you ask me.' McGregor's voice sounded stronger than he looked. 'I think you've saved my life, Mirabelle. Thank you.' He squeezed her shoulder. 'I'm not sure I'll ever be able to thank you enough.'

Vesta got to her feet, grasping Mirabelle's arm.

'Now, given we're the walking wounded, which way is the best to get out, do you think?' he said.

'Back through the coal cellar,' Mirabelle replied. 'Fewer stairs. It's at the front of the building.'

McGregor nodded. 'Come on,' he said. 'Let's get out of this place.'

Two minutes later, as the three of them stumbled blinking onto Queen's Road, Mirabelle could see that McGregor was still trembling. The three of them must look in a terrible state, she thought. The coal cellar had been filthy. Still, given what the pair had been through, it could have been worse. McGregor had a livid scar on his cheek and bruises on his wrists. Vesta was subdued and looked as if she had been beaten.

'Mirabelle, I can't thank you enough,' said McGregor, his voice hoarse with emotion.

'You need to drink something.' Mirabelle put her hand on his arm. 'Water. Tea. Both of you. You're in shock.'

She didn't want to be thanked, she realised. She only wanted to get further away. There was something disturbing about the lodge even if Mr Tupps would never be returning to it. It was as if the building might reach out and pull them back in. She wanted to ask McGregor what he thought of it all. What did grown men get out of arcane ceremonies, books about magic and stuffed birds? Were they so desperate to feel important that they'd do anything? It was superstition gone mad She pushed the thoughts away. Getting her friends something to drink was the priority now. There was a pub across the road towards the front. It wasn't open yet, but a thin, pasty-faced woman with her hair wrapped in a scarf was scrubbing the doorstep.

Vesta still hadn't spoken. Mirabelle clasped her hand. 'Come along,' she said. 'We need to get something in you.'

McGregor flashed his warrant card as they approached the door. 'We need water,' he said.

The woman got off her knees. 'We're not really open,' she

replied but she led them inside and poured water into three glasses, which she set on the bar.

McGregor gulped his down. 'That's better,' he said with relief.

The woman filled his glass again. Vesta lifted hers shakily to her lips.

'What happened to you then?' the woman enquired. 'That darkie's in a right state.'

'The Detective Superintendent has had a shock, that's all, and Miss Churchill is unwell. Do you think you might let us sit here for a moment?' Mirabelle said. 'Don't let us keep you.'

'This best not affect the licence.'

'No. Nothing like that.' Mirabelle's voice was reassuring.

The woman shrugged and returned to her bucket and mop. Mirabelle helped Vesta to take another sip. It was going down. Slowly, but still.

'Mirabelle,' said McGregor, 'you must let me do something for you. Let me thank you properly, please.'

'Not at all,' she dismissed him. 'I just happened to be the one who found you. Simmons was out looking all night. He went to the lodge twice. I tell you what, those masons get away with . . .'

'Murder? Not quite. Not ours at least, anyway.'

Mirabelle looked down. She had to focus. She couldn't tell him everything but she could tell him some of it. She put her arm protectively around Vesta, who laid her head on Mirabelle's shoulder like a child. Mirabelle felt a sudden flush of happiness and relief that the girl was all right.

'The truth was that I didn't even know Vesta was there,' she admitted. 'I'm a hopeless detective. As it was, I thought I might be too late and you'd be gone.'

'You saw how we were fixed. We weren't going anywhere.'

Mirabelle bit her lip. It was good he still had a sense of humour.

'Do you think you might call me Alan now?' he asked.

'Alan,' she said. The word sounded strange. 'The thing is, I'm afraid I have quite a story to tell, assuming you want to know. And if you owe me anything because of what I just did, then I'll be cashing in those chips immediately.'

McGregor stared at her. 'You mean I'm not the first man you've rescued this morning?'

Mirabelle shook her head. 'Much worse. There have been three deaths at the Grand Hotel. Mr Tupps, Professor Marsden, who is a don from Cambridge and a member of the Grand Lodge in London, and another chap whose name is Laidlaw.'

'Tupps is dead?' McGregor's eyes hardened. 'I was looking forward to nicking him. What the hell is going on?'

'I think it's over now.'

'Do you know who killed these men?'

'Yes. I know who killed everyone,' she said. 'Or at least I think I do. But if I tell you, I'm hoping you'll forgive me and you'll keep me out of it. Me and the person I was with.'

McGregor drained the water in his glass. 'You just saved my life,' he said, 'and now you want me to perjure myself?'

'Just a little.' Mirabelle couldn't look him in the eye. 'I'm so sorry.'

McGregor wondered if the woman might sell him pork scratchings from behind the bar. He was suddenly ravenously hungry. 'This wasn't what I meant when I said I wanted to take you out for a drink, by the way,' he said, standing up and reaching for the jar of pickled eggs he'd just spotted on the counter. He pulled some coins from his pocket and left them on the bar, pointing out what he'd done to the woman who had looked up from her work.

'I'll do whatever I can but you'd better tell me everything, Mirabelle. And start at the beginning.'

Mirabelle slipped her hand into Vesta's. She stroked the girl's palm soothingly. Then she began to speak.

Chapter 29

Mercy bears richer fruits than strict justice.

McGregor walked into the Grand almost an hour later and announced himself at the reception desk. A bellboy was dispatched to take him up to the penthouse floor. At the top, the boy waited awkwardly at the lift doors.

'You heard what happened?' McGregor asked.

The boy nodded.

'Off you go, son. No need to hang about. I'll find it from here.'

The suite was busy. A photographer was taking shots of the bodies, two pathologists were engaged in measuring the wounds, and Robinson was bent over the fireplace, smoking a cigarette and gazing at the cooling embers.

'Sir.' The inspector stood to attention. He flung his cigarette into the grate and then put out his hand as he realised what he had done. 'Sorry,' he said. 'I'm just surprised to see you. Are you all right? We didn't know where you'd got to.'

McGregor motioned Robinson to follow him into the hallway and around the corner. He checked left and right up the corridor to make sure no one was around. Then he grabbed the inspector by the lapels of his jacket and pushed him so hard against the wall that he could feel the man's ribs reverberate.

'I'm only going to ask you once,' he said, 'and I'm hoping you're not completely bent. Why did you remove the journalist's body?'

'What journalist?' Robinson's voice was tinged with panic. 'None of them was a journalist.'

'On Monday, Robinson? Remember Joey Gillingham?'

The inspector nodded furiously. 'Oh yes. Sorry, Sir. I was thinking about, well, today. In there.'

'Why did you remove Gillingham's body?' McGregor pulled back his fist.

Robinson noticed the bruises around the Superintendent's wrist and the determination in his eyes. His breath smelled of stale egg. Robinson hesitated. 'It was the matchbook,' he said. 'I know it sounds stupid. It was in his pocket.'

McGregor nodded. That was right. Gillingham's pockets had contained cigarettes but no lighter or matches. 'Go on.'

'It was from the Connaught Rooms. Next to the Grand Lodge. There was a mason's mark scrawled inside. We didn't know what had happened, and I just thought it was best to move him. In the end he wasn't even on the square.'

'Jesus!' McGregor's eyes flashed with fury. 'You pull anything like that because of your stupid club ever again and I won't have you demoted, I won't have you fired, I'll rip out your gullet. Whatever loyalty the bloody lodge inspires, your first duty is to the force, do you understand? We have six bodies now, Robinson, and if I'd known on Monday that Gillingham had been to the Grand Lodge or near it I might have stopped at least some of these unnecessary deaths, you son of a bitch. You withhold evidence from me again and I'll kill you.'

Robinson lifted his hands in surrender.

McGregor let go of his deputy's shoulders. 'You can walk out now if you want, but from now on if you're playing, you're playing on my team, got that? Let your weird friends at the lodge find you another job – it's your decision but it's a decision you need to make. Do you understand?'

'It's not weird, Sir, it's just a club. We do charity work . . .' Robinson stopped protesting under McGregor's gaze.

'Have you ever been in the basement of your precious lodge?' the Superintendent pressed.

'The basement?'

McGregor sized up the lad. He clearly wasn't aware of whatever Tupps had been up to. 'You're pretty low in the pecking order, then?'

'Well, yes, I suppose so, Sir.'

'From now on, Robinson, you remember that. You owe the police more than the masons and you owe me absolute loyalty. I'm your mother and your father, do you understand? You make another mistake like that one and you're worse than out.'

Robinson looked miserable. 'Yes, Sir.' He reached into his pocket and pulled out a notebook.

'You're going to fill me in?' Coming from McGregor's lips it didn't sound like a question.

Robinson held the little book out to McGregor. 'No, Sir. I'm giving it to you. This is Joey's notebook. I just found it in the personal effects of one of the victims.'

'Let me guess. The man with the tweed suit, the moustache and half his head blown away?'

'How did you know?'

'Oh, you'd be surprised. One of our fresh crop of victims kidnapped me yesterday and probably intended to kill me.' Robinson did not look as perturbed by this information as might be hoped. McGregor continued. 'We need to find all known associates of the man in there. The one who was shot. His name, I believe, is Laidlaw. I'm interested particularly in a gentleman seen yesterday in his company and indeed in the vicinity of one of the other victims – a Professor Peter Marsden. The man we're looking for is tall and was last seen wearing a black suit and a bowler hat. They met in Cambridge. You need to liaise with the nick over there and have them collect some statements. Then we need to see if we can find the fellow. He'll be here or hereabouts. He's an associate of Laidlaw's.'

'There had to have been someone else in the room.' Robinson pointed in the direction of the suite. 'I've been thinking about it. None of the victims died slowly enough to be the last one standing. None of them were bleeding out. Someone walked away.'

'You're a genius, Robinson. A veritable mastermind. Right. So, find me this fellow – the known associate. That seems a good place to start.'

'And you think he killed all of them?'

'No. I reckon Laidlaw killed Gillingham and the two other men in the room today. Tupps killed Mrs Chapman and Captain Henshaw, and I suspect the missing associate was the one to pull the trigger on Laidlaw this morning. All right?'

Robinson looked bemused. 'Why?'

'I'm not sure, but your stupid club is up to its neck in it all. You can count on that. Along with a spot of blackmail here and there and an illegitimate child. It started with Mrs Chapman. She found out something that your fellows wanted to keep secret. She had a document for sale. Something that implicated the masons, or at least something important to them. Don't panic. It isn't your lot. It's some chaps from London or even Scotland.'

'All freemasons are brothers, Sir. It's a brotherhood.'

'Very brotherly. All these bodies,' McGregor spat. 'Mrs Chapman tried to sell the document to Gillingham. He was killed, then she was killed. The document fell into the hands of Giles Tupps, I think, who was meeting these gentlemen in order to sell it on. God knows what's happened to it now.'

'The ashes in the grate, Sir. They look like very high-quality paper and maybe some rope.'

'Right. What we need is this fellow in the bowler hat. I'm sure he will be able to help us with our inquiries.'

'Yes, Sir.'

'I'll stay here to oversee things and liaise with the Scottish police. Laidlaw, as you might surmise, is from north of the border. You can leave that to me. Your job is to find the chap who's gone missing. He's potentially very dangerous. Can you handle it?'

Robinson nodded furiously but stayed rooted to the spot.

'Well, get on with it, man!'

McGregor leaned against the wall. His skin was clammy. He felt slightly sick. But he was here – alive – and in charge of the investigation. Thank God Robinson was relatively clueless. He looked at the notebook. He'd better ring Simmons, he supposed. It wouldn't be so easy to hoodwink the old sergeant even with ninety per cent of the truth. He wondered what notes Joey had taken about this whole affair – the notes for which he'd been killed. One way or another he'd see to it that Mirabelle could copy out the notebook for her client, though the book itself was evidence and would have to be retained.

McGregor thought about that moment, sitting in the dark, muscles aching, when he'd heard her voice. He'd felt elated and yet he'd half-hoped that it wouldn't be her. He didn't want her to be in danger, but then she was drawn to these situations. She was good at them. Perhaps he'd fallen in love with Mirabelle Bevan. Then he shook his head, dismissing the notion. It had been an emotional day, that was all. He headed for the suite. He'd better get down to work. If he could prove five out of the six murders then he would be happy. And she'd given him the truth, or enough of it to do that.

Ida Gillingham arrived promptly at McGuigan & McGuigan a mere two and a half hours after receiving Mirabelle's telegram informing her that her brother's notebook had been found.

'I got the train straight away,' she said and drew a handkerchief from her handbag. Today, it was a silk one with little bluebirds along the edge and bunches of flowers in the corners. Ida dabbed her nose. Mirabelle observed the girl. She didn't appear bereaved at all, even if she was sniffing. Perhaps she suffered from hay fever.

'Where is it, then?' Ida asked.

'The police have your brother's notebook, Miss Gillingham. It's evidence. They are on the trail of his killer.'

'Well, that's no good to me,' Ida objected. 'I came all the way down here to pick up Joey's tips, didn't I?'

'Mr Turpin is seeing to it for you.' Mirabelle tried not to show her distaste. 'He's had a copy made. He'll be back in the office soon. Tell me, Miss Gillingham, can you decode Joey's notebook? It's written in code as far as I understand.'

Ida drew herself up in her chair. 'Oh, I can read it all right. It's the same code Joey and I used when we were kids. It's a family code, see. No one else can make it out. Our dad used it and all. Before he was killed in the war.'

'I'm so sorry.'

Ida stared pointedly at the door. 'I hope Mr Turpin hurries up.'

'Might I suggest you don't provide the police with an accurate translation should there be anything in the notebook about your brother's last days, Miss Gillingham. Anything to do with his work. Just in case they ask.'

Ida fixed an uncompromising stare on Mirabelle. 'I generally don't tell anyone nothing unless I have to,' she nodded.

It certainly seemed that way. Mirabelle was about to reply when she heard Bill's steps outside the office door. He had a distinctive flat-footed gait. The result of years on the beat. She let it go.

'Afternoon, ladies.' He tipped his hat as he came in followed by Panther.

Mirabelle noted the little dog ignored Miss Gillingham – he had a certain animal wisdom, she thought.

'Well, now.' Bill reached inside his pocket. 'I got your winning slips, Miss Gillingham. The sergeant released them. And here's a transcript of your brother's notes.' He put the slips into Ida's outstretched hand and laid a small sheaf of notepaper on the desk in front of her.

Ida surveyed the notes. Her lips moved as she read the first few lines carefully. 'Good,' she said. 'What do I owe you?'

'Fifteen per cent, like I said, and if you throw me a racing tip, Miss, that would be lovely.'

Ida reached into her handbag and brought out a small black purse. 'I make it eight pounds, near enough.' She leafed through the slips with one hand and pulled out a white fiver and some change with the other. 'Thank you, Mr Turpin. And I can commend you to, let me see, Nearula. It's not much of a tip but if you put on money both ways he'll place almost any race. It's his third season, see.'

'Thanks,' Bill said uncertainly.

Ida bounced to her feet.

'Do you need any help finding Tony Grillo?' Bill offered. 'He's the man who'll honour Joey's betting slips.'

The girl eyed Bill suspiciously and shook her head. 'Good afternoon.' She nodded at Mirabelle and made for the door.

Bill sank into his chair and started making notes. 'Even I would know to back Nearula. Honestly! Shall we put in for an office sweepstake, do you think?'

'What do you mean?' said Vesta.

'My cousin Denny's hard of hearing.' Bill grinned and held up the list he'd made. 'And Miss Gillingham moves her lips when she reads. I caught four horses' names for meetings taking place this weekend. I'll nip down and get a racing paper, and we can search them out, eh?'

Mirabelle smiled. It had been such a miserable day – thank heavens for Bill. There was something indomitable about him. 'You can lip-read?'

'I learned to do it with Denny when we were nippers. I got the makings of a corking accumulator here. Ten bob each and we'll walk away with a small fortune – if you're game, ladies?'

'Let me fetch my purse,' insisted Mirabelle, reaching for her handbag. 'This one's on me.'

While Bill was away the women relaxed. It seemed odd somehow to get back to normal so easily. Vesta closed her eyes. The office felt right. When she opened them again Mirabelle was leaning across her desk.

'It's over, I promise,' she said quietly. 'I shall let the troubles of strangers be. At least I'll try to. I can't believe that I didn't realise you were there. I should have looked after you better. I apologise.'

'No. I sent you home,' the girl pointed out. 'I won't do that again. It's not as if anyone else noticed, is it? Not even Charlie.'

'Perhaps there's a downside to being so independent. Are you going to tell him?'

'And scare him half to death? No. No, I'm fine.'

'If you need someone to talk to . . . later, I mean,' said Mirabelle awkwardly.

'I know.' Vesta held her friend's eye. 'Thanks. I appreciate it.'

The sound of footsteps hammering on the linoleum outside broke their conversation. Charlie burst into the office. Delighted, Vesta jumped from her chair straight into his arms. Charlie looked surprised. 'Are you all right, Miss Bevan?' he said, peering over Vesta's shoulder.

Mirabelle looked up. 'Of course.'

'And the other lady?'

'She's gone home. She'll spend the summer with her mother, I expect.'

'But you didn't . . . I mean, you weren't hurt, were you?'

'Don't be silly. We got out long before there was any trouble. It seems to me there was a falling out of thieves after

267

we left the building. I've spoken to Superintendent McGregor and he's said he'll keep our presence at a very low profile. I'd be obliged if you'd do the same. And this is for you.' Mirabelle handed back the key to the suite. 'Thank you. As it turned out, it was a life-saver. It's Vesta who's had a tough afternoon. It's Vesta you need to look after.'

'Baby?' Charlie asked, putting the key in his pocket.

'Just paperwork,' she said. 'It's Friday afternoon, Mr Lewis, and we have relaxing to get on with.'

'Well, let's get to it, honey.' Charlie grinned.

Vesta turned to Mirabelle. 'All right?'

Mirabelle nodded. 'Off you go. Have a lovely weekend. That's what it's all about.'

Vesta reached for her jacket. Charlie helped her to slip it on. While his back was turned, Mirabelle mouthed 'Marry him' and demonstrated the relevant finger on her left hand.

'Friday night is our night in, Miss Bevan,' said Charlie, oblivious. 'I'm going to cook up a storm.'

Vesta linked her arm through Charlie's. Then she turned towards him. 'I've got something to talk to you about tonight.'

Mirabelle could swear the girl almost purred. It was a sound she was very glad to hear. I'll look forward to hearing about this on Monday, she thought. And to seeing the ring.

'Baby,' she heard Charlie say as the couple disappeared through the door, 'I could talk to you all night. What's on your mind?'

A fine drizzle was dropping gently on The Lawns when Mirabelle opened the curtains in her bedroom the following morning. On the pebbles three children in wellington boots were carrying plastic buckets up and down from the water's edge on some kind of mission. Mirabelle watched them for a few minutes and then took her umbrella from the stand to walk up to the bus stop.

'Overcast,' said a woman who was already waiting. In a plastic mackintosh and fur-lined ankle boots she was taking no chances. It was a comment that required no reply.

On the bus, the air was heavy with cigarette smoke and damp clothes. There was an air of general gloom as if the week of good weather had been a clerical error that had now been resolved, turning out in no one's favour. A large puddle was forming outside the greengrocers and the bus splashed through it.

At All Saints in Patcham Mirabelle disembarked. Down the road, a cloud of steam was rising from the bakery's chimney. She put up her umbrella and turned in the opposite direction for the church. Inside, a small congregation had formed. Ellie Chapman wore a navy coat. She was clutching a handkerchief in one hand and a single pink geranium in another. Beside her, Vi stood with her arm around a man to whom she looked so similar that he had to be her brother. Their coats were streaked by the rain. Half a dozen older ladies in an array of squelchy summer hats stood around silently. Mirabelle joined them, nodding in Ellie's direction.

The vicar referred to neither Captain Henshaw's confession nor the parentage of Mrs Chapman's youngest child. Nor did he refer to the fact that he was burying a murder victim. Ellie sobbed into her handkerchief as she threw the geranium into her mother's grave, and Mirabelle smiled as Vi reached out and touched her sister's arm, only for a moment, but still. These were the people who were left, Mirabelle thought. Perhaps it was better that they knew everything now. At least they might understand more about each other and try to build something out of their broken secrets.

'Thank you for coming, Miss Bevan.' Ellie shook Mirabelle's hand at the door, after the service.

'If you ever need anything . . .' Mirabelle found herself saying.

'Thank you,' Vi grinned, her hand on her swollen belly.

Their brother had a firm grip as he shook her hand. That was a good sign. Perhaps the Chapman children would be all right. The funerals that would take place next week would be more difficult. Mrs Henshaw must be distraught, she thought, and for that matter, angry.

She raised her umbrella and stepped out. A slight breeze had started. It blew the drizzle sideways. Mirabelle raised her eyes to see if anyone was waiting at the bus stop. That was always a sign that the service was due. And then she saw him. He had parked just along from All Saints and was standing beside the car with his hat pulled down. He raised a hand in greeting.

'Miss Bevan,' Superintendent McGregor said. 'I thought I'd find you here. I wondered if you'd like a lift or if I might take you to lunch.'

Mirabelle reflected. She had nothing else to do. 'It's a miserable day,' she said with a smile.

'But we're alive,' McGregor parried.

'What will you do about that horrible place?' Her voice was low. She had been thinking about it.

'I'll kick it upstairs, that's what,' McGregor said. 'That way the creepy so-and-sos will have to deal with their own. And I'll tell them if they don't, I'll alert the press. But my job's to solve the murders and that's all but done, isn't it?'

'I don't expect you'll ever find the man in black, you know.'

'Exactly why I put Robinson on the job. There's no point in wasting valuable manpower. No, it's over, thanks to you, Mirabelle.'

'Well, we're even then,' she smiled, taking his arm as he opened the car door. On the front seat there was a brown paper parcel.

'To say thank you,' he said.

'You didn't have to.' Mirabelle slipped inside and laid the parcel on her knee. It felt strange to be treated like this.

McGregor skirted the car, put down the umbrella and climbed into the driving seat.

'You saved my life,' he said.

'What on earth else would I do?' She didn't want to appear ungrateful. 'Shall I open it?'

He nodded. She pulled aside the string and the paper parted. Inside, a small bottle of perfume nestled next to an envelope.

'Shalimar,' said Mirabelle. 'Thank you.' Perhaps it was time to try something new. In the midst of life we are in death, the vicar had said. Maybe there was no mystery, no secret to everything. Maybe there was only this.

'I hear it's difficult to get these days. Even in Burlington Arcade,' McGregor said.

Mirabelle smiled. So McGregor had found Fred's hideaway. Of course. She picked up the envelope and flicked it open. Inside were two tickets.

'I hope you like tennis. It's the Championship at the All England Club. It started this week, but the tickets are for the final next weekend. We could drive to Wimbledon, if you like. They mix a fantastic fruit cup, I hear.'

'I didn't know you were interested in tennis.'

'We don't play much in Scotland, but I like to watch. Not a Fred Perry among us. Maybe one day. It's an American tipped to win.'

'Yes, there's a Danish contender, too, isn't there?'

McGregor shrugged shyly. 'Hungry?'

Mirabelle nodded. She thought she could manage something. 'Thank you, Alan.'

'I know a place with an open fire,' he said and started the engine.

Questions for readers' groups

1. In the digital age what can really be secret?
2. How have women's roles changed since the 1950s? What progress has and hasn't been made?
3. If you were Vesta would you marry Charlie?
4. What is the difference between history and nostalgia?
5. How long did the shadow of World War II hang over the nation? Does it still?
6. Is Elsie's murder more or less shocking than that of Joey Gillingham?
7. Would you rather live in Britain in 1953 or today? Would the answer to that question be the same if your skin was another colour?
8. What most successfully evokes the 1950s for you? The tastes, the sounds, the smells, the fashion? What makes a story feel as if it is from an earlier era?
9. Is Superintendent McGregor worthy of Mirabelle?
10. What are the ethics around making a vow of loyalty to the freemasons or any other organisation? Do those ethics hold if the vow of loyalty is to a monarch? A country?

Author's note

The quotations and misquotations used to open each chapter are taken from the following sources: 'Secret: a matter not meant to be known by others' (generic dictionary description); 'Murder is always a mistake – one should never do anything one cannot talk about at dinner' (Oscar Wilde); 'Choose a job you love and you will never have to work a day in your life' (Confucius); 'Nothing flatters a man as much as the happiness of his wife' (Samuel Johnson); 'Women are like tricks by sleight of hand' (William Congreve); 'The secret of getting ahead is getting started' (Mark Twain); 'Actions are visible though motives are secret' (Samuel Johnson); 'To investigate a problem is to solve it' (from 'Investigation may be likened to the long months of pregnancy, and solving a problem to the day of birth. To investigate a problem is, indeed, to solve it' by Mao Tse-tung); 'Practice forms a man to do anything' (Boswell); 'The richest legacy is honesty' (William Shakespeare); 'Look at yourself before condemning others' (Molière); 'Friendship is a slow ripening fruit' (Aristotle); 'Trust not too much to appearances' (Virgil); 'A tragedy need not have blood and death' (Jean Racine); 'Things do not change; we change' (Henry David Thoreau); 'Breakfast is the most important meal of the day' (traditional); 'Charity begins at home and justice begins next door' (Charles Dickens); 'The only good is knowledge' (Herodotus); 'The human race is governed by its imagination' (Napoleon Bonaparte); 'Above all, be armed' (Macchiavelli); 'Wickedness is its own punishment' (Francis Quarles); 'Suspicion is a heavy armour' (Robert Burns); 'A journey is the best medicine' (From 'Let me recommend the best medicine in the world: a long journey at a mild season through a pleasant country in easy stages' by James Madison); 'The law is reason free from passion' (Aristotle); 'Friendship is a partnership' (Aristotle); 'Curiosity killed the cat' (traditional); 'Every good act is charity' (Molière); 'Well begun is half done' (Aristotle); 'We die only once and for such a long time' (Molière); 'Our antagonist is our helper' (Edmund Burke); 'Mercy bears richer fruits than strict justice' (Abraham Lincoln).

Turn the page for a taster of the next
Mirabelle Bevan mystery

British Bulldog

A thing is not necessarily true just
because a man dies for it.

6.45 p.m., Monday, 8 February 1954
Brighton

Mirabelle snapped off the light at McGuigan & McGuigan Debt Recovery and locked the office door. Her breath clouded in the freezing air as she took the stairs down to the deserted street. It had been a cold winter and the weather had been front-page news in the national papers since before Christmas. Further north the winter skies were crystal clear and there was heavy snow, but it felt like a long time since the clouds had parted in Brighton. An unrelenting dampness had settled over the city. On East Street the sky was forbidding. It had been dark since five o'clock. Mirabelle often worked late, especially at this time of year when there was little to go home to and the office was busy with post-Yuletide commissions. She looked up and down the street, her fingers already numb inside her silk-lined leather gloves. If she chose the route along the front she'd get back more quickly to her flat on the Lawns, but the seashore could offer no protection from the biting northeasterly that cut through the city like a shard of ice. Sizing it up, she turned towards town. The streets were silent and eerie, the lamplight hazy over the damp pavements.

On Duke Street she realised she was being followed. A man carrying a briefcase fell into step behind her. She could hear the segs on his heels clicking on the paving stones, his pace distractingly out of time with her own. She crossed the road, making for North Street, and hazarded a quick glance over her shoulder. The fellow was wearing a dark woollen coat with the collar turned up and a bowler hat. The outfit was respectable enough but she couldn't quite make out his face. Near the corner she loitered, peering into the black window of a ladies' outfitters and hoping he'd pass. He did not. In fact, disconcertingly, he headed straight towards her. Mirabelle stiffened. She wished she was carrying an umbrella – the ideal everyday weapon for seeing off an assailant. Instead she concealed the office keys in her clenched fist in case she had to strike and run. Endeavouring to stay calm, she reassured herself that if she had to she could probably wind him and get away. The man tipped his hat and smiled.

'Excuse me, but are you Miss Bevan? Miss Mirabelle Bevan?' he asked pleasantly.

His voice was educated, cultured even. Mirabelle relaxed a little, though she kept the hidden keys turned outwards. Looking up and down the street, she could see no one else in either direction. The shop fronts were dark, flecked with fine drizzle, caught in movement by the buttery streetlight. She took a moment to examine the man who had addressed her. He was of slight build and sported a moustache. His neck was muffled by a dark scarf and he seemed somehow rather keen. Mirabelle wished someone else was nearby. It wouldn't be the first time a man who owed money to one of her clients had tried to accost her in the street. Further down the road, the door of a pub opened. A watery wash of light leached onto the stone paving and a tall figure in a shabby jacket lumbered out. He turned the opposite way without even looking in Mirabelle's direction.

'I'm Miss Bevan,' she admitted.

'I didn't mean to alarm you,' the man smiled again. 'I intended to call at your office but there's a good deal of snow up north and my train was delayed. I thought I might as well have a look anyway to get my bearings, and then I saw you leaving . . .'

Now she took a closer look at him, she realised he didn't look like a man who had reneged on a debt, failed to pay his rent, or run up an outstanding bill in a boarding house or any other Brighton establishment. These things could happen to anyone, but you got a nose for people. So what on earth did he want? Occasionally Mirabelle and her colleagues branched into more interesting cases, deserting debt collection for private investigation, but when a special case arose it generally didn't come their way by commission.

'We'll be open again at nine sharp,' she said. Business was business.

'Yes. I see. Only I'm not here about the collection of a debt. It's a more personal matter.'

'You've had a wasted journey, then. We don't take on that kind of thing, I'm afraid.'

The man nodded. 'That kind of thing' meant evidence for use in the divorce courts.

'No, quite. But I don't mean personal to me, I mean personal to you, Miss Bevan. My name is John Lovatt. I'm a solicitor.' He held out his gloved hand.

Mirabelle pocketed her keys and shook it, her hazel eyes unwavering as Mr Lovatt continued. 'The thing is . . . oh, I didn't want to tell you this way, here in the street, but, well, here we are. You've been mentioned in a will. You've been left a rather unusual bequest. Is there somewhere we might go to talk? And have a drink, or dinner perhaps? It's been rather a long day.'

Don't let the story stop here

www.sarasheridan.com

Join Sara and her fans online for the latest
news, events, competitions and more